WINTER Studs

RUTH D. KERCE ~ RUBY STORM
DIANA HUNTER

ELLORA'S CAVE
ROMANTICA PUBLISHING

ONE NAUGHTY WINTER NIGHT
By Ruth D. Kerce

Kyle Winter is in love with his best friend, but there is no way he's going to tell her and risk that friendship.

Kayla Robard is in love with her best friend. Has been forever.

With Christmas looming, Kayla decides it's time to tell Kyle how she feels. Then Kyle uncovers another secret — Kayla's need for bondage and submission — and his desire for her burns too strongly to ignore. Now they must decide if they're going to risk it all for the intimacy and wild indulgence they've been seeking for years.

A DEVIL IN WINTER
By Diana Hunter

Kevin Devlin Winter is a transplanted Texan, living and working in upstate New York, though his heart belongs in the Lone Star State. When his brother calls and tells him their parents have decided to take a second honeymoon over Christmas, Kevin finds himself alone and lonely during the holiday season.

Although he doesn't have a clue how he will spend Christmas, he certainly hadn't planned to kidnap Anna, the younger sister of his former girlfriend. Nor does he expect the sparks that fly when he ties her up and takes her home!

WINTER'S ROSE
By Ruby Storm

Kody Winter has arrived in Texas—and not for a simple visit. He's back for good and the reason is the sexy woman he's never forgotten.

Though Rose Leighton is blindsided when he suddenly appears after six years, she struggles to remain aloof at all costs. She's done with tears, and she's finished with Kody's special brand of heartache. But Rose never counted on her blistering physical reaction to his presence nor Kody's conviction that they are made for one another.

Kody has the patience and determination to win back the girl he left behind. He won't hesitate to use the passion they share. Whatever it takes...

An Ellora's Cave Romantica Publication

www.ellorascave.com

Winter Studs

ISBN 9781419956287
ALL RIGHTS RESERVED.
One Naughty Winter Night Copyright © 2006 Ruth D. Kerce
A Devil in Winter Copyright © 2006 Diana Hunter
Winter's Rose Copyright © 2006 Ruby Storm
Edited by Pamela Campbell.
Cover art by Syneca.

This book printed in the U.S.A. by Jasmine-Jade Enterprises, LLC.

Trade paperback Publication January 2008

WINTER STUDS

ഌ

ONE NAUGHTY WINTER NIGHT
Ruth D. Kerce

ഔ

Chapter One

ᔓ

Kayla rushed around like one of Santa's less-spirited elves on a sugarplum high, trying to get everything just so. "Hell's bells." Christmas was so not her favorite holiday. Only a major case of the holiday guilts had pushed her into a decorating frenzy.

She wrapped garland around the porch railing and set out artificial holly in a pot beside the door. The outdoor lights she briefly thought about hanging over the garage didn't work. She threw the string out, along with a bag of old candy canes that had melted together sometime during the summer.

"Lucked out. Praise the inadequacies of crappy light assemblers." She breathed a huge sigh of relief. The thought of tacking anything up so high gave her the heebie-jeebies. And candy canes were not her favorite decoration. Their little necks always broke when she handled them. Talk about depressing!

Anyhow, for someone who put off decorating until the last minute, she hadn't done half bad. "Looks festive. Well, pretty much."

Now she was tackling the front door.

For the umpteenth time, she checked her watch. "Darn it." *Kayla Robard – running late as usual.* They'd chisel that on her tombstone, for certain. Mentally chastising herself, she made her first resolution for the new year. "I will manage my time better from now on."

Holding a nail against the wood, she hammered at lightning speed. She didn't have much time left to get everything together before her best friend Kyle Winter was due to arrive.

11

The hammer glanced off the nail and banged her thumb. "Ow!" Pain exploded up her hand, and before she could stop it, a very unholiday-like word escaped her lips. "Oops, sorry," she said to no one in particular. She didn't suppose any holiday nasties were waiting to whisk her down to the dungeons of hell just because her language might be a bit off-color. Still, it didn't hurt to make certain and issue a quick apology. Served her right anyway. She should have had her mind on what she was doing and not on Kyle. She raised her hand to her mouth and sucked at the wound.

Self-consciously, she glanced over her shoulder, expecting to see nosey old Mrs. Crumbly standing on the porch across the street, shaking her head in disapproval. Thankfully, the stoop remained empty. In fact, the entire neighborhood looked uncharacteristically void of activity, except for two small children trying in vain to form snowballs out of icy slush at the end of the block.

A wire pricked Kayla's skin, and she glanced with disdain at the circle of fir hanging from her arm. She'd never understood the purpose of putting a wreath on the door. However, she'd conform to the tradition. But she did so only because the traditions of the season meant so much to Kyle. And Kyle meant so much to her.

She hung the decoration, trying and failing to get it straight. Something round shouldn't have a top and a bottom. She stood back, trying to gauge which way it would hang best. If whoever designed the wreath hadn't loaded it down with poofy ribbons, she could stick it up any which way. "I should have picked a plainer design. I'm not the poofy type."

As she eyed her handiwork, the cold seeped into her bones. She pulled down the sleeves of her thin sweater, but it didn't stop the shivers. At least the really ferocious winter storms hadn't moved in yet. After another unsuccessful wreath adjustment, she gave up. So it hung a little lopsided.

"Good enough." Her thumb still throbbing, she cursed the evils of hammers and holiday decorations and dropped the tool into the box at her feet.

Yes, she knew she needed a major attitude adjustment. But after her parents died, her enthusiasm for the holidays pretty much died too. She would try to make her home feel festive, though. Maybe, eventually, the spirit of Christmas would return to her soul.

A cold breeze hurried her actions, and she rushed inside to get warm. "Brr." She shut the front door and entered the utility room. Pushing aside a pile of junk in the packed closet, she located the stepladder and carried it into the entry. "One more chore." After positioning the ladder carefully below the wooden archway leading into the living room, she slowly climbed the three steps, muttering repeatedly, "It's not that high. It's not that high." If she kept saying the words, maybe she'd convince herself of their truth.

She hated heights—ever since she was seven and that little dweeb Lindsay Taylor pushed her off a slide. Teetering dangerously on the top step, visions of broken limbs assailed her. She breathed deeply to calm her nerves, reached up and secured a stiff, artificial sprig of mistletoe to the beam.

The poor branch was nearly leafless from old age and as hard as a head full of hair spray. All the little white berries had long since fallen off, leaving the mistletoe naked and not very Christmas-looking. The mistletoe's sad state made her wonder why she risked life, limb and good sense to hang it. She shrugged. "Oh well." Anyone with an ounce of holiday spirit would recognize what it was.

She carefully stepped down the ladder, her legs shaking like a pair of rubbery noodles. "Done." Relieved to be on steady ground again, she looked up and studied the sprig. She'd never even received any Christmas kisses under the thing. "Too bad." Her relationships usually didn't span the holidays. Strange, now that she thought about it.

She probably should have thrown the mistletoe out long ago with the other Christmas decorations she'd tossed. But mistletoe was another traditional holiday decoration Kyle insisted she have.

If not for him, she would have gotten rid of every last bit of her holiday items by now. Christmas was his favorite time of year, and she hated to see the disappointment on his face whenever he stopped by and her house looked barren of holiday cheer. For his benefit, she did what she could to make it seem like she enjoyed the season as much as he did.

With another glance at the mistletoe, Kayla did acknowledge that somewhere deep down she hoped one day to have "that special someone" to try it out on. Unfortunately, "that special someone" she had in mind only viewed her as a good friend.

She returned the stepladder to the closet then walked into the living room. The small Christmas tree, tiny box of multicolored bulbs, and sleeve of silver tinsel atop the coffee table caught her attention. "Shoot!" She had forgotten to decorate the scraggly tree. She'd promised Kyle. But she didn't have the time or inclination right now to do a decent job.

Every year she bought a new artificial Christmas tree, each time purchasing a smaller one, not wanting to put in the effort to decorate the previous year's larger version. This year the tree was tiny, the smallest she'd been able to find. Still, as little as it was, the job seemed enormous, so she'd put it off. The tree still sat on the coffee table after a week, waiting for her to spruce up its bare limbs.

She doubted she'd even bother with a tree next year. Maybe she'd just put out plastic poinsettias and bake Christmas goodies. That was festive enough for her, even though Kyle would complain. She didn't know why he cared how she decorated for the holidays anyway. He always drove down to Texas to spend Christmas with his family. But he'd said once that she would never heal emotionally if she kept ignoring what caused her pain.

Unfortunately, the holidays not only brought the pain and memories to the surface but also left her feeling raw and vulnerable.

Memories.

During her first year of college, her parents had died in a plane crash right before Christmas. As an only child, the accident had left her feeling totally alone in the new school so far from home.

After taking care of the funeral arrangements and putting the house on the market, she'd returned to school to finish her studies and grieve. She'd had nowhere else to go.

Tears gathered behind her eyes. She missed her mother's nurturing and her father's quirky sense of humor and comforting hugs. She'd shed many tears over the past ten years. Memories of joyous Christmas pasts, never to be seen again, made depressing holiday companions.

If it weren't for Kyle, she wouldn't even acknowledge the season at all. It would be easier to handle that way. But he was like a little boy when it came to Christmas. How could she disappoint him? Especially after he'd been such a good friend. Without his strength, caring and companionship, she'd probably be a bag lady right now.

A quick glance at the clock told her the hour was growing late. She'd better put the cookies in the oven if she wanted them ready in time.

Kyle would be over soon to unclog her bathtub drain. It had become a ritual for him to do that for her once a month. Her long hair clogged many a pipe, and she never did have much luck with drain cleaners or getting it out herself. She was a total klutz with things like that.

Okay, so maybe she could get the hair out herself if she really wanted to try, but it gave her a perfect excuse to ask him over. He'd come over just to hang out if she asked, but she knew he really couldn't pass up a damsel-in-distress call. It went against his nature.

All Kyle ever asked in return for his monthly de-hairing service was to sample some of her baking. Her heart did a funny little tumble as she recalled him asking for his Christmas cookie reward.

It thrilled her to know that someone enjoyed her sweeter-than-sin creations. Most people ran for the antacid when she brought out her goodies.

Not Kyle. He was her biggest fan. He loved everything she baked, no matter how sweet. Getting sugar-shocked was one of his favorite pastimes. *The lovable lug.*

She fluffed the pillows on the couch then decided to drag out the vacuum cleaner for a quick carpet run. The machine only picked up every other piece of lint. She needed to ask Kyle to de-hair the roller while he was here. And the sink in the kitchen was leaking a little too. She shook her head. Sometimes she worried that she depended on Kyle too much. But he enjoyed tinkering, so she knew he wouldn't mind getting her all fixed up.

When she'd first met Kyle three weeks into her freshman year at college, they'd immediately clicked. Most likely because she loved horror flicks, and he could never find anyone to go with him to one.

The type of women he dated didn't care to be scared more witless than they already were. Okay…that was catty. She knew it, acknowledged it and still thought it.

Kyle could do much better than those boob-babes he had a tendency to date. Kayla didn't know where he found them, and frankly, she didn't want to know.

Back then, she'd sneak peeks at him, admiring his body and almost-too-rugged-to-be-handsome face. She had often fantasized about stripping him bare and having her way with him — still did. What was the harm? Between her fantasies and her vibrator, she slept very well at night.

Their classmates had suspected her feelings, because they were relentless, always making fun of her. And Kyle always came to her rescue. *Her hero.* He'd call them immature idiots then buy her a large cone of chocolate ice cream at the Student Union.

She didn't know what she'd do without him.

Now they were both out of school and owned their own spaces. Her job as a computer analyst provided a fairly good income. Along with what was left of the settlement she'd received from the airline, she'd been able to afford the move from an apartment to a real home.

Kyle had landed a good position in a brokerage firm and found a nice condominium not far from her, but Kayla knew a handyman lurked inside him. So whenever a problem cropped up, he was the one she called.

The phone rang, disrupting her thoughts. She turned off the vacuum then plopped down on the sofa and picked up the receiver. "Hello."

"Hey, baby. You naked?"

Laughter bubbled up inside Kayla as she recognized the male voice. The greeting that had started out as a joke long ago was now a friendly routine, and the familiarity warmed her heart. "Aren't I always?"

"I wish."

"Where are you, Kyle?" She twisted the phone cord around her finger, needing something to do with her hands. Even through the phone line, she ached to touch him. Kayla had vowed back in college not to let Kyle know about the deep feelings she harbored for him. She couldn't compete with the beauties he dated, so she'd never tried.

Fear also played a large part in her decision. Their friendship was special and any move to change the relationship could damage what they had. She didn't want to take the chance.

Each year, though, her feelings became harder to tamp down, which made her antsy and unsure of what to do. She supposed the fact that they were both older now and neither of them had married made her wonder if there might truly be hope for them if she made a move.

"I'm on my way over as we speak," he answered. "I'm running a few minutes late. Didn't want you to worry. I know how you are." He chuckled.

"I refuse to apologize for caring about your welfare." Although Kayla was perpetually late, Kyle rarely was, so she always worried when he didn't show up on time.

She hoped he didn't have car trouble again. He was saving up for a black XT-347 with red trim, or some such car with a bunch of letters and numbers in the name. The engine of his current heap kept going out, blowing up or making alien-like noises. The car's back bumper had fallen off twice this month alone!

He couldn't afford the new car quite yet. He wanted to pay cash. So he kept repairing Lemon Drop, as he called it — such an appropriate name for the ailing yellow car. Maybe next year he'd have enough saved.

"Why are you late? Is it the car?"

"Nosey, nosey, nosey," Kyle answered, his voice laced with humor.

She couldn't help but smile. When he clicked his tongue loud enough for her to hear over the phone, she knew he wasn't going to tell her. She could just see him shaking his head, a cute little grin on his face, the dimple in his left cheek begging to be kissed.

The man had way too much charisma for his own good. She'd seen him talk his way out of traffic tickets, into sold-out shows and around set-in-stone rules and regulations. He always got his way. Little did he know that she'd fantasized more than once about him getting his way with *her*.

The distant sound of his voice brought her back to the conversation, and she realized she hadn't been listening. "Sorry, I missed that. What?"

"I said you'll find out when you see me. I'll be there in a bit."

"Okay. I'm going to want the full story, gory details and all. See ya soon." She hung up and leaned back against the sofa cushions, letting the knowledge that he was on his way soothe her holiday depression.

She felt so blessed to have him as a friend. After her parents died, she withdrew into herself, not socializing at all. Now she didn't have many friends left and no family. Kyle helped to fill the void. Much to her delight, he wasn't above acting or looking like a silly fool just to make her smile.

Last year, after Steve dumped her—one more casualty in a long line of failed relationships—she'd called Kyle the same night and cried on his shoulder over the phone. She swore to him that the fates never wanted her to be happy.

Bright and early the next day, Kyle had appeared on her doorstep, dressed like a clown in striped baggy pants, a red nose and big purple shoes. She'd laughed until her stomach ached.

Then he had taken her to the carnival and won her an armful of stuffed animals. They'd spent the rest of the night naming the assortment of puppies, bunnies and cuddly bears, which resided in her bedroom to this day. She loved Kyle for doing that, for caring. He always knew how to make her feel better.

She glanced at the mistletoe again and allowed herself to dwell on the fantasy that had filled her days and warmed her nights for years. She hadn't been with a man in too many months to count, and her hormones were stuck on permanent stand-by. If only some sliver of opportunity would arise for her to express her innermost feelings to Kyle without damaging their current relationship...

He was, and had always been, the man she wanted.

"Oh, well." Dismissing the mistletoe, undecorated tree and her thoughts, she pushed up from the couch. She needed to get back to work. She rolled the vacuum into the closet then entered the kitchen.

The cookie dough she'd mixed up earlier sat in a large bowl on the center island, waiting for her to do her "finger magic" as Kyle always called it. His favorite phrase for her baking endeavors. Thank goodness the dough didn't need to be chilled, or she wouldn't even be this far along.

Carefully, she shaped the cookies by hand, each with a simple Christmas design. Trees, stars, angels, reindeer — the most difficult. The poor animal turned out looking more like a sick hippo, much to her disappointment.

She thought about tossing the reindeer-wannabe back into the bowl then changed her mind. Kyle would laugh at it and she loved to hear him laugh. The warm, deep sound always made her ache to throw her arms around him and lose herself in his exuberant passion for life. "Geez, I'm on hormonal overload here. I've got to settle down." If she didn't, she feared she might just jump Kyle as soon as he came through the door.

She shoved the pan into the oven.

While the cookies baked, she arranged the decorations. She planned on using red and green sprinkles and vanilla-flavored icing for the toppings.

Kyle loved vanilla. When she'd found out shortly after meeting him, she changed her body spray to vanilla, secretly hoping to spark his interest without being obvious.

He'd never noticed.

"Subtlety doesn't work with men, I guess."

Before the first batch of cookies finished baking, the doorbell chimed twice. Her heartbeat kicked up a notch. Kyle's signal.

She rushed out to the front door and pulled it open. "Hi!" The sparkle in Kyle's eyes and his smile brought a familiar joy to her heart. Too bad she couldn't stay to fully enjoy it. She grabbed the front of his jacket and yanked him over the stoop. "Come in. I've got cookies!"

Chapter Two

ຄຽ

The sight of Kayla always made Kyle's heart beat a little faster. The flour dusting her clothes and hair brought a grin to his face. As she rushed out of sight, he heard a ding and gnawing hunger grew inside him. She was baking her special sugar cookies. He'd smelled the treats the moment she opened the door.

He drew in a deep breath. *Vanilla.* The aroma lingered in the air, making him even hungrier for the cookies…and for Kayla. Somehow, he associated that seductive scent with her.

"Are those cookies for me, I hope?" he called out to her, his stomach rumbling in anticipation.

"Only if you unclog my drain," she answered back. "You're going to have to work for your reward. I swear, one of these days I'm cutting my hair short and getting rid of the problem altogether. What's the mystery about why you were late? You know how secrets drive me crazy. And why are we yelling back and forth? Come into the kitchen so we can talk."

The thought of Kayla cutting her luxurious hair didn't sit well with him. She was always threatening to hack it off. Since she hadn't done it yet, he hoped she wasn't serious. She'd be beautiful either way, but her long hair affected him on some primitive level he couldn't quite explain. Many times, he'd discreetly touched or smelled her hair when she stood close. Sensations of possession, along with the desire to pull her into his protective embrace, had shot through him each and every time.

"I'll be there in a sec. Did you know you left your toolbox out on the porch?" he asked, raising his voice so she could hear him clearly.

"Oh, did I?"

"Yeah, I stumbled right over it. Almost did a nosedive into the rose bushes." He added in a low voice, "Again."

He rubbed his backside, remembering his fall into her garden last summer, after tripping over a large jar of sun tea she'd forgotten to bring in. He laughed now, thinking back on the whole slapstick event. But it hadn't been funny at the time. She'd had to pull thorns out of his butt.

"Sorry about that. Can you set it in the entry? I'll put it away later."

"I know where it goes." He knew Kayla's home almost as well as his own.

They were practically family. They'd known each other ten years now. He could tell her how she'd organize a room even before she did it.

Since college, he'd watched over her and she'd watched over him. Like family. He had his parents and two younger brothers, but they lived in different states, so having someone nearby who cared about him was a really good feeling.

Besides, nobody looked after him like Kayla did. He cherished all the little things she did for him—baking special treats, listening to his complaints about work and women, making him laugh when he felt right on the edge of losing it and just being there for him no matter what.

Kayla was his anchor. He didn't know what he'd do without her. The possibility of her someday not being there for him, once she had her own family to care for, ripped at his heart.

After fighting with a stepladder that kept trying to bang him in the shins, he found a spot for the toolbox in the utility room closet. Then he dragged the surprise he'd brought for Kayla from the porch into the entry and closed the door. He peeked toward the kitchen, hoping she would stay put for a while. With one last tug, he got the surprise from the entry into the living room. He propped his present in the corner, tossed his gloves and jacket on a chair, and then joined her in the kitchen. "Don't you dare."

She looked up from the pan she'd pulled from the oven. "Don't what?" The pan clattered on the stovetop as she set it down. She immediately grabbed the next pan and slid it into the oven.

"Don't cut your hair." He stepped up beside her and laced his fingers through her long auburn tresses. Soft as satin. He could touch the luxurious strands forever. "Your hair is too beautiful to cut. I've always loved the way it flows over your shoulders and down your back like a curtain of coppery-red mist."

He often wondered how her hair would feel trailing across his bare chest, down his naked body, over his hard cock. *Damn.* Erotic images flickered through his mind. His fingers tightened slightly and then eased to massage her scalp.

When she looked up at him strangely, he jerked his hand away and stepped back. What was he doing? Kayla was his friend — his best friend. He shouldn't touch her like that or say such things, no matter how long he'd ached to do so. He didn't want anything to jeopardize their relationship. He knew how vulnerable she felt these days. The holiday season must be making him sentimental and thinking of love.

Love? Shit. Where had that come from?

He wiped a hand over his face, slowly acknowledging the truth. He'd known for some time that his feelings for her ran deep but he had never put that particular word to them. At least, not seriously.

Love.

The realization shook him to the core.

"You better see to the drain," Kayla responded in a shaky voice, placing her oven mitt carefully on the counter. She avoided his gaze and stared down at the baking pan, a frown on her face. "I want to glaze some of these cookies before they cool off too much."

"Yeah, all right." He hesitated, and when she said nothing more, he turned and headed for the bathroom, grateful for the reprieve. His surprise could wait. He needed to get his emotions and his body under control first. Kayla must think him nuts for touching her hair like that. And for saying that goofy line about "coppery-red mist". What a lame-brain.

When he reached the bathroom, he leaned a hand against the doorframe and tried to diffuse the heat of desire burning inside him. If he'd stayed in the kitchen much longer, he would have grabbed Kayla, stripped her bare and sampled more than her baking, once and for all. "A fantasy come true," he murmured.

Taking a few deep breaths, he grudgingly acknowledged that stripping her bare was an exaggeration. Kayla would have the final say in that matter. "But it's what I want to do."

Visions of permanence and having a family with her filled his dreams at night. Not to mention a plethora of sexual visions. At first, he'd just thought they were insignificant images in his head and perfectly normal given their close relationship, except they'd persisted and even escalated, and now...

Now he was ready to admit, at least to himself, that he'd been in love with her for years. He'd hidden his feelings from her and from himself. The thought of letting her know how he truly felt and the possibility of her rejecting him terrified the crap out of him.

He entered the bathroom and turned on the tap. His cock pressed almost painfully against the front of his jeans as he eyed the opposite door that led into her bedroom, making the bathroom accessible from both sides of the small house. He didn't need to be thinking about Kayla's bed right now. Or the two of them grinding away on top of it. He needed a cold shower in the worst way. Unfortunately, at the moment, he'd have to settle for a frigid splash in the face.

* * * * *

Hands trembling, Kayla spilled sprinkles all over the counter. She blew out a frustrated gust of air at her clumsiness and wiped the mess into the sink.

That wasn't heat she'd seen in Kyle's gaze...was it? Her imagination must be working overtime, playing nasty tricks on her vulnerable psyche.

She closed her eyes, remembering the feel of his hand in her hair, his fingers massaging her scalp. Reliving it in vivid detail.

He had such strong hands and gentle fingers. She wondered how it would feel if Kyle touched her skin like that, especially with no clothes in the way to hinder his progress. Her body grew warm at the thought, and a slow throbbing in her pussy turned her muscles weak and shaky.

"Geez." Snapping her eyes open, she shook her head, trying to clear her thoughts and her body's reaction. This was crazy. Her loneliness and fantasies had jumbled her good sense. All he'd done was touch her hair...even though it had been with such tenderness, like a lover would.

The possibilities raised her heart rate and her temperature. Allowing herself one more minute of the fantasy, she catalogued his tender touch in her memory. She would relive the moment every time she daydreamed about Kyle.

A curse from the living room interrupted her thoughts. She shook off the sexy images in her head, set the cookie timer and went to investigate. As soon as she stepped from the kitchen, her breath caught in her throat. "What in the world?"

Kyle stood in the living room, wrestling with a large Christmas tree. Peering between the branches, he smiled sheepishly. "I brought something."

"So I see. Is that why you're late?"

"Yeah. I had a heck of a time getting the thing strapped to the top of Lemon Drop. The tree kept rolling to the side and falling off, like it had someplace better to go." He chuckled. "I brought some decorations too. They're still in the trunk. I'll cart them in later. You probably don't have enough bulbs and stuff for something this big. That thing you have on the coffee table looks more like tumbleweed. *This* is a tree. You've got a perfect spot for it in front of the window, right next to the sofa. I'll set it up in the stand for you, you go finish the cookies, I'll go ahead and clean the drain—get that out of the way then we'll take it from there. Okay?"

He was talking so fast, making sure she wouldn't protest the tree, that Kayla had to smile. He knew Christmas was an especially sad time for her.

"Go on now. Don't burn my cookies. You wouldn't want to see a grown man cry, would you?"

Kayla laughed. "No, I wouldn't want that. I'm going."

"So far so good," Kyle muttered, relieved that Kayla hadn't insisted he toss the tree out the door. He manhandled the monstrosity into position. He was making a mess with the needles, but it would be worth the pick-up and vacuum duty. Her machine probably needed de-hairing anyway. It always did.

As he studied the tree placement, determination filled his soul. Every year at Christmas, Kayla went into a depression. This year was going to be different. He'd made up his mind, and nobody was going to change it.

Since his parents had canceled their normal plans for everyone to spend Christmas at the Circle KW Ranch in Texas, he was free and clear to be with Kayla this year. While his parents were away on their second honeymoon, creating more memories for themselves, he'd be creating some memories of his own.

He hadn't told Kayla yet about being able to spend Christmas with her. He planned to surprise her. He'd already arranged for presents and a festive meal to be delivered to her house—no small feat on Christmas Day. To ensure arrival, he'd used part of his car fund. Lemon Drop would be safe from the junk heap a while longer.

Maybe after one good Christmas, Kayla would finally accept his invitations to spend special occasions with his family. Every time he asked, she refused, insisting that she didn't want to intrude, which was ridiculous.

He wanted her with him. He hated picturing her home alone on the holidays. Besides, Christmas never seemed complete without her. A part of him felt so lost when she wasn't around. He'd already spoken about the situation with his parents, along with Kevin and Kody, his brothers. They had all agreed she should be included. Each of them had met her at some point over the years. They all adored her.

This year, he was determined to make a good holiday for her, even if he had to dress up like Santa Claus and bounce her on his lap in order to make her smile. That thought made *him* smile.

* * * * *

A large tree to decorate. Kayla practically groaned at the thought. It seemed like such a waste of time. And worse than the decorating was the un-decorating.

Maybe after the holidays she'd just throw the whole thing out, bulbs and all. She shook her head. No. She couldn't do that. She didn't have the heart to disappoint Kyle after he'd gone to so much trouble for her. Just in case he bought her another tree next year, she'd store the decorations in the garage.

She knew he was only trying to make her happy, but sitting all alone in front of a large, brightly decorated tree on Christmas Day wasn't something she looked forward to.

"I think you did it this time, Kayla," Kyle called from the bathroom a few minutes later.

She set the timer for the current batch of cookies and went to join him. She spared a glance at the tall Christmas tree next to the sofa. Grudgingly, she had to admit it didn't look half bad, though the back branches dug into her blinds, like the tree was trying to crawl out the window. She'd have to ask Kyle to move it out from the wall a little.

Almost afraid to look, she stepped up to the bathroom door and peeked inside. "What did I do? Is it irreparably damaged?" That would be just her luck. She chewed at her bottom lip, calculating the cost of calling in a professional to do repairs.

"You've created a hair rat." With a needle nose pliers, he pulled a glob of long, wet, soapy hair from the drain. "Disgusting, isn't it? A few more days and it probably could have slithered out on its own."

"Oh, yuck."

Chuckling, he stood up. "I think we might need to clean the drain twice a month, so it doesn't get this bad again. However, you're all fixed up for now, clean as a whistle. Where are my cookies?"

Kayla laughed, relieved she wouldn't have to call in a plumber. She'd splurged the last couple of months redecorating her bedroom, and since she'd used most of the remaining airline settlement to pay off the house, now money was tight.

She liked the idea of Kyle coming over twice a month, even though she doubted the drain needed cleaning that often. They'd been so busy with their jobs lately they hadn't seen enough of each other to satisfy her.

Thank goodness for long hair. Kayla twirled a strand around her finger. No way was she cutting it anytime soon. A hairy drain was too perfect an excuse to get Kyle over here.

Besides, her hair was her only halfway decent asset as far as she was concerned. *A curtain of coppery-red mist.* Kyle's words played over in her mind and she smiled.

She was always threatening to cut her hair because it seemed the right thing to do with her drain getting clogged all the time. But she was tired of always saying and doing the right thing. She wanted to do what made her happy, to take more chances in her life and not care what others thought.

Unfortunately, she was a big chicken at heart and usually shied away from anything that might raise an eyebrow. She intended to change that. It had become her number two New Year's resolution, right behind her "better time management" promise. And even though the new year hadn't arrived yet, she figured now was as good a time as any to start. With Kyle.

Thinking about her decision, her palms grew sweaty. Her mouth went dry, and her stomach did a slow roll. Okay, not good signs. But expected. She swallowed hard. *Be confident and just do it.*

If Kyle gave her that little indulgent smile he reserved for people whose feelings he didn't want to hurt, she'd never live through the pain and embarrassment. Oh, he'd make up a good excuse and turn her down easy then probably do something silly to make her laugh, but it would still be a rejection just the same.

She took a deep breath and plunged ahead before she could change her mind. "Come back into the kitchen after you clean up. I'll get you a plate of goodies, unless…" She let the sentence hang, knowing Kyle would pick up on it.

"Unless?" He rolled "the rat" in some toilet paper and tossed it in the trashcan by the sink.

Kayla's heart pounded against her ribs. "Did you see what was on television tonight?"

"*Virgin Vixens from Mars.*"

"I'm serious, Kyle." He wasn't making this simple.

"So am I. It's on one of the pay stations at nine o'clock. It's part of the babe-o-rama marathon."

She cast her gaze to the ceiling and frustration almost stopped her from going forward. Making eye contact, she determined not to back off and continued more brusquely than she'd intended. "I'm talking about something much more substantial. *A Christmas Horror-Day*, the uncut version." Her voice softened. "We could order pizza and have cookies for dessert, then maybe tackle that tree. You know me and trees. I don't think I can handle decorating it myself." Her stomach churned as she waited for his answer.

He hesitated, and suddenly she felt like a fool. It was Saturday. He probably already had a date for tonight. "I'm sorry. You have plans later with Heather, don't you?"

Tall, blonde and built. Heather was his latest in a long line of admirers. The queen of the silicone boob-babes.

She was certain Heather's chest size measured only slightly less than her IQ. Jealousy surged through her. She fought back the ugly emotion, knowing she had no real claim on Kyle's time and attention.

"Well, actually…we broke up last week."

"You did? You didn't tell me." A surge of hope lifted her spirits then curiosity won out. "I thought Heather was a keeper. You went out with her for almost four months. What happened?"

Too boring, too loud, too clingy. He always had some silly excuse for dropping his lady friends and moving on.

"I don't know." He shrugged. "It's just hard to find someone to really connect with these days. None of the women I've been with have measured up to—" He broke off in mid-sentence, and his face flushed.

Blushing? Kyle was blushing? Kayla couldn't believe it. She suppressed a chuckle, waiting for him to finish his sentence, but he remained silent.

Confusion filled her. She studied his features as his gaze darted around the room. A tantalizing thought struck her, and she wondered if he had been about to say, "None of the women I've been with have measured up to *you*."

Immediately, she dismissed the silly thought.

31

He'd most likely meant to say "measured up to *my standards*" but figured it sounded bad and changed his mind at the last minute about voicing the words aloud.

Her gaze sought and finally held his. He still didn't say anything and looked so uncomfortable that she decided to let the subject drop. She averted her eyes toward the new Christmas tree. Sometimes not looking directly at a person made discussing a sensitive topic easier.

"Well, then," she started tentatively, "how about tonight? Would you like to stay?" She really didn't want to be alone, not this close to Christmas.

He'd be leaving for his parents' ranch soon. Her heart constricted and sadness gripped her like a vise. This might be the last time they'd have together until he got back.

Besides, the least he could do after saddling her with that huge tree was to help her decorate it.

Kyle turned and rinsed his hands in the sink. After a long, silent moment, he answered. "How can I resist an offer like that? Delicious food, good movie...beautiful company," he paused again, "and the promise of some great homemade dessert. You're on."

Did he just say she was beautiful? She swallowed the lump of emotion clogging her throat. "Wonderful," she croaked, then swallowed again to try to clear the scratchiness from her voice.

Happier than she'd felt in a long time, Kayla flashed him a smile. "I'll order." She turned toward the kitchen, giddiness rising inside her.

"Kayla?"

She turned back, pasting a bland look on her face. She didn't want Kyle to read too much into her expression. *Oh my.* She marveled at how sexy and at home he looked, casually leaning against her bathroom door, wiping his hands with a towel. But he had a wary look on his face. "Yes?"

"Do you believe in Christmas traditions?"

She shrugged. "I used to. Why?"

At her answer, Kyle's eyes changed from sweet, light cinnamon to a hot, deep chocolate. He stood staring at her like she was one of her goodies, ready to eat. The image more than intrigued her. Her pulse raced, and she self-consciously moistened her lips.

Kyle's gaze dropped to her mouth and her legs almost gave way. He might as well have been kissing her, his stare was that intense. She half-expected him to blurt out some punch line to ease the tension. He didn't.

He set the towel aside and pushed away from the door. A smile tugged at his lips, which only served to increase the sexual energy in the air. He pulled her over to the living room entryway.

"I'm a big believer in traditions." Kyle slid his arms around her waist and tugged her closer.

Awkwardly, she stumbled into him. The feel of his hard body against her soft curves was exquisite. Her fingers curled around his biceps, and she fought a feeling of dizzy delight. Her heart beat so fast she was certain it would explode from her chest.

He purposely looked up, and Kayla followed his gaze. The mistletoe! They were standing right under it.

With a strength she didn't know she possessed, she wrestled her emotions into place. This didn't necessarily mean anything. A hug and a peck on the cheek. He'd done it before—like when she'd landed her job, and on the day she'd moved into the house, and once when she won a big writing contest in college.

Her gaze met his, and all her emotions broke loose. She saw more than friendship in his eyes. Desire shone bright as the morning sun. She couldn't breathe, couldn't move and definitely couldn't speak. If his arms weren't wrapped around her, she'd melt to the floor.

Before she could find her voice, Kyle's lips landed full on hers. Sweet, gentle, tentative. She was so shocked that she stood completely still, forgetting to respond.

Kyle's mouth caressed hers with such tenderness that she wanted to weep.

He lifted his head and chuckled. "Sorry to take you by surprise like that." He raised a hand to caress her cheek with his fingertips. "It's just that I've wanted to kiss you for a long time. And not because it's a Christmas tradition. That was just an excuse to get you in my arms. I hope you don't mind."

Right then, Kayla fell more completely in love with him than she thought possible. After all this time was he finally looking at her as a desirable woman instead of only a good friend?

His words played over in her mind. *I've wanted to kiss you for a long time.* Even though his kiss had been so loving, his words so sweet, doubt still plagued her. He might simply be trying to make her feel better because Christmas was near and she was all alone.

She forced a ragged breath into her lungs. The only way to truly know his intentions for certain was to ask. "Kyle, what—"

"Shh." Once more, his lips descended on hers. This kiss was different from the first. Hot, demanding, passionate.

Kayla responded like a woman in the desert who'd found a well of water. She drank in the kiss, tangling her fingers in Kyle's hair to hold him close. Their tongues entwined, shooting her passion to a level she'd rarely experienced.

Everything around her faded except the feelings of love and desire coursing through her. Nothing existed in her world at the moment but Kyle. She wanted to stay locked in his embrace forever.

A loud ding in the distance foggily penetrated her brain. She raged against the interruption. Kyle's lips on hers, his hands moving slowly along her spine, felt too good to allow any distractions. She didn't want to let him go.

With a groan of reluctance, he broke the kiss. His breath fanned her hair, and his lips grazed her ear, causing a shiver of delight to race down her body. "You better see to those cookies before they burn."

Kayla nodded. "All...all right." On shaky legs, she pulled away from him. "I won't be long." She turned toward the kitchen and the excitement inside her ran amok at this new turn in their relationship.

She'd felt the desire in his kiss. But desire wasn't love. Her step faltered. She wouldn't accept anything less than love from Kyle. It would hurt too much. She'd shatter into a million pieces if she revealed her true feelings to him and he rejected her heart, wanting only something physical. Friends with benefits. She needed more than that.

When she'd started to question him, he'd interrupted her. Now she wondered, should she ask him about the kiss and his feelings for her at all? Or should she just keep her insecurities to herself and see where all this led?

Her decision could affect the course of their entire relationship. She didn't want to ruin what they had as friends, but she also didn't want to pass up the possibility of what they could share as lovers.

Chapter Three

ഉ

Kyle watched Kayla go and ached at the loss. She'd felt so right in his arms. He wanted to hold her close, kiss her lips, her breasts, the soft plane of her stomach, and plunge his tongue into her pussy until she screamed in ecstasy.

When she'd asked him to stay for dinner and a movie, he was too shocked to respond immediately. All the way over to her house he'd been planning to ask her the same thing.

They had a special connection, so he didn't know why the coincidence surprised him. He should be used to it by now. She always seemed to be one step ahead of him.

Being here with her was like being home, but he wasn't sure of Kayla's feelings. She hadn't responded to his first kiss then practically inhaled him with the second.

Confusion filled his mind but not his body. His body ached for more.

Unable to force his thoughts away from being near her, touching her, making love with her, he hesitated only a moment before following her into the kitchen.

He knew he should go slowly, but he'd waited so long. He hoped her feelings matched his. If not, he was about to make a complete fool of himself. "Kayla?"

She held out a cookie but didn't meet his gaze, as if unsure or embarrassed by what had happened under the mistletoe. "Get it while it's hot."

Her hand trembled slightly, and Kyle felt better. She was just as affected by what was happening between them as he was. He took the cookie, his fingers brushing hers. "I'd rather get *you* while *you're* hot," he whispered, watching for her reaction.

Kayla flushed. She turned her back and began re-arranging the cookies on the tray. "You shouldn't talk like that, Kyle, unless you really mean it."

"I really mean it." He set the cookie down and stepped up behind her. "Feel what you do to me." He pulled her back against him, letting her feel his hard cock and giving him another opportunity to touch her.

"Oh!" She gasped.

He closed his eyes, enjoying her softness pressed against him—a perfect fit. She didn't pull away.

Neither did she rub against him.

Hoping to discover her true feelings, he plunged ahead.

With a tinge of humor in his voice, he whispered, "So tell me, little girl...this Christmas, have you been naughty or nice?"

When she didn't answer, he brushed his hands up and down her sides. He felt her tremble at his touch, and a sense of male pride swept through him at being able to affect her like that.

He'd always known a passionate woman lurked beneath Kayla's usually sweet-as-sugar exterior. He'd seen glimpses of it from time to time.

Whenever she spoke of sex, her sensual side emerged. He loved and hated their conversations about relationships. Loved them, because he saw her softness and vulnerability and it made him ache to hold her. Hated them because she spoke of sex with other men, which caused his stomach to tighten painfully.

She had never dated that much—which was fine with him. The few guys she had gone out with were real jerks and didn't treat her like the treasure he knew her to be.

The thought of any other man touching her sent waves of jealousy through him. Never again, if he had any say in the matter. Kayla was *his*.

If she were willing, tonight he'd explore her sensual side, take their relationship to the next level and hopefully seal their future together forever. It was scary as hell, and he'd be taking a big emotional chance, but he knew the time had come. He needed Kayla as much as he needed his next breath...maybe more.

She started to speak and he held his breath in expectation, but then she turned silent. He nuzzled her neck, and her scent wafted over him, making him want her even more. "Which is it, Kayla? Naughty or nice?"

He knew he was taking the risk of a lifetime. She could rebuff him, slap him, even throw him out. But he had to know.

After the kiss, and from his words and intimate touches, she certainly knew now that he wanted her—no question about it. The next step had to be hers.

Kayla turned in his arms. "Why, Kyle?"

Her question took him by surprise, and he stepped back. "Why what?"

"Why are you talking like this, making these moves all of a sudden? You've never done it before, not with me."

His heart sank. The need to know her feelings had been a mistake. He never should have taken the chance. She didn't want him. If she did, she'd be falling into his arms right now instead of questioning him about his words and actions. He'd just embarrassed himself royally by acting like a complete jackass. How was he going to salvage this screw-up?

"I'm sorry, Kayla. I didn't really mean anything by it. I was just, you know, teasing." His heart broke at the lie, and the words left a bitter taste in his mouth. "And that kiss, well..." He shrugged, unable to voice the untruth.

She spun away from him, but not before he saw the sheen of tears in her eyes. He was the lowest of the low! He should have kept his feelings to himself.

At the same time, he condemned himself for being such a coward. If he were any kind of man, he would just own up to his feelings and let whatever happened happen, not try to weasel out of the situation.

But he couldn't bring himself to do that, to force the issue, like he thought he could. Not if it meant possibly losing Kayla. "I offended you. I'm such a jerk! Please forgive me, Kayla."

When she shook her head, panic gripped his heart like a cold fist. He reached out to touch her then decided against it. He couldn't stand it if she pulled away from him.

"Can we just pretend the last few minutes didn't happen? I don't want to lose you, Kayla." His voice broke. "Please. I'll do anything you want, anything you say."

She turned toward him and bit her bottom lip as if trying to make a decision. The tears in her eyes ripped at his soul.

"Do you love me?" she asked.

Shocked by the unexpected question, he hesitated a tense few moments. "Of course I love you. You know that," he finally responded. For a split second, he'd allowed himself to believe she was asking as more than a friend, but only for a split second.

As if she read his mind, she mirrored his thoughts with words. "As a friend. That's not what I meant."

Her hand slid down the front of his pants, and he jerked in response, bumping into the counter behind him. What was she doing? She popped his top button, and his breath caught, his heart hammering in his chest.

"You asked me a question. Naughty?" With a seductive gaze, she pulled down his zipper. "Or nice?" She tugged the zipper back up and sent him an innocent look. "Which would you prefer, Kyle? And I *do* mean something by it. I love you."

She loved him.

He swallowed hard, trying and finally succeeding in finding his voice. "As more than a friend," he forced out, breathing in large gulps of air. It was a statement. He didn't need to ask. He saw the truth reflected in her beautiful brown eyes.

"As more than a friend," she echoed. "I always have."

Her admission floored him. Now he understood. Her tears weren't because he'd offended her but because he'd said he didn't mean his words—which of course was a lie. He'd meant every word. And now Kayla had said she loved him.

This was better than any fantasy he'd ever imagined. Well…he'd imagined some truly heartfelt, not to mention arousing, fantasies with Kayla. But reality was so much better.

Long-ago memories filtered into his thoughts. College memories. Their friends used to tease Kayla about having a crush on him. Had they been right?

He'd thought they had simply picked on Kayla because she was an easy target and never said anything back, but maybe she *had* wanted him even then. The thought thrilled and excited him.

"Are you going to answer me?" she asked, her hand twitching against his crotch.

With a sharp intake of air, he laid his fingers over hers, still holding the zipper, and guided them downward. "I prefer naughty to nice any day."

When her hand slipped inside to touch his cock, he groaned. "Oh, yeah. Naughty is definitely better."

Kayla curled her fingers around his shaft. "You fit my fingers perfectly, Kyle," she whispered, her gaze locking with his. She eased up on her toes and flicked her tongue across his bottom lip. With a sexy smile tugging at her lips, she stroked his hot flesh, eliciting another groan from him.

Her words and the sound of his name spoken in her breathy whisper almost sent him over the edge. Apparently, baking wasn't the only area where she was skilled with "finger magic". It took him several moments before he was able to speak.

"This is one heck of a Christmas present, Kayla," he answered, his voice harsh with passion.

Kayla pulled her hand out and zipped his pants.

Disappointment flooded through him. Had he said something wrong?

What an idiot! Of course, he had. He should have been more sensitive and romantic. This was new territory for both of them. Not a quick liaison, but something much more powerful. She didn't look mad though...just hesitant, as if she wanted to say something.

"You haven't seen my bedroom since I redecorated, have you?" she finally asked. "I bought a queen-sized, four-poster bed. And I picked up two sets of silk sheets, one in red and one in green."

"Red and green?" Her color choices surprised him. Maybe she actually *was* softening to the holidays.

A blush stained Kayla's cheeks, and she wouldn't meet his gaze. "They were on sale."

He grinned at her embarrassment, until his thoughts refocused on the silk sheets. His pulse picked up its rhythm at the implication. "No, I haven't seen the new stuff yet." But he wanted to.

Her bedroom. Her bed. Her naked on her bed. Him naked on top of her. Inside her. Thrusting hard, fast and as deep as he could get.

His groin tightened painfully as the image flashed before his eyes, and his chest suddenly felt so tight he could hardly breathe.

Kayla took his hand and led him toward her room. She walked slowly and again seemed hesitant. Maybe she was as terrified as he was. This was a big step forward in their relationship. He wanted everything to be perfect for her and for her to have no regrets.

His body was on fire. He ached to fuck her, love her, but he had to give her the chance to change her mind. "Kayla, we don't have to...to...well, you know, if you'd rather not. We can go slower."

At his words, she immediately turned and he saw the hurt in her eyes. The last thing he ever wanted to see was Kayla hurting.

"You don't want to?" she asked in a barely discernible whisper.

With all the tenderness he possessed, he wrapped his arms around her. "Oh, yeah, baby. I want to. The thought of being inside you..." He took a deep breath and shook his head. "There are no words to tell you how that makes me feel." He pulled her close and kissed her long and deep. His hands skimmed the bare skin of her back where her sweater met her pants. She felt soft and warm, causing a need in him so strong that he was awed by its intensity. When he pulled away, they were both breathless.

"Let's not waste any more time, Kyle. I want your cock inside me."

He practically choked at her explicit words. *Oh yeah, baby.*

She led him down the hall and into her room.

Chapter Four

❧

Kayla stood just inside the bedroom door as Kyle studied the re-design. She couldn't tell from the look on his face whether he liked the new room or not. "What do you think?"

"Festive."

"You don't like it?" She pouted. Okay, maybe she had gone overboard with the green and red colors, but not that much. The bed was turned down, revealing the red sheets, which screamed sexy in her opinion. The spread and pillow cases were emerald green. A poinsettia sat on her dresser, and a Christmas decorator rug, with a smiling snowman in the middle, lay in a semi-circle at the foot of the bed.

"No, I do like it."

"You're not just teasing me?" His feelings mattered to her. Though, even if he didn't like the design, she did. More than she thought she would, considering the holiday theme.

"I'm not teasing at all." He turned and pulled her into his arms. "I like the homey, warm feeling of the room now."

"Meaning it was cold before?"

A small smile tugged at his lips. "Are you stalling, Kayla?"

"Yes." She cleared her throat. "I am. Sorry. I'm a little nervous all of a sudden, I guess. I want everything to be perfect."

"Me too."

"Really?"

"Really. I don't want to disappoint you."

"You could never disappoint me, Kyle." She toyed with the front of his sweater. "Um, just so you know. I've never slept with anyone in that bed. You'll be the first."

"Good. I like that. I just wish…"

When he didn't finish, she wondered at his thoughts. "Wish? What?" He looked almost sad.

"I wish that I could have been your first, your only lover." His brow furrowed. "I don't like thinking of you with other men. Them touching you. You touching them."

"Then don't." She smoothed the lines on his forehead with her fingertips. "There's no one in my life but you. No one in my heart but you." And it felt so good to finally be able to say those words aloud to him.

Kyle's lips descended to hers, the kiss soft and gentle. He nibbled lightly on her bottom lip.

Before things got too heated and he drove her completely wild by deepening the kiss, she pulled back. She wanted to change and prepare herself for him.

"Is something wrong?" he asked, a wary look on his face.

"No. I'd just like to freshen up. Do you mind?"

"Oh." He dropped his arms from her waist. "No, of course not. Go ahead."

"I won't be long." After a quick kiss to his cheek, she turned and grabbed a few items from her dresser drawer then disappeared into the bathroom. This would be one night she knew she'd never forget.

Kyle pulled his sweater over his head and tugged off his shoes and socks. He kept his T-shirt and pants on, not wanting to shock Kayla too much when she returned. Not until he figured out exactly how tonight was going to progress. He wasn't certain how quickly she wanted to move. If she came out and spotted him fully naked *and* fully aroused, she might run the other way. Though, hopefully, she'd jump him instead.

He strolled over to one of her bookcases. She loved to read more than anyone he'd ever known. She'd even gotten him interested in some mysteries lately, and he'd never been much on reading for pleasure.

Scanning her shelves, a line of books caught his attention. One full shelf held some trade paperbacks from the same publisher—he could tell by the consistent, though colorful, look of them. The books were written by all sorts of different authors. He found that strange, since Kayla usually stuck to her same few favorite writers, as far as he knew. He pulled out a book, and his jaw dropped open. He flipped the book over to read the blurb on the back. "Damn." After a shocked moment, he slid that book back in its slot and pulled out another. By the time he got to the fourth book, he began to notice a theme. "And I thought I knew everything about you, Kayla."

A smile spread across his face, as he glanced toward the bathroom. "You want an erotic hero, sweetheart? I can deliver." Based on her reading material, he knew exactly how to go about it too. Well, at least, he hoped he did.

He walked over to her dresser and opened a couple of drawers. He wasn't snooping, just looking for something specific. "Ah, perfect." He grabbed his find and stuck it in his back pocket the best he could. He'd often pictured such graphic sexual images in his head, but he never thought Kayla would share his interest.

The bathroom door clicked open, and he turned abruptly, his heart pounding in anticipation. Kayla slowly stepped out. She wore a panty and bra of white silk. And nothing else. Such a beautiful vision. His dick hardened painfully.

"I hope I didn't take too long." She smiled sexily.

"You're worth the wait." Unable to take his eyes off her, he strolled across the room and circled behind her. His pulse raced, and his hands shook from the desire to touch her. "I need to ask you something, Kayla."

"What?"

His fingers stroked her hair. So silky. "What do you want tonight?"

She leaned into his touch. "What do you mean?"

Needing to say things just right, he spoke the words slowly. "Do you want soft and romantic?" His voice lowered, deepened, and his tongue traced the rim of her ear. "Or passionate and wild?"

Kayla's limbs trembled as Kyle swiped her hair aside and kissed her neck. She felt that kiss all the way down to her toes. "Mmm." She'd wanted this for so long. Wanted him for so long. "Passionate and wild." She didn't even need to think about her answer. Her desire ran so deep she felt almost desperate for him.

His fingers fluttered down her arms, causing goose bumps on her skin. He tugged her hands behind her and wrapped something soft around her wrists. Her breath caught, and she tried to pull away. "Kyle, what are you doing?" She'd said she wanted wild but hadn't expected him to restrain her.

"Relax."

When he'd approached her about his feelings, was this his plan all along? Some sort of sexual bondage. People just didn't walk around with bindings. She pulled at the tie to check how tightly he'd secured her. Not bad. She had some give. Again, she tried to turn toward him.

"No. Stand still." He touched her waist. "You trust me, right?"

That one question relaxed her. She was with Kyle. She trusted him with her life, her soul and now with her heart and body too. "Yes, I trust you completely." He'd bound her hands with what felt like a stocking. One of hers? She glanced toward the dresser and noticed the drawer open a crack. She hadn't expected this from him. He'd never said anything about these kinds of desires. But then neither had she. She'd fantasized about him doing something like this to her, but broaching the subject aloud would have been hard for her to do — at least this early in their new, sexual relationship. How had he known her deepest needs? A coincidence?

He stepped in front of her and raised her chin with his finger. His eyes burned intently into hers. "Tonight, your body is mine. You will do what I ask. Understand?"

The best she managed was a nod. Every nerve ending in her body screamed out for him to touch her intimately. To control. To demand and take what he needed, giving her what she needed in return. And then, she might even reverse the situation and demand control of *his* body. But for now, she was perfectly content to allow him the lead.

"I'm yours," she forced out. "To do with what you want." Her voice sounded scratchy and needy, even to her own ears.

He leaned in and kissed her neck again, letting his tongue softly touch her skin. She moaned lightly. It hadn't taken him long to find one of her more sensitive areas.

"Get up on the bed on your knees and face me," he whispered in her ear.

She swallowed hard but complied, only realizing when she started to walk just how rubbery her legs had turned. She climbed up on the bed and shifted to face him on her knees.

He'd popped the top button on his jeans, and the bulge between his legs immediately caught her attention. She tugged at the tie around her wrists. "I want to touch you, Kyle."

"Good. I want you to. Soon." Slowly, he approached her. "You make my dick ache, Kayla. I'm going to fuck you so long and hard tonight, and make you come so many times, you'll never think of another man for the rest of your life."

She almost laughed, thinking that one of his jokes, until she saw how serious he was. Of all the things she thought he might say sexually, that was not on her list. She'd never heard him sound so masterful. She chewed at her bottom lip, wondering what else tonight would reveal about this man she thought she knew so well.

"Did I scare you with what I just said?"

She swallowed hard. "Should I be scared?"

He laced his fingers through her hair and whispered in her ear. "Maybe a little."

Not expecting that response, she gulped and her pulse jumped. His words and actions thrilled her, giving their encounter a more dangerous-feeling edge than she'd expected.

When he stepped back, the look on his face turned primal, almost savage in the reflection of his sexual need. He pulled off his T-shirt and let it drift to the floor. His gaze, obscured for only a moment, immediately returned to her face and intensified.

"If you don't want this, Kayla, say so now, before we're beyond the point of me being able to stop."

She wanted this. Wanted him. So much. "Take me any way you want, Kyle. As often as you want. I need you."

A smile tugged at his lips.

While he stood before her, so commanding, her eyes devoured him. His chest was extremely well-defined. The sprinkling of dark hair across his muscles looked oh-so masculine. The line of hair that led beneath his pants looked even more tantalizing. She'd love to follow that line with her tongue all the way down to his cock and inhale him until he shouted her name and came down her throat.

"You understand that continuing means you submit completely to me?" He brushed her breasts with his fingers, causing her nipples to press hard against her bra.

"Yes." She closed her eyes, enjoying his touch. "I'll submit."

"Open your eyes. Now. I want you to see everything I do to you."

At his order, her eyes popped open. When he mouthed "Good girl" her pussy grew wet and achy. She thought she should say something to him, but she couldn't find her voice.

This was not the easy-going, well-humored man she knew. This was a man on the edge, a man who knew what he wanted sexually and intended to take it, if she permitted.

He unhooked the front of her strapless bra. The back of his fingers brushed her skin, causing a shudder to rush down her body. He pulled his hand back, and the bra fell to the mattress. She heard him take in a ragged breath and knew that he was just as turned on as she was. *Good.* That made her feel more at ease.

"Kayla," he whispered, his voice raspy. His hands rose to caress her bare breasts. He squeezed her mounds, brushing his thumbs across the nipples. "Nice. Plump." He pinched the firm buds lightly. His gaze shifted and, staring deeply into her eyes, he pinched harder.

"Oh!" The thrill raced straight down to her pussy.

Unexpectedly, he grabbed her around the waist, turned her around and forced her down onto her stomach.

"Kyle!" He hadn't hurt her but surprised her so much that her heart pounded a staccato rhythm against her ribs.

He hooked his thumbs into her panties and pulled them off in one quick jerk.

At his move, she gasped. He crawled up on the bed next to her, on his knees. Because her hands were tied behind her, and Kyle's hand now rested on her upper back, she couldn't move. He lightly caressed her ass.

"You're perfect, Kayla. The definition of sexy." He leaned down and whispered in her ear. "I discovered your erotic reading material." His tongue touched her skin.

Her stomach fluttered. She didn't have to wonder what he thought. His actions told the story. Not that she was complaining. Now she knew why he'd asked her the question earlier about what she wanted and if she was certain about submitting.

"Do you want a fucking like in those books?" His fingers squeezed one butt cheek.

"Um, y-yes," she breathed heavily, barely getting out the words. "Please."

"Good. Because that's what I intend to give you. Keep your head down on the mattress." He pulled her to her knees so only her back end was lifted, and crawled behind her, between her legs. His fingers grazed her pussy. "So beautiful and soaking wet. Wet for me. Eager for my cock. Say it. Say you want my cock."

"I want your cock, Kyle." She swallowed the lump in her throat. Her whole body hummed in need and anticipation. When Kyle fell silent, saying nothing more, she began to tremble. She could feel his eyes on her, watching her, calculating his next move. "Kyle?"

Chapter Five

ဩ

Kyle's fingers brushed against her bottom. "I'm going to spank you, Kayla." The words rumbled deeply from his throat, his voice sounding scratchy.

"Spank?" She trembled and hesitated a moment before saying more. She couldn't help but wonder if he often spanked women during sex, or if he'd maybe gotten the idea from her books. "O-okay." She'd never been spanked by a man but had always wanted to try it since college, when she'd overheard two girls in her dorm giggling about their experiences.

"Don't tighten up, just stay relaxed."

Sounded to her like he had experience with this. At least he'd know how to do it more effectively, she hoped. She relaxed as best as she could.

His hand slapped her ass.

The sharp sound sliced through her, and her pussy clenched. *Oh my!* The feeling was more intense than she'd expected.

His fingers fluttered across her skin. "More?"

"Um, yes, please," she breathed heavily, wanting to repeat the feeling, to see if it was normal or a one-time fluke.

Caressing her skin, he shifted on the mattress, moving to a different angle. "You needed a man to treat you like this sexually, didn't you?" He smacked her ass again, a little harder.

"Yes!" With any other man, she'd never allow such actions. "I've craved it for so long but never trusted any man enough, until you. Again." The vibration of his slaps warmed her whole body. "Spank me again."

"Kayla," he choked out and smacked her ass again. "You're so hot."

She moaned. "Don't stop, Kyle. Harder." She wanted more intensity. She needed that rush of erotic feeling through her body.

His barely audible groan caressed her senses. "I'll give you all you need." His hand landed on her ass repeatedly now, harder and faster.

"Ah, ah, ah." With each smack, her pleasure grew. "That makes my clit ache, Kyle."

"Damn. You're driving me crazy." He landed a few more sharp slaps then massaged her cheeks. "Pretty pink butt. Let's see how wet that made you, baby."

Very wet. She felt his tongue on her inner thigh. Her muscles jumped at the moist contact, and she almost came right then.

"Tell me what you want," he demanded, his fingers brushing her intimately.

The spanking, along with his no-nonsense tone, made her pussy drip. "I want you, Kyle."

"No. Tell me what to do with my tongue. I want to hear you say the words."

"I, um, want you to lick me." Like he didn't know. But saying the words aloud upped the intensity level. She realized he understood that and intended to push her to her limits tonight.

"Where should I lick you, Kayla?"

Her desire grew, and frustration rolled through her. She needed to be sexually sated. But Kyle seemed determined to torture her, build her tension, her carnal urges, until she begged for release. And he was doing a good job of it too. "Lick me between my legs." *Now.* She loved a man's tongue lapping at her pussy, especially a man who enjoyed pleasing a woman orally.

"More specific, Kayla. Where between your legs?" His tongue touched her inner thigh, halfway to her knee. "Here?" He moved to the other thigh, a little higher and licked her skin. "Or maybe here?"

Needing his tongue inside her, she whimpered. "Lick my pussy. You know that's what I want."

He slapped her ass. "Nastier! Say it. Say it now." Again, he smacked the same cheek, the sound almost as sharp as his voice.

Her clit throbbed so painfully that she couldn't think straight. "Tongue-fuck my cunt!" she practically yelled, feeling ready to topple over the edge. She sucked in a labored breath. "I can't believe I said that," she whispered.

He chuckled. "Such language."

She raised her head. "You're the one who wanted me—"

"Quiet." He smacked her butt again—the same cheek as before.

"Ouch, enough. That's starting to sting."

"Then do as I say, Kayla. Now head down. Submit." Their gazes locked, and when she made no move to do so, he arched an eyebrow. "No?" Without breaking eye contact, he spread her butt cheeks.

"Um, w-what are you doing?" She wiggled her hips. Never had he acted so demanding with her. She knew he'd completely change if she protested, but she had no desire to protest...yet, for she actually liked this more controlling side of him. His forceful manner intrigued her. As long as he kept it in the bedroom.

"Put your head down, like I told you. Except instead of licking your pussy, now I'm going to finger-fuck your ass. You *will* learn to submit to me." He sucked two fingers into his mouth.

She trembled. He had great hands with long, strong fingers. Still, she didn't lower her head. Closing her eyes, she inhaled a large breath, letting it out slowly, wondering what he'd do to her for not complying. While her eyes were closed, she felt something wet drip into her hole and decided it best not to think where the moisture came from. When his finger circled the opening, her eyes snapped back open and locked with his.

"When you don't submit," he pushed his finger deep, "you bear the consequences."

"Oh!"

While holding her stare, he pumped his finger back and forth. "Like that?" He stroked faster. "Do you like that?" he demanded.

"Yes." When he pushed deeper, she gasped and hung her head.

"Hey, baby, you started this. Look at me! Or another finger goes in."

She didn't look at him.

"Your decision." He worked another finger inside her ass, fucking her hard.

She moaned at the total control he took and the pleasure he gave. When she felt him try to work in a third finger, she whimpered. No way could she take three.

"Relax. Help me get it in." He stretched her with the two fingers already inside her, until she was able to take a third. "Oh, yeah. You like it up the ass, don't you?" He pumped his fingers fast, hard and deep. "Put your head down, baby. I'll make you scream."

She breathed heavily. "Yes, Kyle," she whispered, lowering her head. *Submitting.* She felt helpless, unable to do anything else. Not wanting to do anything else.

His fingers fucked her ass with more power than she'd ever expected or experienced before. She couldn't stop moaning. She felt his hair brush along her thighs then his tongue lapped at her pussy, stroking her wet folds. He sucked her clit into his mouth and drew gently on the bundle of nerves.

"Ahhh!" She screamed. He'd gotten her so hot and worked up from his words and actions that she came hard. Spasms gripped her body. Only Kyle's tight hold on her hip kept her in position. "Kyle!" Too explosive. She couldn't breathe, but she never wanted it to end. If he could make her climax like this, she'd allow him to do anything he wanted to her body. Anything. "Oh, yes!"

He showed her no mercy. He continued licking her and pumping her ass with his fingers as she screamed again and again, until her body was spent and the pleasure finally ebbed. She collapsed on the mattress.

* * * * *

After Kyle cleaned himself up, he sat on the edge of the bed and stroked Kayla's body. Holding a warm, moist washcloth he'd brought from the bathroom, he gently wiped the cloth along her thighs and between her legs, cleaning and soothing her skin. Breathing heavily, her hips jerked slightly at the contact.

Kyle's cock throbbed. He needed to be naked, to be inside her. Having Kayla under his control sexually, making her come multiple times, was such a rush. She was sin in the flesh and possessed an adventurous side he'd never suspected.

He discarded the washcloth then leaned down and licked her ear and neck. "I love it when you scream my name in ecstasy." And hearing her speak so explicitly was a major turn-on for him. He hadn't really thought she'd do it or allow him to spank her so hard before finally saying enough. And the way she'd responded to being ass-fucked provided a new set of erotic images in his head.

She remained motionless on the bed, continuing to breathe heavily. He untied the stocking and rolled her over. She still didn't move much, and her eyes held a glassy look.

Being able to do that to her made him feel powerful, sexually and emotionally. He positioned her the way he wanted on the bed. He tied both her wrists to the headboard, making sure her arms rested comfortably on the pillows. "Ready for more?"

She opened her mouth, but only a small squeak came out.

Macho stud alert, he thought with a smile. He'd worn her out. Well, she hadn't experienced anything yet. "Just lie there and let me fuck you until you come again." His hands glided over her stomach and hips, caressing her silky skin. Now that they'd gone this far, he considered her as his in every way, for the rest of their lives. He'd fight for the right to keep her with him against anyone or anything that threatened to tear them apart. He couldn't wait any longer. He shoved his pants down and kicked them off. His eyes locked on Kayla's, but she didn't meet his gaze. She was staring at his cock.

He lowered his hand and slowly began stroking himself. Her eyes widened. She glanced up at him, flushed then looked back down at his cock as he fisted himself faster. But his hand wasn't going to finish this job, not while Kayla lay there tied to the bed, with her mouth, pussy and asshole available. "Condoms?"

"Um, in the drawer."

"Lube?"

"Lube?" Her wide-eyed stare flew to his, and she looked more than a little wary. "I think there's a tube in the drawer too. Why?"

"I'm not finished with your ass yet, Kayla. I intend to stick my cock in that tight hole tonight. And my cock's going to feel so much better than my fingers, believe me. But I'm thick, really thick, as you can see for yourself, and I don't want to hurt you." He slowed the rhythm of his hand.

"I...I've never allowed a man to do that with his cock."

Never? His heart stammered. *Damn.* Now he really couldn't wait to push his cock up that hole of hers. "Oh, that's perfect, baby. My dick will break you in so much better than anyone's fingers. I love coming up a woman's asshole. And knowing my cock is the only one ever to penetrate you there is so hot. It's going to be an incredible experience."

"For you."

"And for you. You'll see. If you can take three of my fingers, I won't hurt you as long as you're wet enough."

She didn't pause in her response, and a smile actually tugged at her lips. "Okay. I trust you."

"Good." Her trust meant everything. He wouldn't disappoint her. "I want you to lick my cock and balls then suck my dick like it's your last meal. Make me crazy, Kayla, and I'll make it more than worth your while." He got up on the bed and straddled her chest.

Kayla wasn't sure if she'd survive this night. Her heart pounded so hard, and her adrenaline ran so strongly, that she might never come down off the high. Kyle's cock brushed against her lips. She breathed deeply, inhaling the scent of him. His purplish-red member was longer than she'd expected and much thicker than any man she'd ever been with. He knew just what he wanted sexually and what he was capable of giving in return. No wonder women always whispered about him and panted after him. Her tongue eased out and licked the wide tip, drawing his musky taste into her mouth.

"Nice. Lick it again."

She licked the tip thoroughly, swirling her tongue around him and lapping at the clear liquid. Decadent. She felt like some captured sex slave tonight, doing the bidding of her Master.

"Ah, so fucking good." He moved forward, giving her access to his balls. "Suck 'em. Easy."

Lightly, she sucked on his sac. She felt his body tremble and flicked her tongue over his flesh.

"Oh, Kayla. That's great, baby! Let me feel your tongue again. Oh, yeah. One more time. Ah! Okay, stop for now. Or I'll end up coming all over your face."

She didn't care. She just wanted to see him come. But he kept control, not giving in to the desire she clearly saw on his face.

He repositioned himself and she slid her tongue along the underside of his cock. Almost before she realized, the head of his cock was between her lips, and Kyle pushed inside. She took everything he gave her, enjoying the look of near pain in his eyes.

Slowly, he fucked her mouth, moving his hips back and forth in a gentle rhythm. "Yeah, Kayla. Eat my fat dick. Suck it good, baby. Look into my eyes. That's right. Ah! The sight of my cock sliding past your lips, with you tied to the bed and looking up at me, is so damn erotic."

Kayla's fingers curled against her palms. She wanted to touch him so badly. She also wanted his cum in her mouth. She sucked harder. When he eased back then pulled completely out of her, she whimpered. She tried to reach him with her tongue, but he inched away.

He fumbled with the condom box, finally yanking it out of the drawer. He grabbed a packet from inside. She watched him tear open the square and roll on the protection. Her heart lurched. The time had come. In another moment, Kyle's cock would be inside her pussy.

He grabbed her legs and draped them over his forearms. "If you only knew how many times I've fantasized about fucking you."

Really? She hated to think about all the years they'd missed out on by not admitting their attraction to each other.

Holding onto her hips, he thrust into her in one powerful surge.

"Oh!" He filled every inch of her pussy and stretched her muscles for more.

"Damn, Kayla. Your cunt feels incredible wrapped around my cock."

He labored for control. She saw the effort on his face. She'd already come. She wanted him to experience a release too. "Come, Kyle," she encouraged, lifting her hips.

"No." He groaned. "Not yet." He centered himself with a large breath then began fucking her fast, pumping his hips against her almost savagely. "Deeper," he growled. "I need to get deeper."

Pleasure rippled through Kayla. No man had ever fucked her like this, so forcefully, so thoroughly. "Yes, Kyle!" A strong orgasm exploded inside her. "Oh!" Her back arched and she screamed.

Kyle continued thrusting into her. "Beautiful, Kayla. You're so beautiful. Keep coming!"

"Yes! Yes!" She shook, unable to control her actions, until she finally collapsed on the mattress.

Kyle stopped. He tugged her bindings loose and began to pull out of her.

"No, wait. You didn't come." Her voice came out slurred. She sounded exhausted, even to herself. She tried to wrap her legs around him, but he pushed her thighs aside.

"Shh. I want to come up your ass, Kayla. Roll over for me." He urged her onto her stomach.

As she turned over, her stomach fluttered in anticipation.

His fingers massaged her cheeks. "I hurt so badly for you, Kayla. I want to shove my dick up this sexy hole and fuck you like a wild man until I explode. But I need you to enjoy it. Beg me for it, Kayla. Beg me to butt-fuck you with my cock."

She heard him rattle the box for another condom. She didn't think she could move, much less talk. All the muscles in her body felt completely relaxed and totally useless.

He used a tube of lube from the drawer to prepare her asshole, and she presumed his cock too. Although she couldn't see behind her. He spread her cheeks and circled the hole with his finger, which felt like it was also covered by a condom this time.

"Time to completely de-flower this hole, baby." He dipped his finger just beyond the rim. "Let me do it."

She sighed, wanting to experience it all. "Yes. Do it, Kyle." She forced her voice out louder, so he'd know this was indeed her decision, and she wasn't simply trying to please him. "Fuck me with your cock."

"Yeah, baby. You're going to love this." Slowly, he eased his finger deeper inside.

Tensing slightly, she sucked in a deep breath. *Only his finger.* She wanted his cock. Kyle hesitated until she relaxed. With another finger, he penetrated her pussy, stimulating her in both places. "Oh, nice, Kyle."

"Ever have any fantasies of getting double fucked?" he asked.

"Yes," she answered, before she could stop herself.

For a moment, he didn't respond. "By two men or by one man and one woman?"

She smiled slightly, deciding to play with him a bit. "What about two women?"

A groan rumbled from his throat. "Don't put that image in my head. I'll come before I'm ready." His fingers moved faster, thrusting back and forth. He leaned down and licked one butt cheek. "I'd love to see two women going at you, Kayla, holding you down and licking your cunt and tits. Fuck, that would be hot. But no other man will ever touch you." When she moaned, he pulled his fingers out and shoved a pillow beneath her hips. He spread her ass and pushed the head of his cock against her hole, but he didn't penetrate. "Beg me!"

He sounded so desperate that she couldn't refuse, not that she wanted or planned to. "Fuck my ass, Kyle. Please. I need your cock inside me. Now."

"Yeah!" He pushed forward, and the head of his cock popped into her. "Ah, man!"

"Oh!" So thick. His shaft slid further inside, and she gasped. Really thick.

He moved his hips slowly and gently. "Am I hurting you?"

"No," she whispered in a breathy voice. She just felt full, stretched to her limit.

He moved a little faster, using short strokes. He leaned over her. "I'll never forget this night, Kayla. The first of many more."

She nodded. "Many more. Yes."

Fucking her a little harder now, he reached beneath her and pinched her nipples.

Kayla's muscles clenched.

"Ah! Damn. Your ass just squeezed my dick like a vise. I'm beginning to think you like it rough, baby. Let's see if you do." He pinched her nipples again, harder.

"Kyle!" An orgasm rolled through her. She jerked her hips, forcing his cock deeper up her ass.

"Oh, fuck!" His body stiffened, and he came hard, shouting her name over and over.

Chapter Six

እ

Kyle stretched and yawned. The early morning light filtered in through the window. He reached for Kayla, but she wasn't beside him. He sat up and raked a hand through his hair. The bathroom door stood cracked open and the room appeared empty. He frowned and looked at the clock. Barely seven o'clock.

He wondered if Kayla regretted them being together last night and that's why she wasn't still lying next to him. Maybe he should have made love to her gently and slowly, shown her just how much she meant to him. But he'd given her the choice, and she'd picked wild and passionate. He smiled. They'd gotten wild all right. "What a night."

Tossing back the covers, he decided to take a quick shower then look for Kayla. They still needed to decorate that tree. And he was starved. He needed a good breakfast.

He glanced down at his cock and laughed. "What the hell…" A red, fabric ribbon was laced around the length of his shaft. He tugged on the end, but that just pulled it tighter.

"Need help unwrapping that?" Kayla asked from the doorway.

His eyes snapped up and he immediately felt his cock stir. She stood there completely naked. "Morning, gorgeous. You often walk around naked in the middle of winter?"

"I turned up the heat." She stepped forward. "Besides, I'm not completely naked."

When she moved in front of him, he noticed pink icing around her nipples. "Mmm. Looks delicious. Are those for me?"

She nodded.

He sat on the side of the bed and pulled her between his legs. His tongue swirled around one nipple. "Sweet." He squeezed her breast and licked off the rest of the icing then sucked the nipple into his mouth. A taste of vanilla filled his senses. He could suck her tits and bite the fleshy nipples all day.

When his teeth scraped her, she moaned.

He bit down slowly.

"Yes…" Her fingers tightened in his hair, and she arched into him.

Oh, yeah, she likes this as much as I do. He massaged her ass and bit her nipple a little harder. She tensed, and he flicked his tongue over the hard bud to soothe her flesh. Delicious. He pulled back. "Is your butt sore?"

"Some."

He frowned, though he couldn't say he was surprised. He'd put her ass through quite a bit. "Sorry."

"That's all right. I enjoyed it." She leaned over and whispered in his ear. "And, yes, I do like it rough."

His pulse jumped at her words, which echoed the thoughts he'd voiced aloud last night. *How rough?* He wondered but didn't ask. He already knew she liked having her ass spanked and fucked hard, liked her nipples bitten and pinched and enjoyed being restrained. His cock ached at the memory of all they'd done together. He looked forward to more. He also looked forward to making sure she understood just how much he cared. This was about so much more than sex.

He licked the icing off her other breast, lapping repeatedly at the nipple.

Pulling away, she sank to her knees in front of him. "I see your cock is awake and ready to be serviced." She kissed the tip.

"Paying proper respect. I like that."

She pointed a finger at him. "Don't get into this control thing too much, mister."

He chuckled. "You love it, and you know it. Now, are you down there to do some good or are you just teasing me?"

"Definitely not teasing. I want to taste your cum, Kyle. I haven't gotten the chance yet." She tugged at the ribbon but didn't remove it. She secured the fabric out of the way, around the base of his cock, which had now grown rock hard. Her hands massaged him eagerly.

"I have no problem with that." He laced his fingers through her hair. "I'd love to come in your mouth. Will you swallow?"

"Every drop. I promise." She leaned down and flicked her tongue over the head of his cock. Her tongue licked at the slit then glided down along the underside of his shaft.

The erotic sight and feel made Kyle's heart pound. She was phenomenal. When her lips sank over him, he groaned. She bobbed her head up and down, taking him deep then pulling back to just around the tip of his cock. It surprised him how much she was able to take into her throat. His fingers tightened in her hair. "Suck it hard! Yeah, like that." She took direction quickly and without protest. He loved that.

He felt his body tightening and tried to delay the climax by thinking of something else. It didn't work.

Ready to come, even after such a short while, he thrust his hips forward. He groaned as the climax overtook him. "I'm holding you to your promise, Kayla. Ah! You miss even one drop and I'll punish you good." As soon as he said that, several drops trickled down her chin. "Damn it, Kayla. You did that on purpose, didn't you? Now suck and swallow!"

She glanced up at him, and he saw humor in her eyes. Okay, she wanted punishment, she was going to get it.

Just thinking of punishing her made him come even harder. "Oh, yeah!" He didn't think he'd ever stop spewing down her throat. Except for those few drops, she took it all. Finally, he fell back on the bed, totally spent.

Kayla crawled up beside him. He looked to be asleep. Good. She scooted off the bed, wanting to take the time to freshen up in the bathroom. She'd never made a man come like that. It was great.

When she returned, she stretched out beside him again. He'd be leaving for Texas soon. Would he still want to be with her after he returned? She didn't like that he was leaving so soon after they'd started a sexual relationship. Her fingers fluttered down to his groin, and she pulled the ribbon loose. She smiled, remembering how long and hard he'd come in her mouth.

Suddenly, he grabbed her and tossed her onto her back. She screeched. "You fiend! I thought you were asleep."

"I was. I think. Or maybe I just passed out. Wow. That was great. I've never come that long before, Kayla." He lightly kissed her lips, but then his brow furrowed. "Except..."

She frowned. "Except?"

"There's that little matter of your punishment."

"Oh." She chuckled and felt her face flush. "I know you were just kidding about that. You don't have to feel funny about saying it. I understand what you were doing. How about I fix you something to eat, then we decorate the tree? I think I'm actually in the mood. Believe it or not."

"I wasn't kidding, Kayla." His face turned serious. "I *will* punish you."

Her stomach clenched, and she felt her pussy grow moist. Her mouth opened but nothing came out. She'd hoped but hadn't actually believed...

He held her arms securely against the mattress. "Your ass is too tender to take any more right now. But your nipples could probably take a little torture. And I imagine your clit could use some roughing up too."

"Um…"

"I'm not asking, Kayla. It's going to happen."

Her heart lurched then pounded hard against her ribs. She trusted him to not really hurt her. But now that she'd told him she liked it rough, he might get the wrong idea and try to go too far. Rough was a relative term, after all, and as it was, she'd allowed him more control than any other man. Not that she hadn't enjoyed it. She had. Tremendously.

His eyes burned into her, and she trembled in anticipation, wondering if she should say something or just wait and see what happened. She decided she couldn't stay completely quiet. "Wh-what are you going to do to me?" If she knew, she could relax. Maybe.

"I'm going to make you scream, then make you beg for mercy."

She gulped. "Kyle…"

He leaned down to whisper in her ear. "I won't hurt you. Well…not much anyway." He chuckled.

She'd exhaled the tight breath she was holding, until those last four words. Now her nerves kicked back into high gear.

"Relax. You look like a deer caught in headlights." Kyle licked one of her nipples. He kept his hands wrapped tightly over her arms, holding her down. His tongue circled her areola.

Her breathing turned shallow as she waited for whatever punishment he had in mind. She'd never, in her wildest fantasies, imagined he'd share her interest in sexual kink. Well, maybe she'd imagined it. She'd just never allowed herself to truly think he might engage in it with her.

"While looking at your books, I came across something interesting."

"What?" Those books contained all sorts of interesting tidbits. He'd certainly have a lot to choose from.

"A stiff, leather-looking bookmark, with one end shaped something like an arrow and pouched out a little."

Her brow furrowed and then she nodded. She remembered. A promotional item from some contest she'd won. She didn't think it was leather though. It looked like it but felt more like some sort of vinyl to her. Besides, she'd just recently dropped it in some hot water by accident, and it had dried off nice and easy. No damage. The bookmark proved too bulky to put between pages. Even so, she'd kept it as part of her collection. Why would he be interested in that?

Pushing up from the bed, he retrieved the item from her bookcase. When he turned back toward her, he slapped the thicker end of it repeatedly against his palm. "An interesting tool with all sorts of uses, don't you think?"

Tool?

"Spread your legs, Kayla."

"W-why?" She cleared her throat, hating her nervous stutter. It's not like he could fuck her with it. Even though it had some bulk to it, the bookmark was still way too thin.

"Did you hear me?" His eyebrow arched. "I told you to spread your legs. If you don't do it, I'll tie them open."

Oh, goodness. She about swooned at the thought. Did she dare allow herself the vulnerability? "Okay, Kyle. Tie them," she whispered.

His eyes widened and then his jaw tightened. "Fuck," he ground out under his breath. He stalked over to her closet and removed several long scarves that hung on the other side of the door. With a searing look in her direction, he returned to the bed.

"Remember, you asked for this." He wrapped one scarf around her knee, pulled her leg wide with her knee bent and tied the scarf onto the bed frame. Then he did the same thing with her other knee. Then he wrapped her wrists and tied them to the headboard. He grabbed a pillow and pushed it under her hips. "Tightly tied for truly tempting torture," he muttered, not cracking even a hint of a smile at the alliteration.

Tied with very little give, she thought, testing the bindings.

He stood staring down at her, his breath coming fast and hard. He leaned over her and spread her pussy wide with his fingers. "This gorgeous cunt belongs only to me now." His eyes locked with hers. "Confirm that, Kayla, or I'll leave you here while I go eat something less enjoyable but more filling."

"No! Don't go. My, um, cunt belongs to you, Kyle. Take it. Make me come. You know I don't want anyone but you touching me."

A smile tugged at his lips. "Good. That's exactly what I wanted to hear." He dipped his head and with his tongue, he licked and rolled her clit until she sighed and murmured her pleasure. Then he sat beside her, took the stiff bookmark and slapped it against that bundle of nerves.

"Kyle!" The sting shot through her body, up to her nipples and down to her toes.

He slapped her clit again.

"Oh!" Her pussy clenched and she jerked, but the ties gave her no chance of escape.

"Relax." He leaned over and lightly licked her clit, soothing the flesh.

Her mind and body warred with each other. Her body loved the excessive stimulation. Her mind warned her against engaging in such activities.

Kyle lifted his head and stared into her eyes. "You're so hot, Kayla. I love how responsive you are. If I had a video camera, I'd film this for us to watch later. More? Or is that all the punishment you can take?"

Once the shock of what he'd done faded and she'd ignored the warning from her brain, she nodded, wanting to try it again. "Yes. More." Her body shook with need. And with Kyle, she felt free to express those needs without shame. "My breasts too."

"Ah, yes. Don't want these beautiful nipples to feel neglected." Kyle leaned over her breasts and sucked a nipple into his mouth. He bit down slowly and gently then released the bud and repeated the move, biting a little harder each time.

After about the fifth round, she caved. "Enough, enough!"

Releasing the bud, he caressed her breasts. A low chuckle escaped his throat. He licked the nipple, easing the fire she felt.

"Nice." Since he'd stopped when she said, she felt at ease to allow him the freedom to go further if he wanted. "I need to come, Kyle."

"I know, baby. Let's see what we can do about that." He smacked her clit with the bookmark again as he pushed two fingers up inside her pussy. "Come!"

"Ah!"

"Come!" He gave her another slap, while pumping his hand hard.

"Ah!"

After a third smack and command, she screamed and thrashed on the bed, pulling against the ties.

"I'm coming!"

He kept up the intense stimulation on her clit and inside her cunt. "Come hard, Kayla!"

Her body convulsed and she could hardly breathe. Her clit ached, but she continued to come. "Ooo! Ooo! O-oh!"

"You're creaming a river, Kayla. Keep going!" Kyle continued slapping her pussy fast and hard, but not savagely or without control. His fingers thrust deeply.

All she could manage was a whimper as her body climaxed repeatedly. The thrill rushed through her like an out-of-control roller coaster. The combination of pain-pleasure was an experience in sexual discovery beyond anything she'd ever known.

Finally, he stopped slapping her cunt and pulled out his fingers.

Only then did she stop coming.

He puffed out a large breath. "Damn, Kayla."

She collapsed. She felt drained, sore and satisfied. Completely spent, she couldn't speak or move.

"Just lie there. I was afraid to continue any longer, even though you were still coming. You're going to hurt enough later as it is, most likely. Let me take care of you. Soothe your skin as best as I can, so you don't get too sore."

Her eyes fluttered closed. *Too rough.* She'd loved it, but he was right. She'd pay the price later, when her body protested the treatment. Still, at the moment, she had no complaints. And even if they never repeated what had happened, she'd definitely remember those mind-shattering orgasms for a long, long time and know that Kyle was the man who gave them to her.

Chapter Seven

🔊

Kyle sat in one of Kayla's comfortable, overstuffed chairs and stared at the Christmas tree. He'd decorated most of it himself, just leaving the star and a few bulbs for them to do together, later. He figured Kayla would appreciate most of it already being done.

After making her come, he'd run a warm bath for her and helped her into the tub. While she soaked, he'd changed the sheets on her bed then made them something to eat, and he had her take some over-the-counter meds to help further relax her and take away any aches. He'd put her to bed and creamed her body, applying extra to her nipples and a soothing balm to her clit. Now she was napping.

He'd loaded the dishwasher then had taken a shower and decorated the tree. He liked taking care of things for Kayla. He liked taking care of Kayla.

Still… Good thing he planned to leave and not return until Christmas Day to surprise her. She probably wouldn't be up for another bout of sex until then. And if he wasn't around, he wouldn't have to fight his urge to take her again.

Next time they made love, he intended it to be a soft, slow and sensual joining. He'd loved her wildness. What man wouldn't? But he also wanted to experience a gentle closeness and coming together with her.

He checked his watch. He still needed to make some final Christmas arrangements but didn't want to do it here. She might overhear. Besides, if he didn't leave soon, she'd get suspicious. He left the same time each year for his Christmas visit to the Circle KW. She knew his schedule by heart.

A smile spread across his face. They knew each other so well. And now Kayla was finally his. Man, he loved that woman! He hadn't felt this happy and settled in years.

"Kyle?"

At the sound of her voice, he turned and jumped up from the chair. "What are you doing out of bed?" She looked pleasantly mussed and extremely well-loved, but her eyes still looked a little tired.

She tugged her robe more securely closed. "I didn't want you to sneak out while I was asleep. I know you need to leave and get packed for your trip."

"I'd have said goodbye."

"I know, but I wanted to be awake for it." A small smile tugged at her lips. She glanced over at the tree.

"I left some bulbs and the tree topper for us to do together. I was going to stick around long enough for that."

"The tree looks really nice. You did a good job."

"Do you mind me decorating most of it without you?"

"No. I don't think I'd have been up to helping with the whole thing."

He pulled her into his arms. He needed to touch her, needed to make certain she was all right. "How are you feeling?" Concern rolled through him.

"I'm okay." She rested her cheek on his shoulder.

"Sore?"

"Not so much. But, um, Kyle?"

"What is it, baby?" He heard a strange tone in her voice that he couldn't identify.

"Do you think I'm...weird?"

Weird? He pulled back from her and raised her chin with his finger, trying to look into her eyes. "What are you talking about?"

Shrugging, she attempted to walk away, but he stopped her. She patted his hand but didn't look at him. "It's nothing, Kyle. I'm sorry. I shouldn't have brought it up."

"Kayla? You know you can talk to me about anything."

Her eyes finally met his. "Well, it's just... The way I climaxed from..." She shook her head as if unwilling or unable to complete her sentences. She nibbled at her bottom lip.

Ah, he understood now. He saw it in her troubled gaze. "From my punishment of you?"

She nodded. "Is that totally messed up?"

He took her hands in his. He wasn't used to hearing her voice insecurities, so it had taken him a moment to figure out what was going on. "You enjoyed it. I enjoyed it. It was rough, but nobody really got hurt." His brow furrowed. "Right?"

"Right," she immediately agreed. "It just stung mostly. You stopped before it got bad. I don't think I'd have come like that if I was in any real pain."

"Good. So, we had fun. That's all that matters. I want you to continue to feel open with me sexually and every other way. I want to meet your needs. You've certainly met mine and more. You're a wonder, Kayla. Don't ever think otherwise. Now, let's finish up this tree."

A blush tinted her cheeks, and she reached for a bulb.

Working silently and contently, side by side, they finished up the tree. After Kyle put the star on top, Kayla turned on the tree's lights. "Beautiful. Thanks, Kyle." She slid an arm around his waist, snuggling close. "This has been a wonderful couple of days."

"I wish I could stay longer to enjoy it."

She smiled. "You need to go, I know."

"Yes. Unfortunately." He walked with her to the door, thinking maybe he should just tell her the truth and stay. They could watch a movie, then crawl into her bed and sleep the rest of the day away. But he really wanted to surprise her and also give her a little time alone to think about the change in their relationship. Gently, he kissed her lips. "I'll be back before you know it."

"I'll miss you."

His heart clenched. "I'll miss you too."

* * * * *

Christmas Day

Kayla sat on the sofa, looking up at the tree. She'd flipped on the lights earlier. They sparkled beautifully. But the colorful bulbs also made her sad because they reminded her of the man she loved.

She missed Kyle, the big lug. Silly really. He'd only been gone three days. They'd gone much longer without seeing each other before, but now it seemed different and much harder to face the days without him.

Underneath the tree sat a wrapped present for him for when he got back. They'd be spending New Year's together. That would be nice although a long, lonely week stretched between now and then.

She glanced out the living room window. Snow. Not heavy. Just enough flakes to look and feel festive. Thank goodness she'd finished all her errands for the week. She hated driving on snow and ice.

The doorbell chimed, bringing her out of her thoughts. "Who in the world could that be?" She wasn't expecting anyone. She walked to the door and looked out the peephole. "Who is it?" she asked when she didn't recognize the man standing there.

"Special delivery."

Hmm. "You're not wearing a uniform." This guy could be anyone. Uneasiness crept up her spine.

"If necessary, I was told to use the code word — punishment."

"Geez!" She was going to slap Kyle silly. She pulled open the door, trying her hardest not to blush.

The man handed her a medium-sized box, told her to have a nice day and then he was gone. Just like that. No knowing looks or smart remarks from him, so Kyle probably hadn't explained what the code word signified. Not that she thought he would talk about their sexual activities with others. At least the goof was smart enough to know she wouldn't open her door to a stranger without some sort of assurance of safety. She slammed the door closed and locked it.

She sat on the sofa and tore open the brown package. An envelope sat on top of a brightly wrapped present. The words "Open me first upon arrival" were scribbled on the front in Kyle's handwriting.

Eager to read the contents, she ripped open the envelope and slid out the letter. She unfolded the lone piece of paper.

Kayla,

I miss you, sweetheart, and can't wait to hold you in my arms again. Put the boxed present under the tree. I don't want you to open it until I'm beside you. There's another present waiting for you on the porch. Look for it right away, before it freezes.

Love, Kyle

"On the porch?" Why didn't the delivery guy give it to her with this one? She put the wrapped present under the tree next to the one she'd put there for Kyle. Then she headed for the door to see what was on the porch.

First, she checked out the peephole but saw nothing. She unlocked and opened the door a crack. No package that she could see. She pulled the door wider and stepped out to look around.

Someone grabbed her from the side. She shrieked. "Kyle!" Her heart raced from fear, then surprise and excitement. She slapped at his arm. "You scared me to death. What are you doing here? You're supposed to be in Texas." She fell into his arms and snuggled against his chest. "I'm so happy to see you."

"Me too." He held her tightly, burying his face in her hair. "You smell and feel fantastic. Come on. It's cold out here."

They went inside, and Kyle shucked his leather jacket. He hung it in the utility room closet then grabbed her and spun her around the entryway.

She laughed and cried at the same time, her emotions overwhelming her. "Why aren't you in Texas? You didn't cancel, did you? Your family will hate me if you did that just to spend the holiday here with me."

He wiped away her tears. "Calm down. You know my family is crazy about you. And no, I didn't cancel. They did. The folks are on a second honeymoon so the rest of the family is just doing their own thing this year."

"Are you telling me the truth?" Studying his eyes, she wondered. But even if he wasn't being truthful, it was too late for him to make Christmas in Texas now.

"Yes, I'm telling the truth. I wanted to surprise you. Surprise!"

She laughed. "Well, you accomplished your goal." She couldn't voice how happy she was to see him. "Where have you been the last three days?"

"Around. Arranging things. Letting you rest and recover. With both of us having a couple of weeks off work, I thought you'd enjoy a few days of alone time."

"I think I'd rather have had more Kyle time." She used to cherish her alone time, which he knew, but that didn't seem so important now.

"Also, I figured you might need a few days to think about things. Our relationship, specifically. Are we okay?" A wary look crossed his face.

"Oh, yes." Her heart pounded. "Are we okay on your end?"

A wide grin split his face. "Most definitely."

The tenseness in the air faded into joy. She felt like hugging the stuffing out of him. "Why did you send that delivery guy, Kyle? You could have brought the package to me yourself."

"I thought it was more fun that way. And, also, I was kind of taking the easy way out, in case you'd changed your mind about us. If you'd refused the package or not come out after opening it, then I was just going to leave you alone until after the holidays."

"You really thought I might not want to see you?"

"I just wanted it to be your decision. I didn't want you to feel obligated to continue what we'd started, if you all of a sudden had second thoughts."

"Oh, Kyle. You never have to worry about that."

He visibly relaxed and a teasing tone entered his voice. "You sure opened that door fast when the delivery guy gave the code word."

She laughed and felt a blush creep up her neck. "You're incorrigible."

The doorbell rang. "Oh, good," Kyle said. "They're here."

"They?" Oh, goodness. Her thoughts went to what he'd said about him and his brothers being on their own this year. He hadn't invited Kevin and Kody to come *here*, she hoped. She was so not dressed for company, just in her sweats. And she had nothing in the house for a proper Christmas dinner. And no dessert except for her homemade cookies.

Kyle pulled open the door and three men entered. Not his brothers. They carried cartons and boxes. He directed them to the kitchen.

"What's going on?" Delicious odors wafted to her nose. Food?

"Christmas wouldn't be complete without a turkey and all the trimmings."

"Turkey?"

"And pies. Enough to last us the week. And also some champagne for us to toast the New Year."

"You did all this for me?" Tears misted her eyes. How he'd managed to arrange deliveries on Christmas Day, she couldn't imagine.

"I brought a few personal things with me. They're in the car, if you don't mind me staying the week with you. But if you do—"

"No, no. I don't mind. That sounds wonderful." Having Kyle all to herself for an entire week was a dream come true. This was one holiday season she'd never forget.

Chapter Eight

 හ

Kyle sat on the couch massaging Kayla's sock-covered feet. A sense of contentment and peace wrapped around him. The multi-colored lights on the tree twinkled and holiday music played low in the background. "I'm stuffed."

"Me too." She patted her stomach. "I'm going to have to exercise double-time to get all this extra weight off. And I hate to exercise."

"We'll do something aerobic together. It'll be fun." He winked, thinking up various erotic ways to work off the calories.

Kayla laughed. "I can see your mind working, thinking up deliciously nasty positions for us to try."

He wagged his finger at her. "You know me too well. But I like that."

"Me too. It's comfortable but thrilling at the same time. This is the best, Kyle. I'm so glad you're here with me this year. Though I'm sure you miss your family."

"Maybe next year, you, me and my family will all be together."

"Maybe." She smiled. "Now when do we get to open our presents?" she asked, an excited look on her face.

"Look who's revved up about getting a present. I'll have to buy you presents more often. I like seeing you excited. Anytime you're ready, we can open them."

"Good." She pulled her feet out of his lap. "Let's do it now."

He laughed. "Okay." He grabbed her present from under the tree and gave it to her. "You first."

With a big smile on her face, she ripped open the package. She pulled out a short, sheer red nightgown with a red thong. "Oh, it's beautiful, Kyle." She fingered the material. "Something for both of us to enjoy." She giggled. "And it's my size too."

"I peeked in your lingerie drawer. Somehow, it reminded me of you — beautiful, sexy and soft to the touch."

"Is that a line?" She grinned up at him. "Because that's not bad. You softie." She leaned toward him and kissed his cheek.

"It's simply the truth. There's more. Keep looking."

She pulled away some paper in the box. "Oh! Two books. And I don't have these yet. Kyle, these are great! How did you know?"

"I looked on that to-be-bought list you have tacked up beside your computer in your bedroom."

"You're resourceful."

"When I need to be. There's one more thing on the bottom, but I can return it if you want." He wasn't sure how she'd react to the last gift.

After setting the books aside, she peeled back another layer of paper and just stared into the box.

He held his breath.

Tentatively, she reached inside and drew out the foot-long, thin black object with strands dangling from the end. "Is this a—"

"A small crop, made specifically for sexual pleasure." His voice lowered and came out scratchier than he'd intended. "Just in case you get in the mood again." He cleared his throat.

"Oh my." She leaned forward and kissed him slowly and thoroughly. When she pulled back, she whispered against his lips. "Thank you, Kyle. I love all my presents and will use all of them."

He swallowed hard at the intensely sexual look on her face. "Are you sure?"

She nodded. "I'm looking forward to reading you some sexy passages from those books, putting on that red nightie and letting you show me how to use this sex crop. My body is already tingling in anticipation."

Fuck. She knew just how to get his cock harder than steel without even touching him. "Good." He took in a deep breath then slowly let it out, getting his body under control. "I figured the books were keepers but wasn't sure about the other stuff." Especially the crop. But he could tell she genuinely liked what he'd bought her. He'd wanted to make her happy and keep a smile on her beautiful face. This was a special holiday he hoped she'd remember as the beginning of their new life together as lovers, and, if he had his way, as a lifelong couple.

"Open your present now, Kyle."

"Okay." He reached for the box and tore off the wrapping. When he saw the picture on the side of the box, he laughed. "I can't believe it. Did you get this before or after the other night?"

"After. Where do you think I got the idea? Besides, you know I'm a late shopper. And you're so impossible to shop for."

"Thanks, sweetie. A video camera." He pictured her bound to the bed, dressed in the red nightgown, minus the panties, her ass bared to him as he stood over her with the crop, all the while getting every move on camera for them to watch later at their leisure. "All sorts of ideas are flickering though my head."

"Oh I'm sure."

They both looked at each other and smiled.

"It's going to be a fun week," Kayla said, "putting to use all our new toys."

Kyle set the box aside. "I'll read the instructions on that thing later. We'll definitely put it to use soon and often. But right now, I need you close." He wrapped his arms around her and kissed her gently.

They lay back on the couch, holding each other. Kyle's hands slipped beneath her sweatshirt to cup her bare breasts. He loved how she went without a bra around the house when she wasn't expecting company. He massaged her breasts, brushing his thumbs across her nipples.

"Nice." She kissed his neck, letting her tongue trail along his skin.

His hands slid around to massage her back then slipped down into her sweatpants and underneath her panties to caress her butt. Perfectly round and fleshy. Made for sexual pleasure. "Are you all recovered?"

"Completely. And ready for more."

The woman was insatiable. He loved that, for his sex drive was just as strong.

She pushed up his sweater and pulled it over his head, along with his T-shirt. She nibbled lightly on one flat nipple then the other, dragging her fingernails down his sides at the same time.

"Yeah, baby." Twitching, he felt the thrill all the way down to his cock.

She reached between them and slowly lowered his zipper. "Let's see what this package down here looks like. Good enough to eat from what I remember."

A growl rumbled from the back of his throat. Urgently, he tugged her sweatshirt over her head and tossed it to the floor. He cupped one breast and leaned forward to roll his tongue around the hard nipple. Vanilla. Whatever lotion she used on her body, he loved the way it made her skin taste. He sucked gently, treating her other nipple to soft tweaks and tugs with his fingers.

"I can't get enough of you, Kyle." Pulling away, she jerked down his pants and briefs and helped him shuck them all the way off, including his socks. "I'd keep you naked and hard all day long, if I could," she told him.

Sounded good to him. "Take your bottoms off," he grumbled, needing to feel her bare skin against his.

She slipped off her pants and panties then straddled him. "Do I need to turn up the heat?"

His fingers curled around her hips as his gaze zeroed in on her pussy. "You're not going anywhere. We'll generate plenty of heat right here." He reached out to finger her clit, circling the hard bud. Her cunt was already soaking wet. His fingers caressed her gently.

"Oh!" She pushed against his hand.

After several strokes, he pulled his hand away and sucked her wetness from his fingers. Glancing around, his brow furrowed. "We need a condom. I think I have one in my wallet."

She reached down for his pants and rifled through his pockets for his wallet. "Here."

"Thanks." He opened a flap and pulled out a foil square. "Yep, got one. Make me harder, baby. Use your mouth on me."

As he tore the packet open, she scooted down and licked the head of his cock. "Mmm." Her hand closed around him and she pumped up and down, getting him fully hard and ready to fuck.

"Yeah, that's good." When she pulled back, he rolled on the condom, needing to make love to her more than anything right now. "Climb on."

With a contented sigh, she sank down on top of him, enveloping his cock deep inside her. "Ooo…big. I love how thick you are."

Her words pleased him. Locked together as close as two people could get, he realized just how deeply his love for her ran. "Your pussy is so warm and tight, Kayla. I could stay like this forever."

With her palms resting softly on his chest, she moved her hips slowly.

He caressed her hips and thighs. Just looking at her made his heart ache. She was everything he wanted and needed in a woman. She leaned over him and he kissed her tenderly, touching his tongue to hers. His fingers tightened around her hips and he urged her to move just a little faster.

Pushing herself back upright, instead of only slightly increasing the pace, she began riding him frantically. "Oh, Kyle! Fuck me! Harder!"

Damn. She was one wild female. He grabbed her hips tightly, trying to slow her down. "Easy, baby. Make it last."

"I can't. I need to come."

"I know. Me too." Badly. But he didn't want this to end, not so soon.

With a groan, she eased up, following his instructions. "You make me crazy. Let's see if I can return the favor." She leaned over and nibbled on one of his nipples, then bit down hard.

"Oh, man!" His hips jerked up and his hands slid back to firmly grip her ass. Her pussy contracted around his cock and he almost lost it. "Ah!"

Raising her head, she looked into his eyes. "I want to watch you come, Kyle." She rotated her hips. "Come for me."

His fingers squeezed her ass. When she leaned over to kiss his lips, he brought one hand up to hold the back of her neck. He pushed his hips up hard, driving his cock deeply into her cunt. "Mmm."

She broke the kiss just as his body tightened and the climax swept through his body. "Kayla!"

"Yes, Kyle. Come!" Her pussy contracted over and over as she stared into his eyes.

He felt the orgasm grip her, saw her eyes dilate. She gasped, coming right along with him. Looking into her eyes as they both climaxed made him feel connected to her on a deep emotional level that could never be broken. They twisted and undulated against each other, riding the waves of pleasure.

Finally, she collapsed on top of him and they lay together, breathing heavily.

Epilogue
Circle KW Ranch
Christmas, One Year Later

∞

Kayla stared down at the small black box. She shifted on the bed. Kyle had dragged her into his room for some privacy from the crowd downstairs. Now that they were a couple, she didn't feel like an intruder at his family get-togethers anymore and had attended several.

In fact, this Christmas she was having a marvelous time with his family. They treated her like one of their own.

After he'd tugged her into his room and they'd sat down on the bed, he'd pulled this box from his pocket. She knew what it was, or at least, she hoped. When her gaze met his, he looked as nervous as she felt.

"Go on. Open it," he told her, his voice sounding shaky.

With her heart pounding harder than she thought it could, she slowly opened the lid. *Yes.* A gold band with a diamond in the center, surrounded by small red and green gems, twinkled at her. "Oh, Kyle."

Gently, he removed the ring from the box and took her hand in his. "Marry me, Kayla? I want us to spend the rest of our lives together."

Tears misted her eyes. As he waited for her answer, she felt his fingers trembling. Or was it her fingers trembling? She wasn't certain. "Yes, Kyle. Yes!" she answered, before they both passed out from the excitement and anticipation.

She'd loved him for what seemed like an eternity. "I'll marry you." She gazed into his eyes, knowing they would enjoy a long life together. This union would work. Her dream had finally come true.

A wide smile split his face. He slid the ring on her finger and gathered her into his arms. He kissed her gently. Their tongues touched and she sighed, never wanting to let him go. When they finally did separate, she gazed down at the ring.

"It's so beautiful, Kyle. Does your family know you were planning to do this today?"

"You bet. They're probably down there climbing the walls right now, waiting for us to join them so the celebration can begin. Provided you accepted, of course. I think they're more nervous about this than I am...was. My mother probably has all the wedding details already worked out in her head. I hope you don't mind too much."

"I love your mother, Kyle. Your whole family. They make me feel like I belong."

"You do belong." His mother doted on Kayla like a daughter and his father had taken her under his wing, showing her how everything worked at the ranch. His brothers had appointed themselves her personal protectors and already promised her they'd beat him to a pulp if he didn't treat her right.

"Was there really any doubt about my answer?"

He shrugged. "I didn't want to assume too much. None of us did." He enveloped her in his arms and whispered softly in her ear. "I love you so much, Kayla. You are my soul. For now and for always."

"Oh, Kyle. I love you too." Her heart soared. She held him tightly, savoring his words. Kyle often teased her about being naughty. Kayla figured she must have been very nice for Santa to give her the best Christmas present ever—Kyle's love and his commitment to her for the rest of their lives.

"Let's go show the family."

"Yes, let's," she agreed. Hand in hand, they left the room, and Kayla knew in her heart that she'd never feel lonely again.

Also by Ruth D. Kerce

⁊ℴ

Adam 483: Man or Machine?

Diamond Studs (*anthology*)

Virgin Seeks Bad-Ass Boy

Wanton Temptation

Xylon Warriors 1: Initiation

Xylon Warriors 2: His Carnal Need

Xylon Warriors 3: Flames of Arousal

About the Author

၆၁

Ruth D. Kerce got hooked on writing in the fifth grade when she won a short story contest—a romance, of course. And she's been writing romance ever since.

She writes several subgenres of romance—historical, contemporary, and futuristic. Her books are available online in many internet bookstores. Her short stories and articles are available on several websites. She has won or placed in writing contests and hopes to continue to write exciting tales for years to come.

Ruth welcomes comments from readers. You can find her website and email address on her author bio page at www.ellorascave.com.

Tell Us What You Think

We appreciate hearing reader opinions about our books. You can email us at Comments@EllorasCave.com.

A DEVIL IN WINTER
Diana Hunter

ഌ

Trademarks Acknowledgement

Chapter One

ഇ

"Ow, Kevie, that hurt!"

Kevin Winter frowned at the half-naked woman in his arms, his plans for a long evening of making love to a beautiful woman unraveling faster than sledding plans in a mid-winter thaw. Pushing the silk blouse farther off her shoulder, Kevin tentatively wrapped his lips around her nipple again and pulled on it as gently as he could. A slap on the head and another squeal told him all he needed to know. This evening was going nowhere. If she couldn't take a little pull on the nipples, then tying her up and fucking her silly was never going to happen. Stifling a sigh, Kevin Devlin Winter sat up on the couch and ran his fingers through his sandy brown hair.

"Sorry, Mandy. You have really sensitive nipples, I guess. Just like your supersensitive skin."

Although Kevin had lived in upstate New York for the past seven years, when he was irritated, his Texas twang tended to become more pronounced. At the moment, it sounded as if he'd never left the Lone Star State.

Mandy pouted and Kevin frowned again. Just what was it he had thought cute about that lower lip?

"You're just so rough, my little Texas cowboy. You need to be more tender-like." Coquettishly, she ran her fingers up his arm and twirled them in the curls of his sandy hair.

Kevin shook his head. "Mandy, I can't touch you. I run my hand along your side and you tell me you're ticklish. My tongue so much as touches your nipple and you go through the roof. I don't know how to be more 'tender-like'."

He didn't mean to mock her, but his voice took on her airheaded mannerisms. Mandy, however, was too busy pouting to notice the unintended slight. "Kevie, dearest...I can teach you."

"Maybe later, Mandy. The mood's gone now." Gesturing down to the open fly of his pants, he showed her the proof that he was no longer interested. Mandy reached for his cock, her long nails scratching against his thigh. Kevin had had enough. Standing abruptly, he zipped his jeans and settled himself before turning to her.

"Mandy, you're a beautiful woman and I'm sure you'll make some guy very happy. But right now, that guy isn't me."

"Oh, but, Kevie, we were having such a good time!"

"Ke-*vin*. My name has a consonant at the end of it. I'm sorry, Mandy. But you deserve someone...more tender-like."

Turning on his heel, Kevin grabbed his coat and hurried out of the brownstone apartment building. Once on the street, he stopped and slid his arms into his worn leather bomber jacket, tucking his hands in the pockets to keep them warm in the early winter chill before heading down the sidewalk, his lonely figure moving from pool to pool of light along the dark city street.

Mandy had caught his eye when she came to deliver mail to his office. Bright and perky and not too smart. Just what he needed. A woman perfect for a fling who would help him forget Pam Montgomery, the only woman he had actually entertained thoughts of marrying. Unfortunately, Pam found someone else before he had gotten around to asking her to marry him. Kevin had seen his former girlfriend and her new beau making eyes at each other over prime rib yesterday at Eddie's Chophouse, and it rankled to see how happy she was.

Mandy had been his solution. A quick office fling to drown his sorrows and show everyone he still had what it took. An empty beer can sat in the middle of the sidewalk and Kevin kicked it, listening to its empty roll along the pavement. It was as hollow as he felt.

"Quit that racket down there!"

A voice shouted down from a second-story window. Kevin bit back the retort that sprang too fast to his lips. His snappy replies usually got him in trouble. Instead, he bent down and retrieved the now-dented beer can, dropped it in the trash can at the corner and headed for home.

*   *   *   *   *

The number blinking on his answering machine told Kevin that he had only one new message. He toyed with the idea of not retrieving it until morning, but then decided he'd better listen to it. Might be something important. Probably wasn't, but it might be.

It wasn't.

"Hey, little bro. Give me a call when you get home from wherever it is you are right now. I got news for you."

Kevin checked the clock. Only ten o'clock. The date had been even more disastrous than he'd thought. He picked up the phone and dialed his brother's number. It only rang once before Kyle answered.

"'Ello."

"Kyle? Me. Returning your call."

"Good. Was afraid you'd have some hot date and wouldn't call 'til tomorrow."

Kyle's voice had lost none of its native accent, but Kevin could tell right away that something was wrong. There was a somber note in his tone that was unusual for his upbeat older brother.

"Well, the hot date turned out to be too ticklish for my tastes. She'll have to remain just the mail girl for me."

"Kevin, Kevin, Kevin." Kyle's voice took on a patronizing sound Kevin knew well. "Don't you know the old saying? 'Don't get laid where you get paid.' Office affairs are never a good idea."

Kevin grinned. "Yeah, you should know. Seems to me you've had your share."

"Voice of experience, boy. Voice of experience." Kyle dropped the banter. "Listen. This isn't really a social call."

Kevin mirrored his brother's seriousness. "I didn't really think it was. What's up?"

"It's about you coming home for Christmas."

"I know...I haven't bought my plane ticket yet. I will. I just haven't gotten around to it yet—"

"That's just it." Kyle's voice stopped him. "You don't need to come back to Texas for Christmas this year."

Kevin's mouth opened, but no sound came out. He shook his head to clear his ears "What? Whadda ya mean, don't come home for Christmas?"

Kyle's long sigh sounded tired. "There's no point. Mom and Dad have decided they want a second honeymoon. So they've booked a cruise and turned us loose for the holiday."

"Why would they do that?" Kevin's numbed mind still wouldn't work.

"It is their fortieth. Whether we want to admit it or not, they're allowed to go on another honeymoon if they want to."

"I know. But why do they have to go on a second honeymoon at Christmas?"

"Well, their anniversary *is* the twenty-sixth."

Kyle's news was the second disappointment of the night and Kevin wasn't in the mood.

"I know when they were married, big brother." He smirked as he imagined his brother's gritted teeth on the other end. Kevin knew he hated that nickname, but he wasn't in the mood to be polite. "I also know that cruises leave ports all over the world at all different times. They didn't *have* to be gone for Christmas day."

"Look, Kev. Stop killing the messenger, will you? I'm not happy about this either, but there's little we can do but be happy we have parents who are still in love and who want to spend time together."

Kevin dropped the receiver to his side and stared out the window at the black northern sky. Snowflakes fell against the pane, making wet kisses against the glass. Visions of escaping to the warm zephyrs of the Texas hills faded. His yearly trip to touch his roots and bring order into the chaos evaporated just like one of those snowflakes would under the warmth of the Texan sun. Sighing, he put the phone to his ear again.

"Sorry. This wasn't a good day. I really was looking forward to being with you all. Don't suppose you want to get together anyway?"

"Can't, bro. Gonna spend the time here."

"Okay. So I'm not going home for Christmas."

"I'm sure you'll find some hot broad up there to keep warm with."

"Yeah, right. Thanks for letting me know."

With promises to place a three-way call on Christmas day, Kevin dropped the receiver in the cradle and went to submerge his sorrows in sleep.

* * * * *

The first big snowfall of the winter season fell two days later. On a weekend, of course. The city wasn't moving much, so no one was inconvenienced but the shopkeepers. Kevin holed up in his one-bedroom apartment overlooking a snow-covered schoolyard next door where a group of kids waged a snowball fight. He pulled out his infamous "little black book" that wasn't black...and wasn't so little. He grinned unapologetically. What could he say? He liked women.

By the time he got to the "V"s two days after that, he wasn't so sure they liked him back.

"Yeah, so I'm looking at spending this Christmas by myself." Kevin grimaced on his end of the phone. Even to him he sounded like such a loser. "You're going up to your aunt's? Oh, big family gathering. Good for you. Glad you're— Okay. I'll give you a call some other time."

He dropped the receiver back into the charger.

"Not having any luck, I take it." Tony Aretti stood in Kevin's kitchen doorway, his tall frame filling the space like the lanky pitcher he'd been all through school. He had a sandwich in one hand and two beers in the other.

"When did you show up?" Kevin held out his hand for the other beer, and Tony obliged. Even though their lives had headed down different paths in the years since sharing a college dorm room, they had ended up in the same apartment building in the same northern city and still considered what belonged to one, belonged to both. Kevin didn't think twice about the fact that Tony had let himself in while he was on the phone trying to find something to do with his Christmas. He'd walked in on Tony in much more delicate situations. Including one where he'd gotten a glimpse of a beautiful woman with golden-brown hair tied tightly to a chair. Tony had shut the door on him though, and the glimpse was all he'd had of Tony's love life. Of course, that little glimpse had been enough to start a conversation about sexual preferences. Kevin wasn't too surprised to discover his best friend's appetites ran in similar directions as his own. They'd discussed the possibility of sharing at some point, but that opportunity had yet to arise. Tony took a bite from his sandwich and talked around the mouthful.

"I came in at the 'my-parents-are-going-on-a-second-honeymoon' part. Leaves you all alone for Christmas? Bummer."

Tony took a big bite out of the sandwich he'd purloined. Washing it down with a swig from the bottle, he gestured to the family portrait Kevin had hanging over the desk. "Why not get together at one of your brothers' places? Doesn't one of them still live in Texas?"

Kevin drank, morosely surveying his traitorous family. "No, but Kody's going back to mind the ranch while Mom and Dad are away. Made it quite clear, however, that three would be a crowd. He has plans, he says. The fucker. And before you ask, Kyle's staying put where he is. Talked to him again this morning. Says he's saving money. The shits. Both of 'em." He took another long pull.

Tony had the good sense not to laugh at his friend's plight. In college, Kevin had chosen to go by his middle name, Devlin, and his exploits with the opposite sex had earned him the nickname "Devil Devlin". But even back then Devil put everything aside, including women, to go home for the holidays. He'd regale the entire floor with stories of his brothers and their antics. There was the time Kevin had switched the tags on all the presents so his mother ended up opening a miter saw intended for his father, and his eldest brother had received a diamond tennis bracelet. And then the time their parents had put coal in all their stockings and hidden the presents because of a broken dining room window. But Tony's favorite was the story about the time the three boys had sneaked downstairs and found, not Santa, but his father doing more than kissing his mother under the Christmas tree.

"Well, you can count me in among the shits, roomie. I've got a girl and we're spending the entire holiday at her parents."

"I need to get drunk."

Tony stood and stretched. "No, you don't. Devil Devlin needs to get a date, that's all. Spend the day in bed fucking and you won't even miss it."

"Can't get a date." Kevin didn't move from the chair. "That call was the last one in my little book. Am too gonna get drunk."

"Nope. We just drank the last two beers in your fridge. You wanna get plastered? You need to go shopping first." He swallowed the last of the beer in his bottle and put the empty on the table. "But don't worry, Devil. You still have twenty-eight shopping days 'til Christmas."

Tony grinned as his best friend flipped him off, and left him to his own devices.

* * * * *

Kevin saw Pam again three nights later. The day had already been long—he'd spent most of it in meetings getting a new project off the ground. Much as he loved working for old Mr. Sampson, the man just didn't get the hang of new technologies such as IMing and e-mailing. As a result, Kevin felt he'd wasted most of his day in meetings dealing with piddly stuff that could've been handled much more efficiently and quickly with a few e-mails.

Kevin drove out of his parking spot in the company garage and headed for the grocery store. The weekend snow, pushed into piles along the side of the road, had already crusted over with ugly black grime. Not the image he'd had of snow in winter when he'd traveled north for college years ago. Learning to drive on the slushy stuff hadn't been easy, but Kevin had a well-earned reputation as a fast learner and now he maneuvered the slick streets like a native.

The grocery parking lot still had icy patches and some slush. Stepping carefully, Kevin made his way into the store without slipping or getting his shoes wet. He bought the groceries he needed for the week, with a few bags of junk food as nourishment for his wounded soul, and headed back out the automatic doors in record time.

That's when he saw her. Halfway back to his car. Pam Montgomery. His heart jumped like it always did at that first sight of her.

About a head shorter than he was, Kevin considered her to be the perfect size for him. Although currently bundled up in a bulky winter coat against the cold, Kevin still knew that body intimately. He knew how her smooth cheek curved down to the sweet hollow of her throat, the spot where he could feel her pulse quicken when his hands cupped her perfect breasts—each just large enough to hold in one hand without any extra—with tiny, round little nipples he could suck on forever. He knew how her short black hair, at the moment pressed against her cheek by a pink felt hat, tickled his chest when she placed a trail of kisses from his Adam's apple to his waist, and how her talented slender fingers would cup his balls as that perfect heart-shaped mouth encircled his cock.

Kevin watched her cross the parking lot, oblivious to his presence, while memories tormented him. Torn between wanting to make her suffer and wanting to make love to her right there, he decided an aloof panache would be the best approach. Groveling was not his style, although, as he caught a glimpse of those beautiful, shapely legs in thin-heeled boots, he decided he could be persuaded. Affecting an air of nonchalance, he waited until only a car length separated them, before stepping in front of her.

And landed on his backside, the plastic bag of groceries spilling into the parking lot, and his panache flying off into the evening sky trailing laughter behind it.

"Kevin? Is that you? Are you all right?"

Her voice still held the promise of satin nights and spectacular romance. Kevin shook his head in resignation. "Yeah, it's me. And I'm fine." He glanced at his hands, now wet and dirty and brushed them off on his ruined dress pants. "Saw you across the lot and thought I'd drop in."

She laughed, as she always had at his bad jokes and extended a hand. Kevin took it, feeling again the warmth and deceptive softness of her skin. He knew full well the steel rod of control hidden by that softness. A steel rod he'd never gotten around to bending. As he stood, he pulled her into his arms with a practiced move that belied his earlier clumsiness.

"How are you, Pam?"

His voice, no more than a murmur, unnerved her exactly the way he knew it would. Flustered, she took a step back.

"I'm fine, Kevin." He watched her arch her eyebrow as she slammed the steel rod back into place. "And how are...you?" She pointedly peered around him to draw attention to his soaked ass.

"Wet." After weeks of not returning his calls, of ignoring every overture he made to her, she was finally talking to him. Despite his wet clothes, he couldn't keep the optimism out of his voice.

"You need to change into dry clothes before you catch cold."

Kevin shook his head. "My apartment is all the way 'cross town." For good measure, he added a little white lie. "And the heater is broken in my car."

Pam laughed out loud and Kevin grinned to hear the deep, throaty sound that she often told him only he could get her to make.

"Kevin, you are such a liar. My apartment's right around the corner, as you very well know. I suppose you can come in and we can throw your pants in the dryer."

Kevin's heart soared. Score! After weeks of unreturned phone calls, his foot was in the door. He dared to hope she'd broken up with the guy he'd seen her with in the restaurant, but had enough sense to not mention her hopefully former boyfriend. Instead, he accepted her invitation, even offering to return to the store for her and pick up whatever she needed.

"Just a quart of milk and loaf of whole-wheat bread. Thanks, Kevin." Pam turned to go back to her car, but only took a step before turning back to him. "And condoms." The twinkle in her eyes made her meaning clear.

Kevin skated across a patch of ice and practically flew into the store. If he knew how, he would've kicked his heels together, but after his spill in the parking lot, decided not to push his luck.

By the time he reached Pam's apartment, his pants were almost dry, so he detoured through the shoveled snow piled beside the walk to get them wet again. They didn't call him Devil for nothing. He intended to have those pants off his body within five minutes and be in bed with a beautiful woman two minutes after that.

It actually took him a full ten minutes to achieve his heart's desire. Pam answered the door in her bra and panties, a wicked grin on her face and a glint of mischief in her baby blue eyes. They stopped in the kitchen only long enough to drape Kevin's wet pants over a kitchen chair to dry, then headed directly for the bedroom.

She's changed her perfume, Kevin noted, nuzzling a kiss just under her ear as he unclasped Pam's bra and sent it sailing somewhere into the corner of the room. Her willowy figure, hard and firm from years of dance, then karate, followed by judo, Kuk Sool Won and finally kick-boxing, still melted under his touch, so he wrapped his arm around her waist to hold her to him as he indulged his reeling senses.

He'd feasted his eyes on her gorgeous curves as soon as he'd entered, quickly centering in on her pixie-like face, which he captured between his hands and examined in every detail. Unblemished perfection smiled back at him. Not a freckle marred the creamy skin that blushed as he gazed. Some might call her turned-up nose a tad too cute, but he found it perfect for placing a kiss on the end. Beneath, two perfect lips, heart-shaped and made for pouting...or kissing.

He kissed her now, their clothes in a trail from the kitchen to the bed. In his hands, she was compliant, letting him take the lead and lower her to the mattress. A soft light filtered into the room from the kitchen...neither of them stopped to turn on a bedroom light. Kevin didn't mind. He didn't need a light to appreciate her silky skin or the scent of her perfume.

"Oooh, Kevin. You always did know exactly what buttons to push."

Pam's voice, deep-throated and breathless, purred in his ear and urged him onward. His already-hard cock brushed against her thigh, scattering his thoughts until only one remained — get the condom on fast.

She spread her legs for him, fingering herself and grinning wickedly at him as he slipped on the condom and got back to business. No need for lubricant with Pam...she always produced enough of her own to make his entrance smooth and slick.

Her legs wrapped around his back, urging him in. He thought about making her wait, making her beg for him, but he doubted he'd last that long. Her pussy, pink and open and waiting, glistened at the vee of her legs and Kevin needed no further invitation. With the skill of a master, he slid his long cock home. Just the tip at first, teasing himself more than Pam. Her sweet warmth enveloped his cock as he slid it farther inside with each gentle thrust. Under him, her body set up a quick rhythm and Kevin followed right along, loving the whimpers and small cries that came from the back of her throat. Kevin supported himself on his arms so he could look down at Pam's beautiful face, her blue eyes closed in concentration. Her hands gripped his upper arms, using them as leverage as their pace quickened to help his cock bury itself deep inside her. The whimpers turned to moans as each thrust hit home and Kevin pushed her deeper and harder, the scent of her perfume mingling with the scent of her pussy making it difficult for him to concentrate on pleasing her first.

When she came and her muscles tightened around his cock, Kevin still restrained himself, even though he groaned to do it. He helped Pam ride the waves of ecstasy, keeping the beat going and the surf pounding. When she came again Kevin gave in, joining in with Pam, feeling nothing but the intense explosions of relief as his seed emptied into its rubber sheath.

An insistent tapping on his shoulder brought Kevin back to earth. He lifted his head to see Pam's face, just an inch from his own, looking more than a little flushed. She whispered only one word in a somewhat strangled voice. "Off!"

Obediently, Kevin rolled over, his cock reluctant to leave its nice, warm nest between her legs. Disposing of the condom, he turned to find her already dressing.

"What are you doing? You usually like to snuggle a bit afterward." Kevin reached across the bed to touch her arm. She pulled away.

"I'd forgotten what a good fuck you were, Kevin." Pam shook her head almost as if she regretted what she was going to say even as she slid on a silk blouse and started buttoning the small buttons. "I have a date tonight, Kevin. With Robert."

Kevin frowned. "Pam, I just made love to you and you're telling me you're leaving to go out on a date with another man?"

She didn't meet his eyes as she nodded. Turning away from him, she picked a comb up off the dresser, snapping on a small lamp so she could see. The light revealed several half-packed boxes along one wall and a half-empty closet. "Pam, what the hell is going on here?"

"My lease is up at the end of the month, which is fine. I'm getting married."

"Married!? Good God, Pam. What are you talking about? Why the hell did we just have sex then?"

The look of anger she turned on him still managed to turn his blood cold. "We had sex because I felt sorry for you. You looked so helpless in the parking lot and... Kevin, I did love you once."

"But not anymore." His voice was flat.

"No. I told you that months ago."

Kevin's chest felt as if it would explode. "I hope your new husband knows what a slut he's getting. I cannot believe you led me on and had sex with me before going on a date with another man. A man you hope to marry. There's a word for women like you."

Gathering the shreds of his dignity, Kevin turned toward the door, congratulating himself on his restraint in not saying more. Grabbing his shirt from the floor where it had landed, he threw it on, pulling on his still-damp pants without bothering to stop and put on his underwear and socks. Putting on his coat and shoes, he glared back at the bedroom door, wondering if she would have the courage to come out. She didn't.

Feeling about as important and loved as an ant, Kevin headed back out into the winter snow.

Chapter Two

ഔ

Pam haunted his mind. Every woman with short raven-black hair reminded him of the sweetness of her body under his. Every long-legged, high-heeled figure made his back ache where she had guided his strokes as he took her in her bed. Every low, sultry voice over the radio whispered her name in his heart. He was a man obsessed.

"No way." He slammed his palm on the countertop in his kitchen. "There's just no way that was pity sex."

Tony shook his head. "Sorry, bro, but that's what we're calling it nowadays. Look, she admitted that she loved you once. Then the two of you met by accident, you got your pants wet, she had sex with you, then went off on a date with her boyfriend. That's the very definition of pity sex."

"You weren't there. You didn't feel—" *her come around my cock.* He left the sentence unfinished. *At least twice.* Perhaps a third time when he came, but he'd been pretty much wrapped up in his own reactions by then and wasn't really sure. "Look, Tony. She came. A lot. What she showed me was a lot more than what a woman would give a guy she just felt sorry for."

Tony tossed off the last of the beer in the bottom of the bottle. "Whatever you say, pal. I gotta get going."

"You're getting pretty serious about this one, aren't you?"

His friend grinned. Kevin recognized that grin as the idiotic smile of a man in love. He knew that smile intimately. Until Pam had dumped him, he had worn just such a smile. He tried not to feel bitter that his best friend had found what he himself was lacking. Tony threw the empty at Kevin, who caught it and rinsed out the bottle. With an exaggerated stretch, Tony continued. "Yep. I'm thinking this might just be the one I'm gonna take on a little trip to the altar."

Kevin raised an eyebrow in surprise. "You show her the ropes yet?"

Tony's grin turned mischievous. "Several times. She loves it." He shook his head in real sympathy for his friend. "I know you love Pam, Kevin. But she hates the ropes...and you're a master at them. It would never have worked out. You need to get a girl who really enjoys being tied up. There's nothing like it."

Kevin got another beer from the fridge, pulled out the chair and sat down, sliding the bottle across the kitchen table. His own was still half full. "I know. But I want more than just tying a woman up and fucking her. That's in the past."

Tony saluted him with his beer. "To the demise of Devil Winter. May he rest in peace in the vanilla world."

Kevin shook his head in mock horror. "Not that! Never that!" He took a swig from the bottle, weighing his words. "Pam's definitely not into any kink, I'll admit that. She's always been a very straightforward kind of gal, telling me just what she liked in the bedroom and what she didn't." He saw the look in Tony's eyes and added quickly, "No, not like a Domme. Just like...well, a woman who knew what turned her on."

"But what about what turned you on? Didn't she ever ask about that?"

Kevin conceded the point with a shrug. "I didn't care. Being with her is always so intoxicating, nothing else matters. I've got to get her back!"

"Well, just don't become a stalker or somethin'. It's one thing getting bailed out of jail for mooning the president of the college...it's another thing getting bailed out for stalking."

Kevin grinned. "Just how drunk were we that night, anyway?"

Tony held up his beer. "Drunk enough to be stupid." He sat up, the teasing gone from his eyes. "Seriously, Kevin. Leave her alone. She's nothing but trouble."

Kevin tossed off the rest of his beer and put the empty bottle down. "I'm a big boy, Tony. I can take care of myself. And don't worry. I'm not going to turn into some whacko stalker either." He gazed across the room, the memory of her coming around his cock flooding his mind. "But I will get her back. You'll see."

* * * * *

As he sat outside Pam's apartment, however, he wasn't so sure that stalker might not be an apt description of his actions. She was back to not returning his calls. Tonight he'd stopped at the grocery again and on a whim, driven over to her apartment. Her car was parked in its designated spot and the light was on in her living room. Kevin still had her number in his cell on speed dial. With a shake of his head, he decided to give it one last try. If she didn't answer this time, he was done chasing. The phone rang four times before the machine picked up. "Hello, you've reached the number for Pam Montgomery. She is unable to come to the phone at the moment. Please leave your name and a number where you can be reached. Thank you."

"Fuck it." Kevin snapped the phone shut. No point in leaving a message when she couldn't make it more obvious that she never wanted to see him again.

Even though Pam's silence told him she'd moved on and no longer wanted anything to do with him, Kevin found himself thinking of her at odd moments. Having sex with her had been wonderful right up until the moment she told him she was leaving for a date with her fiancé. Each time he thought he was close to accepting that she didn't want him anymore, the words he'd thrown at her when leaving the apartment came back to haunt him. Ending so many months of happiness with an argument just didn't sit well. He wanted —

no, *needed* — closure. One last face-to-face meeting with the two of them holding a sane, adult conversation.

Two nights later Kevin found himself in her parents' neighborhood. On a whim, he decided to swing past their cul-de-sac. If she were there, maybe he could talk to her and put the entire affair to rest so he could move on with his life.

The lightly falling snow of the city became wind-whipped and nasty in the suburbs. Turning off his headlights, he coasted to a stop at the entrance to the dead-end street.

Sure enough, Pam's car, already covered with a fine layer of snow, sat in her parents' driveway. Kevin parked and debated what to do. Her parents had always liked him. Her mother usually made lasagna when he came over for dinner. Did she make lasagna now for Robert? The thought churned his stomach.

Not really having any plan in mind, Kevin turned off the engine and got out.

An inch of snow in the road made walking treacherous, so Kevin kept to the middle of the street, making his way past the silent, dark houses on either side of the Montgomery house at the center of the cul-de-sac. The three houses before him, built in a sort of fake Tudor style, complete with towers and mullioned windows, arced around the curve. It was time to end to all of this.

Kevin's heart stirred when Pam answered the door. If only she weren't so damn beautiful. The few words he'd rehearsed on the way up the drive flew out of mind.

"Kevin. What the hell are you doing here?" She continued without giving him a chance to speak. "I never want to see you again. Ever. Go away and don't bother me anymore or I'll call the police."

"Look, Pam, I just wanted to say—" The door slammed in his face. No sound came from the house and Kevin swore.

He stood on the small porch and shook his head. Just what was his intention here tonight? He'd driven out here on a whim, but Pam's reaction to his coming put everything into focus. An apology. He had just wanted to apologize for the ugly names he'd called her. That was all. Put a civilized end to the whole thing. An end he apparently wasn't going to get.

He stepped off the porch, defeat bowing his shoulders when a scream from inside stopped him. Almost not believing he'd heard it, he paused, alert for any sounds of disturbance. A crash and a second scream split the night air and Kevin bolted for the door. Locked! What was going on in there?

No further sound came from inside and Kevin went into automatic save mode. The woman he still loved was inside the house and in trouble. So were her parents. Without thought, he ran down the steps and headed around the house for the back door.

He got no farther than the side of the house. Little squares of light shone out onto the fresh snow, mirroring the pattern of the divided windowpane of the Montgomery great room. A glance in as he ran past pulled him up short. Pam's dad was righting a puny little chair that Kevin knew from experience wasn't very comfortable. Mr. Montgomery sat down, rubbing his shin, as Mrs. M ranted on about something that excited her. But it was Pam's face that caught Kevin's attention—a face alight, alive, and animated with excitement was in full view. Apparently she was telling them good news of some sort. When she blushed and gestured to her left ring finger, Kevin knew what it was. His shoulders sagging in relief, he leaned against the house.

He hadn't seen her eyes alive like that in a very long time. She really had found her heart's desire and it wasn't him. Suddenly he found he couldn't be angry with her anymore. Pam was Pam and that's all there was to it.

"Don't move."

Something sharp prodded him in the ribs. He didn't move anything but his head. "What do you want? Money? I don't have much, but you can have it."

There was a snort from the figure behind him. A short figure, judging from the position. "What are you doing snooping around my house?"

"Anna?" Kevin turned around. Pam's younger sister stood before him, a stick in her hand.

"Kevin? Are you stalking Pam? Why didn't you use the front door?" Pam's sister turned on her heel and took two steps toward the front of the house. She didn't get any farther. Kevin grabbed her arm and pulled her back.

"Anna, I'm not stalking her. I heard a scream —"

Anna cut him off. "I don't think so. You snuck up to the window to spy on her! Let me go. I'm calling the police." She shrugged off his hand and turned toward the front again. This time, she only managed one step before Kevin stopped her, his hand holding her arm more firmly this time.

"Anna, you don't understand."

"Kevin Winter, you're crazy. I'm going in there and telling Pam to come out here right now and deal with you."

He shook his head, not letting go of her arm. "No. She'll think I really am stalking her. She said she'd call the cops if I didn't leave."

"And you didn't leave. Maybe I should be calling the cops."

"Why?"

"Because you're snooping around here peeking in our windows, why do you think?" She jerked her arm back hard, but Kevin didn't let her go. He had to make her see he wasn't the monster she was forming in her mind.

"It's not like that, Anna. Since I couldn't get in the front door, I was going to try the back— I mean...let me explain."

"Let me go." She gave another yank and Kevin shook his head.

"I'm not letting you go until you promise not to call the police on me."

Anna snorted. "You're screwed, Winter. All the evidence points to harassment on your part. I'm going in to call. The cops are gonna arrest you without question."

Something inside Kevin snapped. He slid one arm around Anna's waist and pulled her closer to him. "I can't let you do that, Anna. This is too important. You'll see."

Pam's sister, only twenty months younger and an inch shorter, also proved to be easier to manage than Pam would have been. Kevin hadn't ever paid her much attention, but knew she wasn't the goddess her older sister was. And apparently not the athlete either. He dragged her across the lawn and across the cul-de-sac, glancing at the houses as he did so. No one looked out, or if they did, they made no sign of it.

Anna squirmed in his arms, but Kevin knew what he was doing. He liked his sex rough at times, pinning the woman to the bed with his superior strength. Always consensual, though. The high that came from a woman who voluntarily let him play with her was incredible. Anna might not be giving her consent at the moment, but then again, this wasn't a sexual escapade. Under the circumstances, keeping Anna under control wasn't difficult at all.

Getting her into the car was. Now she fought like a madwoman, kicking and trying to bite his hand. "Stop it, Anna. I'm taking you back to my place where we can talk like civilized human beings. If I can't talk to your sister, maybe I can talk some sense into you."

He shoved her into the backseat, knowing full well he'd never flipped the child-safety switch off. With it on, she couldn't open the back door. But his mind raced. If she were unbound, she could too easily blind him or knock him over the head as he was driving. Holding her down and working fast, he tilted down the backseat to get to the trunk and grabbed a hank of clothesline, pushing the seat back into place before continuing. "Sorry, girl. But you're forcing me into this. If you hadn't kept talking about calling the police, I wouldn't have to take you with me. But I just want one calm, rational talk with a member of the Montgomery family before I die." He kept talking as he grabbed her wrists and tied them behind her back. If he could make Anna see that he wasn't going to hurt her, maybe he could turn her into an ally. Yeah, and maybe pigs would be flying soon, too.

Satisfied she couldn't do him harm as he drove, he got into the front seat, looking around the neighborhood again to see if anyone had noticed. The two houses on the corner, still dark, were no threat. The two houses to the left and right of the Montgomerys appeared to have lights on, but no one inside. He started the car and turned the heater full blast.

"You're not going to get away with this." Anna kicked his seat.

"I told you. I just didn't want you calling the cops. How did you know I was there anyway?"

"Duh. It's snowing, genius. You left tracks."

Kevin shook his head. "And you followed them armed with nothing but a stick? I don't know if you're stupid or just plain dumb."

"Haven't you figured it out by now, you moron? Pam's in love with somebody else—Robert. Not you. Robert."

"I know that, Sherlock." His voice was sharper than he intended, his anger at Pam finding a target in Anna. "I figured that much out."

Kevin eased onto the expressway, being sure to keep well within the speed limit. Last thing he needed was to be pulled over. Anna didn't reply, which meant she was busy trying to figure out how to get loose. She wouldn't. Kevin knew how to tie knots.

The weather was definitely getting worse. Every once in a while a gust blew snow across the road and his visibility went down to almost nothing. Not much traffic crawled along the roads now. Most sane people were already home. He glanced in his rearview mirror when Anna grunted. Still secure.

At last he pulled into his parking place in front of his apartment building. This was going to be the tricky part. Getting Anna into the car had been a piece of cake compared to getting her out, into the building, up the stairs and into his apartment without anyone seeing. Or hearing. In for a penny, in for a pound.

Kevin popped his trunk and rummaged around in it for a minute before finding what he was after. Unlocking the car, he got in the backseat and shut the door behind him. He had some preparations to make.

"Look, Anna. You're going upstairs with me and that's all there is to it. I can't have you making a lot of noise, so..." He held up the roll of packing tape he'd fished out of his trunk.

"You are not going to put that over my mouth, Kevin Winter. You just aren't."

He nodded, a look of regret on his face. "I am, Anna. I really am." He tore off three pieces, sticking the ends to the back of his hand. Setting the roll on the seat, he leaned over and brushed the hair out of her face. Not short hair, like Pam's, but long, wavy and black as midnight. Hair that would be fun to play with under different circumstances. She shook her head, trying to foil him, so finally he grabbed a fistful of the silky stuff and her wiggling stopped. He slapped a length of tape over her mouth, following quickly with the other two...one slightly above, one below...overlapping and snug, all the while trying not to notice the fullness of her lips. Much more so than Pam's incredible heart-shaped mouth.

"Now, we're going to get out of the car and you're going to behave yourself."

The look she glared at him told him that was a pipe dream, but he'd hope anyway. Thanking the inventor of the keyless entry, he unlocked the car doors with a push of a button and backed out, pulling Anna along with him. Once outside and standing, he took off his jacket and threw it around her shoulders, then checked to see if her hands showed. They didn't. The jacket was huge on her, even over her winter coat.

She had been wearing a knit cap when she'd accosted him outside her parents' house, but that was now on the floor of his car somewhere as a result of all her struggles. At least he hoped it was on the floor. He didn't think it had come off when he was dragging her across the cul-de-sac.

Thankfully, she still had her scarf. The light brown plaid with the red stripe was a pretty common pattern. Pam wouldn't have been caught dead in anything worn by so many other people. Kevin wrapped it around her face and tied it off in the back. Not tightly, but enough so she couldn't push it off. Total time spent? Less than a minute.

Sliding his arm around her waist as if they were lovers, Kevin steered her into the building and up the stairs. The key was in the door when Tony's voice sailed down the hall. "Hey, Kev, gonna introduce me?"

Kevin shook his head furiously, opening his door and practically shoving Anna through. "Later!" he called to his friend, desperately hoping he would take the hint. To be sure he did, he slammed the door behind him.

Anna's eyes shot darts. The apology Kevin was about to give her remained unsaid. She wouldn't hear it now anyway. Instead, he steered her into his living room and gestured to the overstuffed couch. As far as Kevin was concerned, comfort was infinitely more preferable to style and his choice in furnishings showed it. "Have a seat. Here, let me help you." He reached out to take her arm, but Anna pulled away from him, losing her balance and landing on the couch on her side. Muffled noises that might have been screams came from behind the gag and Kevin hurried to pull her upright.

"Anna, are you all right?"

Her bluster faded and tears formed in her eyes. Kevin watched as she sniffed, thrust out her chin, and tossed her hair out of her face. Her composure back in place, she stared him down as if daring him to push her further. Kevin sat back on his heels, readjusting his attitude toward the woman that, until now, he had simply ignored as supporting actress to Pam's starring role.

Anna certainly had spunk. He snorted. A word he never would have used to describe Pam. While the love of his life had let him tie her up and make love to her, Pam had always been pretty placid throughout the entire affair, letting Kevin do what he wanted with little or no protest. Not that he'd pushed her very far. She might not have said anything, but Kevin instinctively knew Pam would never go for any rough stuff.

Anna, on the other hand, stared Kevin down as if her eyes were darts and she could do damage. Funny, he'd never considered how alluring an angry woman could be. Especially one tied up and at his mercy. Far down in the dark recesses of his psyche, an animal stirred. Kevin shook his head. This woman was dangerous on so many levels. Undoubtedly, she could hurt him if she chose. Maybe kidnapping her like this hadn't been such a good idea.

"I'm sorry, Anna. I just couldn't risk having you tell Pam I was there. She already thinks I'm stalking her." Kevin unwrapped the scarf and began gently pulling the tape from her mouth. "Promise me you won't scream and I'll take this off because I am really a nice guy." When she nodded, Kevin realized he didn't know if she was agreeing not to yell or that he was actually a nice guy. Her eyes still shot daggers, so he suspected it was the former.

Kevin kept up a patter, partly trying to quiet the part of his sexuality that had awakened from seeing this woman at his mercy and partly trying to get Anna to see his side of the story. Who knew what stories Pam had been filling her family's ears with?

"I wanted to apologize for some things I said. Pam only wanted me for sex, I know that now. But I also know what she's giving up to be with a guy who has to substitute a fancy car for performance in the bedroom."

Okay, maybe that last was a little too revealing. He yanked harder on the tape than he intended and Anna winced. With a final pull, it came off and Anna wasted no time in telling Kevin exactly what was on her mind.

"What goes on in their bedroom is none of your business, not that you were any better, from what Pam says. Kevin Winter, you let me go right now. How dare you kidnap me? Wait 'til I tell Pam about this."

Kevin sat back on his heels, watching and enjoying her struggle against the ropes that still held her arms. The dark animal paced in the cage and Kevin savored the exertion as one relishes a cut lip. Anna wasn't for him, no matter what his stray thoughts wanted. He let her bluster. She couldn't escape, but then again, he didn't want to leave her tied like that too long, either. At least she hadn't screamed.

"You don't deserve my sister, you deserve to be locked up. You're nuts."

"Not nuts. Just in love." Kevin frowned. "At least I was in love with your sister. I'd have done anything for her."

"Including kidnapping her little sister?"

"You're not that much younger than she is. Only what...two years? And I didn't kidnap you. You're just temporarily detained."

"You wanted to see her, why didn't you just use the front door?"

"I did. She slammed it in my face. No more, thanks."

"Kevin, this is ridiculous. Untie me."

Kevin stood up. "No way. As soon as I do, you'll call the cops. C'mon, Anna. Isn't there any way I can get you to forget this happened? For crying out loud, she had sex with me last Friday night, then went out on a date with Robert afterward. I was angry and said some things I regret. I just wanted to apologize and end everything with a clear conscience. You're blowing everything out of proportion."

Anna's face softened a little. He took that as a sign of hope that she would agree. But then she spoke and her words rattled him.

"Robert has asked her to marry him. They're getting married on New Year's Eve."

Kevin stood still, but his psyche reeled. "New Year's Eve? That is so soon."

"I know. Pam's planning a midnight ceremony with a Justice of the Peace."

"Robert has no idea the trouble he's getting himself into."

Anna snorted. "You sound like a B-movie actor. Give it up, Kevin. You had her for over a year and never thought to ask. Now she's found someone who has. A doctor, no less. Now let me go." She started struggling again, her hands uselessly flailing behind her back. "I don't really care about your relationship with Pam anymore. Kevin, you've got to get me out of this. Untie me!"

He stopped his pacing, once more becoming aware of the bound woman on his couch. Her face had contorted with the effort she was putting into getting free and Kevin frowned. Why hadn't he ever noticed how pretty she was?

"I can tell you one thing, Kevin Winter. Kidnapping me isn't going to help your case. I'm calling the cops just as soon as I get free."

Kevin shook his head. "I told you, you're not kidnapped, only detained." He sat beside her, his fingers undoing his carefully tied knots. She'd been tied long enough and he really didn't want to hurt her, in spite of the fact that she would probably have him arrested.

Anna's voice, still tight with anger, snapped at him. "Semantics. You tied me up, gagged me and forced me into your car. There isn't a court in the world that won't call that kidnapping. The only thing you've got going in your favor is the fact that you haven't tried to rape me."

He couldn't resist. Looming over her, he stared down at her, all traces of kindness and friendship wiped away. He let the animal inside pull at its leash. "Maybe I just haven't gotten that far yet."

For the first time, fear appeared in Anna's eyes, although she quickly masked it with more bravado. "Just try it and I'll kick you in the balls so hard you'll be seeing double the rest of your life."

He chuckled, but there was no mirth in the sound. He threw the animal back into its cage. How had he ever thought he could talk Anna into helping him out? And now he'd pushed her too far.

Kevin's shoulders drooped. The game was over. Anna wasn't going to help him and Pam was lost forever. He undid the last knot and stood up, gesturing to the phone on the table beside the sofa. "Okay. You win. Call the cops."

To her credit, she didn't bolt for the phone. Eyeing him warily, Anna rubbed her arms, letting the blood flow into them as she slowly moved toward the end table. Kevin felt a little guilty. She really hadn't deserved the treatment he'd given her, even if the dark animal inside responded to it. Pam rarely talked of Anna, and when she did, it was in mostly disparaging terms. She never liked any of her younger sister's boyfriends, and Kevin was fairly sure Pam had never told Anna of Kevin's sexual preferences. There was no way she could know how tempting she had looked with her hair tousled and the flush of anger in her cheeks. He would never rape her, but in his fantasies later on…he just might.

Anna picked up the receiver, dialed and listened, her eyes never leaving Kevin's. He made no move to stop her. He wondered if Tony would bail him out of jail for kidnapping or if he'd let him rot. Kevin turned away, aimlessly wandering toward the window that looked out over the parking lot. Absently he noted it had stopped snowing.

"Mom? I'm running a bit late."

Kevin swung around and stared at Anna, hardly understanding what he heard.

"Okay, I'm running a lot late. Sorry. I'll be home in about half an hour. Just didn't want you to worry with the snow and all. Oh, and Mom? I'm bringing a date."

With a self-satisfied grin, Anna dropped the receiver back into the cradle and turned to Kevin. "Now you have to take me home."

"Why did you do that?"

Anna's brow creased. "Why did I do what?"

"Call your parents."

"I'm late for dinner. I didn't want them to worry."

"But I kidnapped you."

She laughed and Kevin decided he'd never heard a sweeter sound. "I thought you 'temporarily detained' me."

"I did." Kevin's mind worked overtime, trying to understand why Anna hadn't called the police as she had threatened. "I mean...yeah, I did. But..."

"But nothing." Anna picked up his coat and tossed it to him. "There's a statute of limitations on this little...incident...of course. But I figure I can hold it over your head for quite some time before it runs out."

"Over my head?"

Anna stamped her foot impatiently and for a moment looked like a little girl trying to explain something to a thick-headed adult. "Stop repeating what I'm saying. I'm not calling the police. Not yet." A devilish grin spread across her face. "I have plans for you, Kevin Winter. For you and for my extremely stupid sister. You tied me up and kidnapped me. I won't call the police, if you do what I want."

Kevin didn't know whether he should thank her or tie her up again. He certainly wasn't the type to take direction well. But then again, rotting away in a jail cell wasn't high on his list of things he wanted to do with his life either. Grudgingly, he had to admit, Anna had the upper hand.

"What do you want?"

"First, you are going to apologize to me. Second, you are going to take me home. Third, you are coming to dinner with me."

"What?" Kevin looked at her as if she'd just lost her mind. "I will apologize. Profusely. That I'll do. Yes, I'll take you home. But I am not walking into that house. Not tonight."

"Why not? You wasted time before, Devil Devlin." At Kevin's surprised look, she laughed. "Yes, I know your nickname. You never knew *me*, but...well..." She laughed again and Kevin decided he liked the sound, even if he wasn't exactly sure what was going on.

"I was a freshman in college and you were the first person the upper-class women warned me against. You were a junior and, I think, had hit on almost all the girls on my floor." She giggled. "And the few you hadn't gotten around to yet couldn't wait for you to notice them."

"Look. I was a bit of a jerk back then—"

Anna shook her head. "No, you weren't. You love women. Correction. *Loved* women. You made each girl feel like she was something special. I saw it time and time again."

"Wait a minute. If we went to the same college, how come I didn't meet you there?"

Anna shrugged. "You never noticed me. But then, I grew up in Pam's shadow...and believe me, she casts a long one. So I'm used to not being noticed." Her grin was lopsided and Kevin was about to protest, to tell her she had a beauty very different from her sister's, but Anna cut him off. "Don't worry. I don't have any complexes or anything because of it. It's just I knew I wasn't your type. Besides which," she paused to flip her hair over her shoulder. Kevin liked the way the blackness caught the light and reflected it back. "I transferred out at the end of freshman year when I changed my major."

"Wow. I have to admit, Anna, not many people can take me by surprise quite so effectively. You're turning into one hell of a surprise."

"Glad I could return the favor." Anna buttoned her coat, which had come undone in all her struggles. "Now, take me home before my parents start to worry again."

"Um, yeah…right. Home."

Anna had blindsided him in more than one way tonight. First his physical reaction to seeing her tied up and helpless, then her calling her parents and not the police, topped off with the information that she had known him much longer than he had known her, made his head spin.

"I'll take you home. But I'm not coming in for dinner. I'm not dressed for it and your parents aren't expecting me."

"You'll take me home and you'll come in for dinner. You wanted to see Pam. I've just given you the opportunity."

Kevin knew when he was beaten. He also knew one other thing—he'd overlooked Pam's little sister twice. She wouldn't be overlooked again.

Chapter Three

Anna Montgomery swallowed hard, forcing her heart to get out of her throat and stay firmly in her chest. If she had planned the evening, it could not have worked out better. At the moment, she sat in the front seat of Kevin Winter's car as he drove her to her parents' house for dinner. The great Kevin Devil Devlin Winter, scourge and blessing of countless women, was under her orders to do what she wanted.

The snowplows had been out, adding a fresh white layer of snow to the piles along the streets. With Christmas almost here, it was a pretty safe bet that it would be a white one this year. Come Saturday, she was headed to the mall to finish up her shopping, crowds or no crowds.

Anna chanced a glance over at Kevin, who glowered at the road as if it were responsible for his predicament. She quickly looked away again, too tempted to laugh. From the moment her girlfriend had dropped her off at the corner of her parents' street and she'd seen Kevin's car, she'd known the fireworks were going to fly. She hadn't, however, quite anticipated the direction of the first volley. There were certainly worse things in life than being kidnapped by Devil Winter. One of these days, she'd have to ask him where that nickname came from. But not yet. First she had to get a certain older sister out of the way.

When Pam had brought Kevin home the first time over a year ago, Anna's heart had fluttered. He still had that lopsided grin, his hair still didn't stay put, and it still gave him that rakish air that had captured the hearts of so many women on campus. And he still could weaken her knees with just a look.

Except he never looked at her. Not then, and not now. Certainly not with Pam in the picture. Until tonight, she didn't think he'd ever really even looked her in the eye. Most people—correction, most *men*—tended to look right through her as if she didn't exist if Pam was anywhere nearby.

Anna sighed. She really didn't hold it against her big sister. She couldn't help being naturally beautiful any more than Anna could help being…well…plain. Where Pam's face was oval, Anna's was closer to round. Where Pam's delicate nose turned up just a bit at the end, Anna knew hers was a straight shot from bridge to tip. And where Pam's figure, kept slim by strict dieting and exercise, could stop men in their tracks, Anna's athletic look was more suited to the baseball diamond than the fashion runway.

She stole a glance at the man beside her. He needed a shave. Probably should have made him do that before leaving his apartment. No matter. She would just spin a story about him growing a beard. A wicked grin played on her lips. Pam would freak out at that. Hell, she was gonna freak already just from him walking in the door. It was all she could do to keep from rubbing her hands together and letting loose a deep, evil laugh. As it was, a chuckle escaped and Kevin, who up 'til now had driven in sullen silence, noticed.

"I'm not finding a whole lot of amusement in this, you know. I hope you realize that."

Anna stuck out her chin. "Well, I am. Pam's going to throw a fit when you walk in the door on my arm and I'm going to love every moment of it." She turned to face him. "Don't you see? As soon as she sees you with me, she'll get jealous and want you back." She kept silent about the second part of the plan already forming in the back of her mind.

Kevin glanced at her as if she'd lost her mind. "That's your strategy? Pretend I'm with you now and hope she gets jealous of her little sister?"

Somehow it sounded awfully Hollywood when he said it. She frowned. "And peeping in windows is a better idea?"

"I need to explain that—"

Anna crossed her arms and settled into her seat with a self-satisfied smirk as she cut him off. "You watch. You'll walk in, she'll throw a hissy fit and by the end of the weekend, she'll be calling you to get back together."

Kevin shook his head. "I'm doing this only because I'm being blackmailed. You know that."

Anna gave him a disgusted look. "Of course I know that. Why on earth would you ever want to actually go out with me?"

Kevin opened his mouth and shut it without saying anything. Twice. Anna went back to staring out the window. She hadn't meant to sound so bitter. In college, she'd made as much fun of Devil Winter as the rest of the girls on the floor, but deep down inside, it rankled that he hadn't thought her worth his time. She'd had her share of boyfriends over the years. The fact that she hadn't attracted this one really shouldn't be such a big deal. Except it was. She frowned as she tried to figure out why.

They turned the corner into the dead-end street and pulled into the Montgomery driveway. Kevin turned off the ignition and gave her one of those you're-not-really-going-to-make-me-do-this looks. She had only one word for him. "Out."

The evening was both better and worse than she had expected. Pam's iciness was predictable. Anna was prepared for the barbs about "castoffs" and "secondhand boyfriends" her sister had thrown at her when Kevin wasn't beside her. She was even prepared for her parents' look of shock when Kevin walked in the door.

But what totally bowled her over was her sister's dissolve into a fit of hysterical crying after Kevin left. That shook her. Was it possible her sister loved the man after all? That would definitely be a problem, as Anna fully intended Kevin to be her own.

Lying in bed later that night, unable to sleep, Anna tried to figure out the precise moment when she had decided Kevin meant more than just a notch in her belt. Was it the moment he held her in the snow outside the living room window? Or later, when he tied her up? She definitely liked that part. The hardest thing she had ever done was to conceal just how turned on she was by his rough handling of her. She had pretended anger, because to admit arousal was impossible.

But wanting she had been. In the dark, under the blankets of her bed, her hand slipped along her breast, lightly pinching her nipple, then pinching harder as she imagined how Kevin would take the nipple in his teeth, biting down until she cried out in aroused agony while her arms were bound behind her.

She smiled that evil little smile she got when she was thinking naughty thoughts. Kevin had shown a remarkable knowledge of knots. No matter how she struggled, she had been totally unable to get free. The thought flushed warmth all through her, straight down to her pussy. Her hand followed the warm trail as she let her mind wander, creating a fantasy she fervently hoped to make come true...

~~~~~

They were in Kevin's apartment, in the living room. As she stood to the side, already naked, Kevin unfolded the couch, revealing a double bed hiding underneath. A sensuous deep red satin sheet was already on the mattress and leather cuffs dangled from the frame, one in each of the four corners. The locks that held them in place glimmered in the soft light cast upon the scene.

Although she wore nothing, she wanted Kevin still dressed in tan pants and a white button-up shirt...no, make that a cream-colored shirt that accented his light brown hair. His eyes, shadowed by the light, bore into the darkest recesses of her being, challenging her to submit to the glorious torture he had planned.

Anna's fingers slickened as her body responded to the images in her head. Both hands were involved now, one set of fingers holding her labia apart, the other taking advantage of the opening to circle her clit...occasionally dipping down to her pussy as her body heated.

"On the bed, spread wide."

She gasped at the words of command from Kevin's mouth, letting her thoughts detour even as she moaned into the darkness of her room. That wonderful, kissable mouth. She wanted his lips to be soft, yet insistent. Gentle, yet commanding. In her dreams, Kevin paused, leaning over her as she lay on the bed, his hands on either side of her...touching her with only his lips...first gently, then forcing his way in, making her give way to him as he possessed her mouth.

Anna rubbed faster, taking short breaths, trying to breathe as she lost herself in Kevin's kiss. Deeper he probed, tasting her as she yielded her body to his touch. A sure touch that knew just how to elicit moans and whimpers of pleasure from the hidden spaces inside.

The kiss ended, yet the tingles grew as he fastened the cuffs around her ankles and wrists, forcing her open to his inspection. She imagined his fingers lightly caressing the length of her body, taking a meandering path over her breasts and stomach...each circle bringing him lower and lower.

He bent down and blew his warm breath on her exposed pussy lips and Anna gritted her teeth to stifle the moan that threatened to escape into the darkness of her bedroom. Her fingers rubbed harder as her imaginary lover slid a finger inside her, his other hand teasing her clit, deliberately pushing her toward the edge.

Kevin's firm touch brooked nothing but complete surrender and she gave it to him, her own fingers substituting for his as she drove herself off the edge of the cliff and into the sky beyond. One gasp, two...she hovered, her entire body tense...waiting...and then the plunge, her body racking with the intensity of her orgasm.

~~~~~

When the swells of emotion passed and she had caught her breath once more, Anna grinned and licked her fingers clean, imagining they were Kevin's and he had commanded her to. Feeling every inch the wanton, Anna stared up at her ceiling, deciding on her next step in the capture of Kevin Winter.

* * * * *

The opportunity came a week later. "The Group", comprised of Beth and Richard and Ave and Tina and herself, often hung out together...going to the movies or out for pizza and wings. Beth had called Anna at work to tell her they were planning to meet at the mall immediately after hitting their respective banks, doing a bit of Christmas shopping and then heading out to see the latest Tim Allen Christmas movie. They'd snack at the movie and maybe do pizza later. Was she in?

Anna was in. Racing into the mall now, she spied three of The Group gathered around the mall's carousel. The landmark, moved there after the local amusement park folded, was a popular meeting place for separated shoppers. Cheery holiday tunes floated from the center of the whirling merry-go-round and Anna grinned to see a father, looking a bit green around the gills, bravely holding his little girl on her chosen horse. A white charger, of course.

Exchanging hugs with Beth, Tina and Richard, she looked around for the last of their companions. "Where's Ave?"

"Late as usual." Beth rolled her eyes as the others grinned. Ave always seemed to run behind. They didn't mind. He was never very late, and always had great excuses.

"I need to head over to the bookstore first." Tina, the organized member of the group, had her list out, checking it twice. "What time is the movie?"

Robert consulted his watch. "First showing's at 6:50 and it's 5:10 now."

"So we need to be in front of the theatre by what...6:30?" Anna could see the wheels turning in Tina's mind as she plotted out her battle plan. When Richard nodded, Tina folded her list with decision. "All right. The bookstore's only around the corner. When Ave gets here, stop by and pick me up?"

They told her they would and Tina headed off.

Anna liked the easy camaraderie of these people who shared an apartment building in common. Ave took his ribbing with typical good nature when he showed up ten minutes later and together they trooped over to find Tina just finishing up at the bookstore. Ebbing and flowing together as their shopping needs dictated, the time passed far too quickly and soon they grouped together in front of the entrance to the mall's movie theatre.

"Anna? How are you?"

Anna's heart leapt. For a moment, her joyful surprise showed on her face...just long enough for both Tina and Beth to notice. With a quick swallow, Anna plastered an aloof expression on her face and turned to face the man who belonged to that beautiful baritone. She extended a cool hand, proud of her decorum.

"Hello, Kevin. I didn't expect to find you here. Of course, I didn't expect to see you the other night, either."

Her veiled reference did not go unheeded. His eyes narrowed as if he expected her to out him right there in front of her friends. But she didn't. She had something far more nefarious in mind. This was not an opportunity to be missed.

Calmly she introduced him around, glaring at the smirks on both Beth's and Tina's faces. Busy casting around in her mind for an excuse to leave the group, she started when she heard Beth invite Kevin to join them at the movies.

"We're going to see Tim Allen's movie, why don't you join us?" Beth smiled at Kevin, but gave a nod filled with meaning in Anna's direction. She started to protest, but Kevin cut her off. "I'd love to. Do you like popcorn?"

Anna fumed as Kevin sailed past her and offered Beth his arm. To her credit, Beth fluttered a little before accepting it, sending an "oops" look over Kevin's shoulder as the two turned to go into the theatre. Grabbing Richard's arm, Anna dragged him through the doors behind them. Two could play that game.

Anna, however, did not count on Beth's resourcefulness. Laden with popcorn and soft drinks, the six lined up coming down the aisle. Beth maneuvered the group so she entered the row first with Kevin beside her. Anna took advantage to go in next, not caring how the others ordered themselves. Kevin's smirk almost made her change her mind.

He was a perfect gentleman all through the movie. Drat him. Not one move on his part. Too bad she'd driven here on her own. Otherwise she'd talk him into driving her home later. At least the night wasn't over.

It was Ave who jumped into the fray this time, asking Kevin if he'd like to join the group in their weekly ritual of pizza and wings at Mario's. The credits rolled on the screen, but Anna liked to watch them all the way to the end. A few filmmakers had taken to giving a little "goodie" to those who stayed to watch, but that wasn't why she liked to watch the names scroll by. Those people had put a lot of effort into making the film and she felt at least one person ought to honor them by reading their names. The others, by now, had gotten used to her oddity and had fun reading some of the more unique names out loud. They were the last six in the theatre when the lights came up and Ave called out his invitation to Kevin.

"Love to. Haven't been there before."

Richard hooted as he made his way into the aisle. "A Mario virgin! We're gonna have fun tonight!"

For over sixty years, the small brick building across the parking lot from the mall had housed the best fast-food Italian restaurant in town, as far as Anna was concerned. Crispy crusted pizzas, calzones, and of course, chicken wings, were the staples of the menu, along with assorted pasta dishes and submarine sandwiches. Mario's had it all.

Anna took her turn shuffling along the seats and into the aisle of the theatre. "Better watch out, their wings are pretty hot."

Tina grinned. "Pretty hot? Try *volcanic* hot." Tina always ordered pizza, saying the wings were just too much for her. Anna could eat about a half-dozen before the heat got to her. Richard, Beth and Ave always ate all twelve in their respective orders. She wondered where Kevin would fit in.

Later, she realized she should've known. The six of them sat clustered around a medium-sized round table, the red-and-white-checked tablecloth barely discernable underneath the piles of plates and wadded-up napkins. Kevin sat beside her, twelve sets of bones heaped on his plate. His fingers had been licked clean, and now he sat back with a self-satisfied smirk on his face. A dab of hot sauce by the side of his mouth gave him a little-boy look and Anna couldn't help but laugh.

"Well, Kevin, I'd have to say you fit right in with this crowd." Richard eyed the pile of bones that matched his own. "You kept right up with me."

"Great. Another one for the hot wing side." Tina put out a fake pout, then polished off the last bite of the last piece of pizza.

"Any time Anna wants to bring you around, you're welcome at our table." Beth's eyes twinkled and Anna tried to kick her under the table.

"Ow! Who kicked me?" Ave peered down, but there were too many legs to tell.

"That was meant for me, dearest." Beth's stage whisper into Ave's ear brought nudges from Tina and Robert. "Anna's trying to send me a message to shut up about bringing Kevin around."

"Yeah, and we can see it ain't working." Anna rolled her eyes.

Kevin just grinned, wiping his hands with one of several wet napkins provided by the restaurant. "Well, any time Anna feels like inviting me, I'll just have to accept."

Anna blushed, wishing the lighting were dimmer so no one could see. This was tipping her hand more than she wanted to. "If you behave yourself, I just might."

She grinned when an uncomfortable look crossed Kevin's face at her emphasis on the word "behave". Score one for her. Feeling like she had regained the upper hand, she dug in her wallet for her share of the bill.

"I've got it." Kevin pushed her hands back. "This one is my treat."

Anna shook her head. "Thanks, Kevin, but I'll take care of my part."

Beth snorted. "Let him pay, Anna. Not every day that a guy offers to buy you dinner." She glared at Ave and Richard, who both held up their hands.

"Sorry, woman. I'm tapped out. Pay your own bills." Robert opened his wallet to show the one and only ten-dollar-bill he had. "Gotta get to the ATM later."

Ave's excuse raised some eyebrows. "I'm paying for Tina tonight. Find some other sucker."

This time Tina's cheeks were the ones that turned bright pink. A chorus of all-knowing "Ohhhs" came from the circle of friends.

"I'm like Richard," Tina protested. "I forgot to go to the ATM after we went shopping."

"Mmm-hmm. Sure, Tina. A likely story." Beth ribbed her, and Anna, glad the attention had been diverted, decided to be gracious and let Kevin pay for her dinner.

Their cars were scattered all over the mall's parking lot so the group said their goodbyes, each guy escorting one of the girls to her respective vehicle. Kevin, of course, took Anna's arm as they called out goodnights. Anna thought of and rejected several comments. All seemed too sarcastic. That was definitely not the tone she wanted Kevin to walk away with. Instead, she walked beside him in silence, every sense tingling to be alone and so close to him at last. From the possessive way he held her, making sure she didn't slip on the icy patches, to the scent of his masculine cologne...every part of him set her heart racing. She was glad they didn't talk. She couldn't be sure her voice wouldn't crack and betray her.

They rounded the corner to see Anna's little runabout sitting all alone in that section of the vast concrete parking lot. She loved her four-cylinder manual transmission for the control it gave her over the road, especially in winter. Light from the lamppost shone down on the car, making it look lonely. In the bright white light, they could see a few random snowflakes settle onto the hood of the car. One landed on Anna's cheek and Kevin paused to brush it away. The act caught them both by surprise and they jumped apart as if shocked. Kevin recovered first. "Please tell me that's your car."

Anna nodded, her heart racing. She wanted him. Right here. Right now. All she had to do was tell him. With his reputation, she was sure he would go back to her apartment and spend the night with her.

She took a deep breath and stayed on safer subjects. She did want him. But not just for a night. Keeping her voice steady, she wondered where his car was. "Where did you park?"

"Over on the other side."

"I can give you a ride over."

"Thanks. I'll take it."

Anna suspected Kevin was going to have trouble fitting his lanky frame into the passenger seat, since she usually kept the seat pulled all the way up so she could carry groceries easier in the back. He was all grace, however, as with one motion, he slid his body partway into the bucket seat, leaned down to lift the lever and slide the seat to a more comfortable spot, then settled in as if the car were made for him. She stifled a sigh and started the car.

It didn't take nearly long enough to drive around the mall and find his car, just as lonely as hers, sitting forlorn in its place. She thought she ought to say something witty, something astute, just *some*thing, but not a single thought came to her except she'd had a wonderful evening. And when Kevin turned to look at her in the harsh light of the parking lot lamp, even that inanity stuck in her throat.

Anna held her breath, her lips parted as her desires tore her in two directions. He still wanted Pam, yet tonight she had a glimpse of what life would be like with him at her side instead of her sister's and she knew she had to make him forget his past entanglements and come to her freely. Tonight, a kiss would be too filled with shadows to be everything she knew he could deliver.

So instead of leaning toward him and inviting his kiss, she leaned back against her seat and gestured to his vehicle with a disengagement she did not feel. "There you are!"

Kevin hesitated as if he were about to ask her something, but apparently changed his mind. He opened his door and called over his shoulder, "Thanks for tonight. I had a good time." When she only nodded, he added, "We should do it again sometime."

Was he fishing? Did he want her to invite him somewhere else? Questions pelted her mind and before she could sort them out, Kevin had shut her car door and opened his. Deciding silence was better than making a fool of herself, she waited until she heard his engine roar to life before putting her runabout in gear and heading back to her apartment.

Anna sighed as she drove down the empty road. All she needed to do was figure out how to turn tonight's fun into more.

Chapter Four

ಬ

Sprawled on the couch in his apartment, Kevin flipped through the stations, looking for a good holiday special. Anything to cheer him up. Tony lay in the recliner, a bowl of popcorn on his lap, getting frustrated with Kevin's aimlessness. "Just pick a station, man. Stop flipping!"

"Nothin' looks good."

"Stop there. Yeah. *It's a Wonderful Life*. You need to see that one. Tonight. You got a shitload of blessings and can't see 'em." He tossed an unpopped kernel at Kevin's head, who only turned to glower at him.

"Yeah, a shitload of blessings. My family's not getting together for the first time ever in my life, the girl I love is gonna get married to some other dude and her sister takes me out with her friends last night and I have a good time. Loads of blessings."

"That last one sounded pretty good, actually." Tony shoveled a fistful of popcorn into his mouth as one commercial gave way to another.

Kevin glowered at him again and didn't answer.

"What?" Tony asked, his mouth full.

"I had a good time." Kevin emphasized each word so his friend would get the point. When Tony only shrugged, he rolled his eyes and elaborated. "I wasn't with Pam. I was with Anna. Her sister. And I had a good time."

"So? Go out with Anna instead of Pam. What's the big deal?"

Kevin shook his head, not answering as the commercial ended and the movie picked up in the middle. Clarence was trying to convince the Jimmy Stewart character that suicide wasn't the answer. As Kevin watched Clarence work his magic, transporting Stewart into an alternate universe, he considered an alternate universe of his own.

What if he dated Anna instead of Pam? Anna was certainly livelier...but Pam still took his breath away with her svelte figure and the way she swung her hips when she walked in those stiletto heels. Of course, she did have a tendency to preen in store windows, but Kevin didn't care. He had enjoyed watching other men give his girl appreciative glances, knowing at the end of the day, her heart belonged to him.

Except it didn't anymore. If it ever really had. He watched as Jimmy Stewart realized the woman he had fallen in love with now didn't even know his name. Kevin had seen this movie dozens of times. Stewart would decide to go back to his life, to pick up the pieces and move on with the woman he loved at his side.

But what if Kevin decided differently? After a few initial tries, Pam had made it quite clear she wasn't going to put up with any of "that bondage stuff" Kevin enjoyed. At the time, although disappointed, Kevin put it aside, thinking it was a worthy sacrifice for love.

Then he'd tied up Anna. The memory made him grin like a fool. While the incident hadn't been a sexual encounter, he couldn't forget the look of her clothed body bound in his ropes, or the fire that spit from her eyes...fire that wasn't always angry. He could swear she enjoyed it.

And the dinner at her parents' house later. Anna had been the perfect hostess, smoothing over things with her parents and ignoring Pam's jibes. The more he'd thought about that dinner over the past week, the more irritated at Pam he'd become. She had treated him like crap, but he hadn't had the option of leaving.

The TV droned on, but Kevin didn't even notice it. Anna had treated him with respect, even when she had been spitting nails at him. She had shown herself to be above all Pam's ludicrous posturing. She had invited him out with her friends, and he'd found he liked being with her. And above all, she hadn't called the cops when he'd kidnapped her. Maybe Tony was right and he was looking at the wrong sister.

"Nah, Anna doesn't want me. She has lots of friends and isn't looking for a boyfriend right now." Kevin wasn't sure who he was trying to convince, Tony…or himself.

As if to prove it to himself, he swung past Anna's on his way home from work the next day. He'd stop in, see if she wanted to go out to get a bite to eat, perhaps make love to her and get her out of his system. That's all he needed to do. Make love to the woman and move on. Just like in college.

Except Anna had other plans. The look of surprise and consternation on her face were not exactly what Kevin had hoped for.

"I'm sorry," she'd replied to his invitation for dinner. "I have a date already."

Feeling like a fool and now a two-time loser, Kevin stopped at the grocery store, bought two half-gallons of chocolate fudge ripple, took them home, ate his way through three-quarters of a gallon of ice cream while watching a basketball game, and finally went to bed.

By Christmas Eve, the early December snow was nothing but a memory. The rain of the past two days had seen to any leftover piles at the ends of driveways, although a few car-high mounds remained in the corners of the mall parking lot. Skirting around the end of one of those black-crusted reminders of the season, Kevin searched for a parking space. He'd already dropped Tony off at the airport for his flight to New York and his big family reunion, listening again to Tony's advice to find a good woman and sleep away the holiday with her. Feeling restless and having nothing better to do, Kevin had decided to go to the one place he knew would be bustling with holiday spirit—the mall.

He wedged his car into a spot made for a much smaller vehicle and decided it was the best he was going to get today. Making himself as skinny as possible, he slipped between the car and the snow pile and headed for the food court. Substituting food for companionship wasn't a habit he intended to cultivate, but it was the only way he was going to make it through the next couple of days. Deliberately, he pushed thoughts of his traitorous family from his mind.

The rows of fast-food restaurants were packed with shoppers taking a quick break. He paused to scan the crowd. Holiday spirit sounded out in the calls to friends, the bells outside the doors, the carols coming from the carousel. Banners of red and green, weighted with golden tassels hung from the skylights. Kevin felt his shoulders relax. How could one stay stressed with so much good cheer in the air?

"Kevin! Hey, Kevin! Over here!"

A hand waved frantically from one of the tables. He headed toward it, unsure who it belonged to and hoping it was someone he wouldn't mind meeting in the mood he was in. Finally getting around the woman with the baby carriage and three kids in tow, he spotted the woman of his dreams, sitting amid an island of shopping bags. Pam Montgomery, an island of tranquility in a sea of chaos.

But her hand was not raised in greeting. Kevin slowed his steps and turned his attention to her companion.

Anna's forced smile as he approached pinched his heart. It was *her* hand raised in greeting and as she lowered it, he realized just how often she must've played second to Pam's beauty. Not quite sure if he was trying to make Pam jealous, or simply trying to make up to Anna for Pam's existence, he bent to Anna first, giving her a light kiss on the cheek. From the corner of his eye, he saw no change in Pam's attitude or expression. Okay, so she wasn't jealous of his attentions to her sister. It was time he faced the fact that his relationship with Pam was really over.

Kevin offered his hand to Pam, who took it regally — friendly, yet distant — as a queen might address her subjects, Kevin thought. With sudden insight, he realized she had always been that way, but he'd been blinded to her shortcomings, so taken with her external magnificence. Seeing the two sisters here now, side by side in such an ordinary setting, their differences obvious, Kevin wondered if he'd been chasing the wrong one.

"Did you just get here?" Anna's small talk took Kevin by surprise when such momentous understandings had been going on in his head.

"Hmm? What? Oh! Yeah, just came in." He gestured to the mound of bags surrounding their small table. "You two've been here a while, I see."

"All finished." Pam smiled up at him with a look that said *I'm better than you because I'm done and you're not. Knowing you, you're just starting.*

Kevin grinned, a sudden need to get even twisting in his belly. "I'm done, too." At Pam's startled look, he turned to Anna. "Finished up last week. But I like the spirit in the stores today, so I thought I'd come out and just walk around a bit."

"Figures you'd be the sort to like crowds."

Kevin almost replied to Pam's snide comment and even as little as ten minutes ago, probably would have. His new revelation, however, had him seeing her in a different light. Instead he turned to Anna. "Are you all done, too?"

She nodded, her eyes narrowing as if she saw but did not understand the change in him. Pam, apparently, noticed it too. With a little wicked smile, she turned to her sister.

"Anna, did you know Kevin had a nickname in college?"

Anna shot a puzzled look at her sister and Kevin shifted uncomfortably. What was Pam up to?

"He was pretty popular with the ladies, from what I hear. Even had a nickname. Want to hear it?"

Anna opened her mouth to reply, but before she could, Pam blurted it out. "Devil Devlin." She sniffed. "Although I'm sure I don't know why. Your name's Kevin. Seems it should have been something derived from Kevin...or something."

Kevin gritted his teeth, but kept his tone civil. "Devlin is my middle name." He turned to Anna. Suddenly it was important that she understand. "When I left home for college, I wanted a fresh start. I was a sort of goof-off in high school, but no one at college knew that. I figured a new name would give me a new start." He shrugged.

"But it was too hard to remember to answer to Devlin. Before the year was out, I'd gone back to using my first name. My frat brothers, however," Kevin paused to grin—a grin that showed the dimple in his cheek that had been the downfall of many a fine lady, "since I'd pledged as Devlin Winter, and had made a reputation with the ladies..."

"You became known as Devil," Anna finished for him. He nodded.

Since every chair in the place was already taken, Kevin couldn't sit down. He stooped instead, crossing his arms across the tabletop, ignoring Pam and looking straight at Anna. "How about I carry your bags to the car and then we take a walk around the mall together?"

"What? You can't. Anna and I have things to do." Pam stood, letting him know the conversation was at an end. She slid her arms into the sleeves of her coat as if she dared him to protest.

Kevin's eyes never left Anna's and he took her hand as she, too, stood. "Walk with me?"

Later, Kevin would have sworn the mall became silent as he waited for her answer. People disappeared from the tables, crying babies no longer existed, and parents no longer scolded. Cheery greetings and grumpy bah-humbugs went unheeded as he waited for Anna to speak. He almost held his breath when she turned to her sister.

"Pam, Kevin and I are going to spend some time together. I'll see you at Mom and Dad's tomorrow morning."

Pam's eyes flashed daggers as she gathered up her bags. "Fine. Leave me alone on Christmas Eve. See if I care."

Anna buttoned her coat and Kevin picked up her bags. His conscience told him to help Pam with hers as well, but the spiteful part of him enjoyed watching her struggle. Once she had them all in hand, however, her natural aplomb took over and even as she stalked away, she managed to look incredibly graceful.

Her parting words, however, nagged him. Kevin turned to Anna. "She's going to be alone tonight?"

"Robert's on call at the hospital. She's getting to see firsthand what it means to be a doctor's wife. Can't tell yet whether she's got it in her or not."

They threaded their way between the tables and out the door of the mall. A cold drizzle had started up and the two hurried toward Anna's car. She popped the trunk and by the time Kevin got the bags stowed, the rain became a downpour. Anna unlocked the car and laughing, they dove for the safety of the dry interior. Since it was Anna's runabout, she took the driver's seat and Kevin pushed back the passenger seat to give his long legs lots of room.

Rain beat a tattoo on the roof of the car as sheets of water poured over the windshield. "Still want to go for a walk around the mall?" Anna nodded toward the weather.

What he wanted was to kiss her. How much time had he already wasted on Pam? Time, he was beginning to realize, which could have been much less aggravating and a whole lot more fun if spent with Anna. This woman had all the possibilities of being someone he wanted to make love to time and time again. Taking a leisurely stroll around the mall was now the last thing on his mind. He shook his head. "I think I'd just as soon stay here as go out again."

Kevin couldn't stop looking at her face. She'd called herself plain before, but she wasn't. Not by a long shot. While Pam had the edge that pushed her into the drop-dead gorgeous category, Anna had a sweeter smile — probably because it was genuine, he realized. Her normally straight black hair, curled now in the damp and currently tucked behind one ear, combined with that straight nose and those full lips to give her an allure all her own.

As the rain obscured the world, Kevin reached out and took her chin, his eyes focused on her lips, knowing they would taste of spring and bright promises. She didn't resist, nor did she stop him when he leaned forward to kiss her. He intended a light kiss, an exploratory one, wanting to be sure she didn't deck him for being fresh. What he got surprised the hell out of him.

Almost the moment their lips touched, the manner of the kiss changed. He couldn't get enough of her fast enough and she couldn't stop giving. Her mouth, soft and sensitive, hungered for him as much as he wanted her. He slipped his hand into the damp softness of her hair as the kiss quickly deepened, their tongues searching, tasting each other at last.

And the kiss didn't stop. He wanted to pull her into him, devour her and keep her nearby where he could taste her any time he wanted. But he had no words for that. So he let his fervent hands talk for him, unbuttoning her coat and sliding in along her waist to revel in the warmth of her body.

Anna moved toward him, abruptly breaking the kiss and the momentum of the moment when the stick shift got in the way. While his head reeled, her face lit up with a mischievous grin and she nodded toward the backseat. "More comfortable back there."

"Making out in the car? In December?" Kevin grinned back. Not one to miss an opportunity, especially when his body had such an incredible response to such a simple kiss, he grabbed the door handle. "Race ya!"

He bolted out of the door and into the back in seconds, Anna only a few heartbeats slower, as she took the time to slip her coat off. Chilled, she shivered as she shut the door and closed out the rain.

"Come here, I'll warm you up."

"I'm counting on it."

Kevin enfolded her in his arms, wondering why he hadn't ever noticed before the delicate shape of her ear or the way her cheeks turned pink when it was cold. "Now, where were we?"

"I believe we were trying to consume each other." She slid her hands under his coat and up along his back.

"Ah, yes. Shall we try that again?" He bent down to kiss her again, softer this time, exploring at his ease every nuance and shape of her lips. Full lips that, until now, he hadn't realized had been made for kissing. The passion of their first kiss had left them breathless. He was determined this time not to rush. Anna let him explore, seeming content to follow where he led.

He couldn't resist bringing his hand up along her side under her sweater, noticing she didn't flinch when he brushed against the spot that seemed to send too many women into fits of giggles. Good. He would have fun finding out where her ticklish spots were, since the obvious one didn't move her. His intent now, however, was higher up...and in front.

The cold made her nipples stand out in the confines of the thin bra she wore. She shivered again and Kevin knew it wasn't from the cold this time. He pulled back to look at her, make sure he had permission before exploring further.

"Don't stop," was all she said, her eyes already dreamy. Yet Kevin sensed she held back still. Not like the kiss in the front seat where all stops were gone. She enjoyed his touch, his explorations, but he could tell there was caution. What was she guarding? Her heart? How many times had she been hurt?

Kevin brushed his fingertips over the top of the raised nipple, seeing her lips part and enjoying the sudden intake of her breath. Bending to kiss her again, he closed his hand over her breast as his lips closed over hers. A piece of whatever she was using to hold him at bay fell away and she relaxed a little into his arms.

Kevin prolonged the kiss, his fingers warming against her skin. He knew his cold hands tormented her, but she didn't push him away. If anything, she moved even closer, pressing into the palm of his hand, encouraging him to knead his fingers over and around her breast.

He needed her all right. Trapped in the confines of his pants, his cock grew uncomfortably large for the too-small space and yet Kevin was reluctant to expose himself to the increasingly frigid air. No, there would be time enough for that later, if he played his cards right.

And at the moment, he was playing the seductive card. Luring her in...getting her excited yet not letting her go too far. Just hints and promises of what could be. All part of the fun of taking a woman to bed. He thought of Anna tied on his bed, vulnerable to his every whim. While he never approached such activities this early on in a relationship—no sense in scaring them away—he had to wonder if Anna might already suspect his predilections, based on their previous encounter.

This train of thought wasn't helping his cock. The incredible smoothness of her skin coupled with the mixture of eagerness and reserve turned him on in a way he never had experienced. With all the other women he'd had, especially those in college, neither his head nor his heart ever got involved. It was straight sex. With Pam it had been different. With her, Kevin had become intoxicated with her beauty.

But Anna had an inner core that baffled him. Even as he bent to taste her nipple, a part of his brain wouldn't shut up. It kept trying to figure out what made her different...and what that meant to him.

"Kevin, where are you?"

Anna's question took him by surprise. He looked up, confused. "What?"

"Your hands are wonderful, but I get the sense your mind is somewhere else. If you don't want to do this, it's okay."

"No! I do want to do this. Really." He squeezed her breast to emphasize his point.

She took his face between her hands. "Then make love to me as if you mean it, not as if you're doing this because you're lonely."

Her voice was gentle, but her meaning clear. She wasn't a substitute for Pam or anyone else. If he wanted to bed her, he had to truly want her—all of her—for herself. No more analyzing. Put up or shut up as the saying went. He pulled his hand from under her clothes and took her hands in his. She deserved truth. All of it. Her fingers were cold and he warmed them with his big mitts.

"I'll admit...I *am* lonely." He tried to explain. "Christmas has always been my favorite time of year. I've always spent it with my family down in Texas, playing tricks on my brothers, opening presents. Going to my aunt's for dinner or else having them over to our house. Lots of cousins and noise and fun. You know. Family stuff."

Anna shook her head. "My family is pretty staid, in case you haven't noticed. No tricks, just a civilized morning opening presents and then brunch. No extended family. Just the four of us."

"No cousins?"

"Both my parents were only children and three of my four grandparents have already passed away. Only one grandmother is left and she's in a nursing home with Parkinson's. We'll visit her as a family tomorrow afternoon, although most of us usually try to stop by once a week or so."

Kevin knew by "most of us" she meant everyone but Pam. What had he ever seen in that woman? Beauty, and apparently that was it. He shook his head. "I'm afraid there's little that's civilized in our Christmas. We take turns opening presents so everyone can see what everyone else gets, but that's about as far as it goes. Grace before meals, yes. But then it's every man for himself." He grinned at the memories. Lots of noise and laughter...and no one went away hungry.

"So why not this year?" She shivered in the cold and Kevin leaned forward to pull her coat from the front seat. As he answered, he wrapped it around her.

"My parents went on a second honeymoon. They got married the day after Christmas forty years ago and this year decided to go on a cruise. They're already sailing on calm seas with balmy breezes."

"Don't you have two brothers? Why aren't you getting together with them? Or with your cousins?"

"Both my brothers made other plans when they found out Mom and Dad weren't going to be home. They mailed their presents out, just like I mailed mine to them. It isn't the same, though." He tried to keep the pout out of his voice, but it came through anyway.

Suddenly Anna laughed, a long laugh that dissolved into a giggle. Kevin stared at her, baffled. What had he said that was so funny? Still, he had to smile—she had an infectious laugh that made him want to laugh out loud, too.

"Sorry." She grinned at him. "I just never realized that the great Devil Winter is actually a kid at heart."

He gave her a wry grin. "Just don't tell anyone, okay? I kinda like my reputation the way it is."

"As a ladies' man?" There was a challenge in her voice.

"As a man who loves women."

"Ever think you'll find the one woman worth giving up all the others for?"

Kevin narrowed his eyes and studied her face. It betrayed nothing. He answered tit for tat. "Someday I'll find her and she won't know what hit her. I'll take care of her, protect her, and make love to her every day. She, in turn, will take care of me, protect me, and let me make love to her every day."

"Sounds like a pretty even relationship."

Kevin frowned. "Why wouldn't it be?"

Anna didn't look at him, but doodled with her finger on her thigh. "I was thinking about those ropes."

Kevin sat back, totally stunned. "What about those ropes?"

"I'd say you were pretty good with them. Now, I might expect such expert knots from a Boy Scout or a sailor, but you weren't either of those, were you?" She looked up at him from under her lashes. Yet it wasn't a coquettish glance, rather a searching one Kevin found himself under.

"No, I wasn't either of those. What are you asking me, Anna?" He decided not to make it easy on her. Besides, his heart was beating too hard for him to take chances. Was she intimating what he thought she was?

She put her chin up, almost as if she were screwing her courage into place. He understood that, whatever she was about to say, it came from a part of her she rarely shared with anyone. When she spoke, he knew he was right.

"If you want an equal partner in a relationship, where do the ropes come in? If you tie a woman up, isn't the dynamic unbalanced? She's there, all tied and helpless and you're there, all macho and dominant."

Her voice shook and Kevin took her hands. "Anna, I won't lie to you. You are proving to be far too interesting a woman for that. Yes, I like to tie women and play with their bodies, bringing them to climax over and over again before...well, before I take them. Still tied up. Still helpless to prevent me."

Her eyes dropped and he put his hand under her chin. It was important that she hear the rest of it. "But that only works if the woman enjoys being tied. She has to give me permission to do what I want with her, or the same act has a very ugly name. And I would never, ever take a woman against her will. Do you understand?"

She nodded and swallowed hard. Clearly there was more she wanted to ask him, questions that would reveal secrets she had never told. Kevin guessed what those might be, but kept silent. Anna had to come to this on her own, or the specter of coercion would always hang over them. He waited with patience for her to find the courage.

"So there are women who enjoy that—being tied up and helpless? And that's not wrong?"

"No, Anna. It's not wrong. It doesn't mean they want to be sex slaves and do nothing all day long but be used by men for that purpose. It means they simply wish to give up responsibility for a while. To rest in the arms of their beloved who will take care of them and give them a wonderful experience. Bondage is a kink, yes…but one shared by millions of people."

Her eyes widened, then narrowed with skepticism. "Millions?"

He laughed. "Okay, maybe hundreds of thousands. Depends on how broad a definition of bondage you want to get into. For me, anyone who ties anyone else up for sexual pleasure gets the label."

Anna nodded. "So when you say you want someone to take care of and to make love to every day…"

"I'm not looking for a sex slave, if that's what you're asking."

She sat back, a relieved look on her face. "It was. I'm still not sure I understand it all, but I do know that…" She hesitated and Kevin gave her the time to phrase what she wanted to say. "I know that night you kidnapped me, well, I was…intrigued by the feeling of being tied."

"In other words, you didn't mind it…and maybe even enjoyed it a little?"

"Yes." She looked up at him quickly, as if afraid that admission would make him think ill of her.

Kevin crossed his arms. "Good."

"That's it? 'Good'?"

He sat forward again, dropping all pretense. Too much rode on the answer to this question. "Anna, do you want me to take you home and tie you up and make love to you?" His heart pounded as he awaited her answer.

"You won't think I'm a pushover if I say yes?"

"No way. I'll think you're a woman of uncommon courage if you say yes."

"Courage?"

"It isn't easy to voluntarily put yourself in that position. I can't do it. Only once when I was learning did I switch places. Glad I did, 'cause I learned a whole lot. But don't want to make a habit of it."

"So you like being the...what's the word? Top?"

He grinned. "You've been doing your research."

She sighed and let it all come out. "For a very long time. I've always had the fantasy, but never the guts to ask anyone. I was afraid they'd think me sick or something."

"Anna." He took her chin again, this time kissing her gently before continuing. "You're not sick. Your fantasies are normal. And I can make them come true."

"Then take me home and make love to me, Kevin Devlin Winter. Before I change my mind and chicken out."

Chapter Five

ဆ

Leaving Anna's car in the mall parking lot over Christmas wasn't an option. Driving separately temporarily cooled their passions and Kevin fervently hoped she wouldn't change her mind and drive somewhere other than his apartment. She was ahead of him in traffic and he lost sight of her shortly after leaving the mall.

On the drive home, he turned over the events of the last hour in his mind, but gave up trying to analyze them. The fact of the matter was that Anna was a far more interesting person than her slightly older sister and Kevin wanted to get to know her better. Much better. Already he was planning which ropes to use and wondering what torments she would allow him.

Her car was parked outside his apartment building. Relief flooded him, then he shook his head. He hadn't realized how much he hoped she would actually be there.

The rain had slowed to a cold drizzle by the time he parked and walked over to her car. She stood beside the driver's door, as if uncertain what to do next. Kevin recognized the signs of a woman with second thoughts and sought to reassure her.

"Anna, before we go upstairs, I want you to think of a traffic light. If at any point you want to stop what we're doing, just say 'red' and I'll untie you and we're done. If you just need to pause a moment, say 'yellow' and if everything's going along just fine, say 'green'. This way, you're in charge, even though you're physically helpless. Does that make sense?"

Her face relaxed into a smile, all traces of nervousness gone. "Yes. Perfect sense. I see now how it's an equal sharing. I give up power, you wield it. But in reality, you have it only because I'm choosing to give it to you."

"That's right." Kevin held out his hand to her. "Ready?"

With new assurance she put her hand in his. "Ready."

Anna followed Kevin up the stairs, a part of her wondering just what the hell she was doing, the other part rejoicing for having scored. Wasn't this what she had always wanted? Even as she asked herself the question, she knew that having sex with Kevin was only a part of the plan. He was falling in love with her just as much as she was already in love with him. He just didn't know it yet.

But he would by the end of the evening. After their last encounter in his apartment, Anna's fantasies had taken a decidedly kinky turn. What she had told him was true, she'd had those fantasies for years, but hadn't ever acted on them. With the Internet, however, she could look in secret and it had proven to be fertile ground for learning about bondage and the whole Dominant/submissive thing. It hadn't taken long for her to realize Kevin's knowledge of just how to tie her up so completely must've come from a similar interest. It also hadn't taken long for her to realize she preferred the submissive role to the dominant one.

Assured that this wasn't some immature power trip on his part, Anna now entered his apartment, ready to let him lead her along an exciting path. Whether bondage was truly naughty or not didn't matter. It felt a little naughty...and that only added to her interest and arousal.

"Let me take your coat?"

Kevin had only turned on one small light just inside the door, but it was enough for her to see the concern in his eyes. Smiling, she handed over her coat, then stood a bit awkwardly. They had discussed the bondage part of the evening, but not the submissive part. What was he expecting of her? For that matter, how far into bossing her did she really want him to go?

"Come on into the kitchen for a minute and have a seat while I…um…get things ready."

She followed him along a short hall and waited while he flipped on the overhead light. Narrow and efficient, it boasted a tiny table with only one chair besides the normal appliances and cupboards. The walls were painted the same light ivory that every apartment manager seemed to buy by the bucketful.

"Would you like something to drink? I'm afraid I have milk or beer. Wasn't really expecting to have company."

He looked so cute as he asked, even though there was no apology in his tone. She shook her head. "No, thanks. I'm fine. I'll wait here 'til you come back."

For a moment she thought he was going to say something, but then he turned and disappeared. She sat in the chair, facing the hallway she had just come down. With the light on, she saw pictures hanging every so often and wondered if they were of art or family. After hearing the wistfulness in his voice about not being with his family this Christmas, she suspected the latter.

In less than ten minutes he returned and immediately Anna saw something different about his demeanor. She'd caught glimpses of it before, but now saw the controlled power unmasked.

Kevin's broad shoulders, hidden under a thin cotton shirt, hinted at a strength Anna suspected from the way he'd manhandled her the night she'd caught him spying. But there was an inner strength that came from him now as well, as if he allowed a light to shine from within that he normally kept hidden. She saw it in the command of his eyes, eyes that would brook no disobedience. As she rose from her chair, her stomach gave a little flip.

Kevin held his hand out to her and she placed her smaller one in his. He pulled her close and her hands flew to his chest as he pressed a kiss on her lips. His muscles, hard-packed and firm, were strong enough to crush her and the thought thrilled her. She answered his kiss with a passion of her own, letting him know she wanted this.

"I'm going to push you tonight, Anna. Push you into places you've never been before. Are you ready?"

Not trusting her voice, she nodded.

"Then take off your clothes."

"Right here?"

"Right here."

Anna stepped away from him, swallowing hard even as she pulled off her sweater and started to unbutton her blouse. His voice was hard, commanding, giving her orders. She wasn't sure she liked it. In her fantasies, Kevin always undressed her slowly, taking his time and driving her to distraction.

But this? Under the cold overhead light in a kitchen? This shouldn't be sexy at all. So why was her heart pounding as she shed the layers of clothing she'd worn for the winter weather?

Draping each item over the back of the kitchen chair, piece by piece Anna showed more of her body to Devil Winter. She was beginning to suspect now where the name came from. His frat brothers must've known his sexual kinks. Who knew? Maybe he'd learned a thing or two from them. When at last she was naked, she stood in the middle of the kitchen, feeling naughty and a bit vulnerable.

Kevin fought to keep his aloof demeanor as he watched Anna disrobe. He knew she had a good figure, but wasn't prepared for the incredible loveliness of her pale skin. Smooth as silk as the saying went, a few freckles scattered about on her arms with one perfectly placed beauty mark on the inner top of her right breast just to keep the eye interested.

The look in her eyes also intrigued him. She was scared, but not of him. At least, he didn't think so. Of her own sexuality? That surprised him. From what she'd said before, he thought her fairly experienced. Of course, that was a relative term. No matter what kinds of sexual relations she'd had in the past, tonight he was going to give her one that would blow away all past encounters.

"Follow me." Keeping his commands short and to the point threw her off guard. That was the point. Keep her slightly off balance. Not a lot, but just enough to keep her on the edge of excitement. Keeping a knot in her belly that threatened to explode into a small orgasm, but not letting it slip downward and over the edge, was part of the thrill for him.

Kevin led Anna into his bedroom, currently lit only by little Christmas lights and one tall white candle. He'd strung the lights a week ago, often leaving a strand on all night long, enjoying the holiday atmosphere. The soft light they cast now provided exactly the romantic setting he wanted. The covers had been stripped from the double bed, leaving a plain white sheet that would be the perfect backdrop against Anna's tied body.

Kevin had chosen this bedroom suite years ago with bondage in mind. Sturdy maple posts at each of the four corners provided excellent anchor points as did the "jail post" head- and foot-boards. She could yank as hard as she wanted...those posts would never give way. As he crossed to his closet on the other side of the room, he told her a bit of his plan for her tonight, knowing it would heighten her arousal.

"Spread-eagled is the most common bondage experience for people, but I want to show you just how sensuous ropes can be by themselves."

Anna's nipples were raised, and Kevin suspected they might be quite hard, but he resisted the temptation to pull her to him. He had a torment planned for those little nubs later. Rummaging in the closet, he found and opened a dark duffel bag, pulling out a hank of thick black cotton rope, almost as thick as his little finger.

Anna still stood by the bed where she'd first come into the room. She'd crossed her arms, rubbing them as if she were cold...or nervous. Dropping the black rope onto the white sheet, Kevin wrapped his arms around her, letting his hands warm the soft skin of her back. She stood as if she were still making up her mind, stiff and a little awkward. Kevin looked down, searching her big brown eyes, giving her the opportunity to tell him "red" and when she didn't say it, he bent down and kissed her.

For a moment, Anna's fingers clutched the front of his shirt, holding on to him...needy...scared...wanting. Then all at once, almost as if a dam broke and years of longing poured out of her, her lips parted and she let him in. Her arms came up around his shoulders as she opened herself, surrendering not only her body to his pleasure, but her soul to his use.

The force of it staggered him even as her surrender fed him. He tightened his arms, holding her, letting her know her trust was not misplaced even as his tongue plundered her mouth, beginning his possession of her.

For possession it was. As his body responded, Kevin knew Anna Montgomery was the woman he'd been in training for all those years. The girls he'd taken to bed in college had just been girls to learn with. With them, he'd honed his skills as a lover and as a Dominant. Skills he'd set aside when Anna's sister Pam blinded him with her beauty.

The woman in his arms now, however, sank into his kiss, reveling in his touch, surrendering herself to him and he gloried in her surrender. The power rush filled him and he took his fill.

She did not pull back as he savaged her lips, her tongue, her mouth. Small noises came from the depths of her throat, he could feel the vibrations all the way to his center. Still he pushed, giving her a taste of the beast he could unleash inside.

And still she gave to him. She kissed him back, her own animal answering the demands of his until finally Kevin pulled back, satisfied that she was not pretending, convinced the woman before him could not only take what he dished out, but could give it back to him many times over. Not for the first time did a part of him stare at her in wonder.

Anna's breath came in shocked and heavy gasps. Holy shit, but Kevin could kiss! Never had she felt so entirely consumed...and yet she understood that kiss had been just a precursor of his appetite. Well, she'd been warned. She waggled her eyebrows at him as he picked up the hank of black rope, wanting him to know she would never back down now. Not after that kiss.

Keeping the rope tied in its bundle, Kevin draped the heavy rope across her shoulders like a yoke. The weight of it surprised her. She had to bow her head to keep it balanced there, like a burden carried by—she smiled—like a milkmaid or a water carrier. Just a beast of burden. An object for use. Her smile deepened to a grin.

"Feel how heavy this rope is? When I'm done, it will caress your body like a second skin."

Anna nodded and Kevin removed the hank of rope. She felt so light with the weight gone...almost as if she could fly. Kevin's eyes hadn't left her and he smiled now to see her understanding.

"Just a simple thing, really. A weighing down...a lightening." Kevin stepped close. "I will weigh you down over and over, not letting you fly until you are ready, little one."

The appellation caused her stomach to tighten. Two small words and her heart flew to her throat. She wasn't little. She was a grown woman. Yet his epithet made her feel like a child.

And wasn't she, when it came to this whole BDSM thing? She'd been tied up exactly once in her life...and that was when Kevin had kidnapped her. Okay, so she'd read a whole lot of stories on the web and had a ton of fantasies. Neither of those made her anything close to experienced.

Kevin had played out the rope, finding the ends, then finding the middle. Stepping to her, he encircled her with his arms, pulling the rope tight against her upper back. "Ready?"

With more assurance than she felt, she nodded. "Green."

"Arms behind your head, then. Don't take them down until I tell you to."

Kevin watched as she put her arms up into that vulnerable position. A little of the guard came back as she did so, which only made him more determined than before that he would prove he could be trusted.

He took his time winding the rope around her. His mind, totally focused on her body, entered a zone where the outside world faded away and time didn't exist. He brought the rope above her breasts and keeping it taut, crossed it around her back again. This time when he brought the two ends around the front, he snugged them up under her breasts, again pulling them tight, constricting her body in the web he wove.

Making an overhand knot to keep them in place against her skin, he decided to make her a part of her own binding. "Put your finger here," he instructed her, watching as she brought only one hand down to hold on to the two ropes so he could tie a second knot. The fact that she returned her hand behind her head when the knot was finished reassured him.

He measured a handlength down to her navel and made another knot, tying the two ropes so he could split them to wrap around her waist before bringing them forward again. He pulled them tight. Very tight. Kevin took advantage of the deep breath he forced her to take and tightened the rope even further.

This time he tied it off around the back, watching her discover she couldn't release all her breath. Nor could she take in another deep breath. The headiness of the sensation unbalanced her and he put out a protective hand. But she recovered first, ending up with her legs slightly parted. Perfect.

For the first time, he inspected her ass. While he'd certainly appreciated it when it was clothed, in its nudity, he realized she had an incredibly spankable ass. Her cheeks, soft and generous, would turn a beautiful shade of pink, should he decide on such a torment for her tonight. Later. Right now he had a different ordeal in mind.

Kevin tied the two pieces of rope together in a series of three knots, each about two inches from the one before, then wedged the tied rope between those beautiful cheeks. She gasped, yet shifted her stance giving him better access. All business, he inhaled her scent, letting the muskiness of her arousal stir him.

He brought the rope forward, parting her already slick nether lips. Pressing the rope upward, he made sure each knot sat directly over a particularly erogenous spot. Once he was sure the rope was set to give the strongest effect, he stood before her, the ends of the rope loose in his hands.

"You can feel how the rope constricts you. It doesn't hamper movement tied this way, but changes motion. You cannot walk as you always have. You breathe differently, stand differently. Can you feel it?"

Anna nodded to him. She tried to say something that got stuck in her throat, cleared it and spoke again. "I like how it feels."

He stepped close, letting his presence overwhelm her as he pulled up on the cords, making the rope dig into her tender pussy. "And do you still like how it feels?"

She knew a challenge when she saw one, but was at his mercy and knew it. The knots bit hard and she couldn't suppress the gasp—no, the moan—that escaped her. Balancing on her tiptoes, her hands slipped from behind her head to steady herself on his chest. He pulled harder and she moaned again.

"Hands up again."

It was a command and she fought to follow it. With her legs spread so she wouldn't topple over, she stayed on her toes as Kevin kept up the pressure. Only when she put her hands back did he relent, chuckling as he secured the rope by tying it to the part that encircled her waist. She managed a breathless "Thank you".

"You won't have cause to thank me when you understand just how nefarious this particular tie is."

She didn't understand, but waited patiently, gradually easing down onto her heels when the rope proved snug but not too tight. Kevin made sure she stood comfortably before going back to the closet and pulling out another hank of black rope. But when he brushed it against her skin, she realized it was a softer rope this time, and not as thick.

"Different ropes have different purposes. This one is better to keep your arms tied behind you."

Anna wasn't sure what she was supposed to do. Should she put her arms down and behind? He hadn't told her to do so yet. Damn. This D/s thing was harder than she thought it would be. Was she just supposed to stand here like a puppet? Or be an active participant in her own binding? She didn't have enough experience to know which she preferred. Okay, she didn't have *any* experience.

Kevin circled her, watching her stand there and try to figure things out. She had to give him that. He seemed to intuitively understand when she needed a minute without her having to resort to the traffic signal. He stopped behind her, his hands resting on her waist. She couldn't help herself. His body was so warm, she wanted his touch so much, she leaned back, resting herself against his chest.

"When you're ready," he whispered into her ear, "put your hands down behind your back."

Taking a deep breath, Anna stood straight again, and lowered her arms. Blood rushed to her fingers and she flexed them, shaking out her arms before putting them behind her.

"Palm to palm if you can."

She could, although she had to bend her elbows slightly to do so. The soft rope encircled her wrists, drawing them together. Involuntarily, her pussy twitched in response.

"Oh, my glory," she breathed. "I think I could come just from being tied up."

Kevin chuckled. "That's the point, isn't it?"

She felt him bring the rope up to encircle her elbows, drawing them together in their turn. The action forced her shoulders back...and her breasts outward into the ropes that held them fast. The double constriction almost buckled her knees.

Kevin caught her, his right arm around her waist while his left still held the rope he hadn't finished tying. Anna was responding beyond all his hopes. This was a woman born to be tied. Her body was perfect for it...just the right angle of curves to hold the ropes in place, her skin such a wonderful pale color that shaded to pink from her own modesty, and a pussy that was soaked and wanting to come just from this simple binding. Oh, yeah. Anna's understanding forced him to take a second look at her. Now her incredible responses to his handling had him already considering a long-term relationship.

"Anna..." He stopped. What was it he wanted to say? But she mistook his question and replied quickly. "Green. Don't stop." She caught her breath.

"Did you come?"

She shook her head as she leaned into him. "No, but I'm close. The knot over my...clit...is..." her voice trailed off, almost as if to use the words embarrassed her. With a start, he realized they did. A part of his brain envisioned a moment when he would force her to say "dirty" words aloud. Embarrassment could be a powerful aphrodisiac when used in the right context. He filed her slight unease away for a future day.

Because if he had his way, there were going to be a lot of future days with Anna. He liked her. And he definitely liked the way she reacted to him now.

"Stand up straight, little one."

He watched her face as he used the affectionate term. Just as before, it made her smile. Later he would use stronger language, but for now, he'd take things slowly. Tying her up was far too good an experience to rush.

He made short work of tying her elbows close...not touching, but close enough that her back was forced into a gentle arc. Coming around in front, he hooked his finger behind the knot just below her breasts and led her across the room to the full-length mirror. She needed to see how beautifully the black ropes complemented her white skin.

Anna gasped when she saw herself bound. The pictures she'd furtively peeked at on the web hadn't prepared her for the stark beauty she saw reflected in the tall mirror. Looking at those women, her body had responded more to their vulnerability than their appearance. But seeing her own face, her own body tied in a webwork of dark rope, with the soft light of the little Christmas lights casting a romantic glow over her skin, she understood bondage had an artistic allure as well. She started as she realized, "I'm the canvas!"

Kevin nodded. "An apt analogy. You have given me your body to do with as I wish. I can outline it and change its shape through the use of ropes. I can even change its color through the use of...other instruments."

"Oh?" His hesitation only made her more curious.

When he answered, his voice was soft, seductive. As he listed the tools he could use on her, she found herself being mesmerized, drawn further into a world she'd only dreamed of. "Through the use of paddles...floggers...whips...canes...even clamps."

She came. Images from the past several moments flooded her mind—Kevin hooking his finger through her ropes and pulling her across the room like the object she was, the knot rubbing her clit coupled with the one digging deep into her pussy, seeing herself as Kevin's canvas and the beauty he had made, feeling her body restrained by those magnificent black ropes. If Kevin hadn't put his arm around her again to steady her, Anna knew she would have dropped to her knees as his power flooded through her in waves of pleasure.

Kevin held her body as her orgasm ran its course. She gasped for breath, her eyes closed and her head thrown back against his chest. He could see the rapid pulse in the hollow of her throat and feel her muscles strain against their bindings. Only when he saw her orgasm subsiding did he reach down to finger her clit under the rope, knowing it would send her body off into another tremor.

She didn't disappoint him. He lowered her to the floor as her body racked in uncontrolled bursts, waiting again until her movement slowed before once more pressing his fingers against her increasingly sensitive clit. Her moans before had been soft whimpers. Now they became cries of anguished pleasure.

Three orgasms in as many minutes. Not a bad way to start a relationship. Feeling pretty proud of himself, he lay on the floor beside her, pulling her into a tight embrace. Her mind needed centering as she came back to reality, and he wanted it centered on him.

"Kevin..." Her voice was no more than a whisper.

"Shh. Don't talk yet. You're safe. I've got you."

He pitched his voice low and soothing, knowing such aftercare was a necessary part of the process. Without it, she'd get too disoriented, unfocused. Or worse, her focus would land on something insignificant. And Anna was too important to him, he realized. He didn't want her thinking of anyone or anything else at this moment. Kevin cuddled her closer.

Only when her breathing slowed to a normal speed did he loosen his grip. He helped her stand, then pulled out his desk chair and helped her sit. The ropes would need to be undone soon...they had served their purpose.

"So. Do you like being bound and forced to come at my will?"

From the look Anna gave him, he wasn't sure whether she wanted to shoot him or kiss him. But then she smiled and his heart lightened. "I think I could get used to it."

Kevin laughed, relieved and gratified at the same time. "Well, that's good to know. Right now, though, I want to take those ropes off you. Since this is your first time being bound..." He stopped at her snort and amended what he was saying. "Okay, since this is your first time being bound for sexual purposes — better?"

"Better."

"Here. Turn around." He waited while she wiggled around so he could get to her hands. As he unbound her, he shared a part of his approach to bondage. "Being restricted is exciting only while the mood is building. The tighter the binding, the more exciting it can be. But..." he paused to wrestle with a tough knot and continued as it came free. "But the tighter the bondage, the shorter the time you can leave your sub in it. Last thing you want is to do damage." He tossed the rope onto the bed and helped her bring her arms forward slowly. She bent them experimentally as he rubbed up and down along them.

"No damage here." She stretched her arms out, twisting her body on the chair. "But these ropes...they don't seem as tight as they were."

Kevin gestured for her to stand. As he untied the length that passed between her legs he explained. "They're not. This particular rope has a lot of stretch in it. One of the reasons I chose it. Looks great and is wonderful for short bursts. Here." He handed her the end of the rope. "You take it out from between your legs. It's gonna feel weird, so be ready."

It did feel weird. She couldn't exactly describe it though. Not painful, yet the relief was huge. Like taking a two-by-four out from between her legs instead of a simple half-inch of rope.

Kevin unwound and unknotted the rest of the rope, freeing her completely from her bondage. Part of her was disappointed. While three orgasms in a row wasn't something to sneeze at, she still had expected…well…more. His talk of floggers and paddles started a flame burning inside her that she didn't entirely understand, but knew she wanted with all her heart.

As Kevin wrapped the big black rope back into a neat hank, she took the time to study him in the romantic light. Had he used that very same rope on them? Not one of the women in school had ever mentioned bondage and Devil Devlin in the same breath, yet he certainly seemed practiced. How many times had she publicly sneered at his college conquests, yet wished she was one of them? And here, tonight, she was. Years after the angst of college had faded, she, Anna Montgomery, was sitting naked in Kevin Devlin Winter's bedroom. She shook her head.

"What's the matter? Is it warm enough for you?"

"Nothing. Just thinking. Bemused, that's all. So…what happens next?"

He glanced at her and again she had the feeling he was measuring her. "You want more?"

Anna blushed. "Well, I can take more, if that's what you mean. I gotta admit, Kevin, I'm just not sure where the line is between submissive and equality."

Kevin spoke slowly, as if he were weighing his words. "I know a lot about ropes and ties and the whole BDSM lifestyle...from the Master/slave extreme to just two people getting together for sex. Where are we on that continuum?" He came over to sit on the bed and face her. Anna didn't speak, understanding that his question was rhetorical, and hoping he'd answer it. Her heart fluttered a little. This had every indication of becoming one of life's "Important Discussions".

"I won't lie to you, Anna. You are one hell of a surprise to me in about a dozen different ways."

"Oh?" She crossed her legs and leaned back in the chair, wishing she could raise one eyebrow.

"Forget Pam. I am. It took me a long time to see past the surface and discover there wasn't much underneath. You surprised me when I kidnapped you and you didn't call the cops. You surprised me at the movie because you were so...charming...and I'd never noticed it before. And you surprised the hell out of me tonight by not only agreeing to bondage, but enjoying yourself to boot." He frowned. "You are enjoying yourself, right?"

Anna hastened to reassure him. "Right. Multiple orgasms? How could I not?"

"So what does this mean for the future?" He stood, holding his hand out to her. She stood as well, putting her hands in his and he pulled her close, wrapping his arms around her. Now that she was free to do so, she let her hands explore the muscles of his arms...muscles she'd only felt indirectly before.

His voice, quiet with meaning, asked the question. "Are we a one-night stand, Anna?"

She answered from her heart. "I don't want to be. I can't say I want to go all the way to that Master/slave extreme, but I do know I want to explore bondage and BDSM and the whole Dominance/submissive dynamic a whole lot more." She put her head down, gathering her courage to step out on the limb. And when she had it, she looked back up, back into those beautiful brown eyes and told him. "And I want to explore it with you. To wherever it leads us."

Chapter Six

೫

"Then let's explore a little more." Pulling Anna close again, he bent down to give her a gentle kiss as a seal on their conversation. He liked holding her. She just seemed to...well...fit.

When the kiss ended and she pulled back to look at him, he saw the mischievous twinkle was back in her eyes and she was, indeed, ready to go again. "All right, little one. On the bed. Facedown and spread."

Grinning, she practically jumped up onto the mattress. Using a set of royal blue silk scarves he'd found in a flea market years ago, he tied her limbs to the sturdy posts of the bed. "Silk must be tied carefully. The more you wiggle, the tighter the knots become until they become almost impossible to undo and have to be cut off." She shot him a concerned look. "Don't worry. I have safety scissors on my dresser. You won't be permanently tied to my bed."

Yet, he added silently, his cock stirring at the thought. With each scarf, he took away a little more of her freedom, a freedom she gave him without hesitation this time. In truth, he didn't want a full-time sex slave. What on earth would he do with one? He thought of a woman, mindlessly existing for only one reason...to give him sex. Okay, it was a great fantasy. But in real life, he wanted someone to talk to, someone to go out to the movies with, someone to tie up and dominate...but only for a little while before she took back her independence and stood on her own two feet.

He wanted Anna. The last scarf in place, he stood back from the bed as the realization finally hit home in its entirety. She might be compliant now, but he'd been on the receiving end of her anger before. She wouldn't just let him roll over her, but would stand up and make her feelings known. Like tonight.

Kevin sat beside her on the bed, his hand freely roaming over her back and shoulders and down to cup the cheeks of her ass as he spoke to her. "I'm going to give you a flogging tonight, Anna. It won't hurt, not at the beginning. Just as different ropes have different purposes, so do different floggers. It isn't so much about the pain as it is about the sensations. Do you have any questions?"

She shook her head, although she couldn't raise it very far off the bed, spread out as she was. Still, she gave him permission. "Green."

He chose a deer hide flogger with soft suede thongs to start. One of his favorites, he liked the milk chocolate coloring of the thongs that deepened to a dark chocolate color on the handle because of the oils of his hand. Taking it now, he lightly ran the tips of the thongs over her back, watching her reaction.

It tickled. Anna shivered in anticipation. A flogging? She'd read about them, fantasized about them, but never thought she'd ever get one. *Sensations*, Kevin said. This first one wasn't so bad, although she couldn't stop flinching, expecting a hard blow at any moment.

But the next sensation still held no force. He dragged the suede over her skin, letting her feel the softness of the thongs. *More like a caress,* she realized. *Almost as if he's making love to me with the flogger.*

Which he was. Understanding flooded her. That's all this was...a different way of making love. With that thought, she relaxed her muscles, letting herself go for the ride Kevin planned for her without analyzing every move.

At this slight force, her skin would not change color. Actually, in the soft light, seeing the color change would be difficult, Kevin realized. He made a mental note to himself. Tonight he'd pull his blows, partly because of the light, partly because he didn't want to scare her away.

It was a new feeling for him. In the past, he didn't really care whether the woman before him was a one-night stand or a week-long romance. While the entire sexual act was always about the woman first...pleasing them was what got him hard...his heart never got in the way of a good fuck.

And it wouldn't tonight, either. As Kevin increased the force of the flogger, he admitted that caring about the woman on the bed actually increased his need to please her, and yet, increased his need to be pleased by her.

You're overanalyzing, Kevin. Stop. Just enjoy the moment.

Picking up a second flogger, leather but with slightly stiffer thongs, he alternated strokes, first soft, then hard, setting up a pattern to lull her into a calm before the storm.

As much as she tried, there was still a part of her brain that wouldn't shut up. It kept a running commendatory going in her head as Kevin's tattoo on her back changed tempo, beating faster, yet alternating between a caress and a slight sting.

She liked this. Almost as good as a massage, and in some ways, a whole lot better. Her skin felt warm...alive. There was a sexual feel to it that kept her interest, but as yet, just lulled her along.

A sudden slap by something much harder made her jump. She cried out in surprise more than pain. It had stung, but only for a second or two before fading into a definite sexual pleasure. In her reaction, she tried to pull her hands down. But they were tied and she couldn't move to protect herself. Her cry turned into a moan of longing.

But Kevin had gone back to the alternate caress and small sting cadence. She would not be lulled so easily this time. A knot of tension formed low in her gut.

If Anna could have seen Kevin's face, her tension would've been a lot stronger. A fire burned in his eyes now. Her vocal reaction to his hard slap awoke the Dominant beast inside and his cock had responded, pushing against his pants, insistent.

But he didn't want to stop the flogging. Not yet. He could ignore his own needs for a while yet. Besides, the more he delayed, the greater the payout at the end. Still, he dropped the soft flogger on the bed between her legs, using only the stiffer one while he undid his pants to give his cock more room.

Where before he'd concentrated mostly on her shoulders and bottom, now he landed blows on the backs of her legs, the inside of her thighs and on her ass. She moaned more frequently now, wiggling in her bindings.

"Wiggle away, my little one. You won't get free. And that thought excites you, doesn't it?"

It did. A lot. That's why she moved so much. Not to try and get away, but to revel in the fact that she couldn't. The tension in her gut moved lower with his blows and now centered itself directly in her pussy. Kevin increased the tempo and the force of the flogger yet again and Anna wondered how much she could take even as she wanted him to give her more. There was only one way out of her dilemma. "Please, Kevin. Make me come again!"

The flogging paused. "You wish to come?"

"Yes!" The word practically tore out of her.

"No."

He said it with such finality, she almost cried. How dare he? How could he take her to this point and not let her come? All he had to do was land that puppy just a little lower a few times and she'd come harder than she ever had before. She knew it.

But before she could voice her protest, he lay on top of her, his weight crushing the air out of her lungs, his warmth enveloping her.

"You have given your body to me to play with as I see fit. Do you want to reconsider that gift?" He nuzzled a kiss along the ridge of her ear.

"No. I want...I want..."

What did she want? She couldn't think straight with his breath so close, his entire body covering hers. Between her legs, she thought she could feel his hardened cock and her pussy flooded, suddenly wanting him inside her.

"You want me to do to you exactly what I want to do to you."

She nodded, unable to talk, her thoughts jumbled as her need grew stronger.

Kevin stood, yanking off his clothes. Lying on her had been a torment. He wanted to feel her warmed skin against his, the softness of her ass against the raised veins in his cock.

Pulling a pillow from the floor where he'd tossed it earlier, he now raised her hips and slid it underneath. For the first time he had a good, clear view of her pussy, the white cream pooled at the entrance giving away all her secrets.

"I want you, Anna. Tell me you want it, too."

"I do. Please, Kevin. I do."

The pleading in her voice was unmistakable. Sitting on his knees between her legs, he placed his cock at the entrance to her pussy, rubbing the tip along the slit to cover it in her juices. The sadistic side of him couldn't resist teasing her.

"Beg me, Anna. Let me hear you beg to take my cock."

She moaned and Kevin knew he was pushing her. But if he'd played his cards right, if he'd read all her signs correctly, then she was at the point where she would promise him anything, would be willing to do anything just to come.

"Yes, Kevin. Please put your cock inside me. Let me feel you take me. Please!"

He shifted position as he slid on a condom and pressed his cock against her pussy. Anna's back arched as she rose to meet him, every part of her urging him in. He didn't need a second invitation. Sliding the tip into her pussy, he paused for her body to adjust to his size. Her pussy was a wonderful tight sheath and he didn't want to tear her. She moaned underneath him.

"Please, Kevin. Hurry. Take me, dammit!"

If he hadn't been so far along his own path to coming, he would have laughed. So much for her submissiveness. Throwing caution to the wind, he slid the rest of the way inside in one swift movement.

Heaven. This must be heaven, Anna decided as Kevin's cock filled her pussy. And when he slid it home, his weight suspended on his arms over her, she arched her back again, wanting to feel every inch of him deep inside.

He set up a rhythm and she tried to follow it. But tied as she was, all she could really do was lie there and take it. She was helpless to stop him. Helpless to help him as he pounded deep inside her.

"Oh, Kevin, I'm going to come!"

"Yes, little one. Come for me now."

She dove off the cliff in a headlong rush. Her body trembled and shook. The great Devil Devlin possessed her body and mind like no one ever had before. Kevin wanted her. He didn't want Pam. He didn't want anyone else. He wanted her. The steady beat of his cock thrusting into her quickened and drove thought from her mind. Together their groans grew louder as the tempo increased yet again.

The tension in her pussy coiled around his cock so tightly she could hardly bear it. And still he drove into her, repeatedly slamming against her sensitive skin to increase the tension even more.

Time stopped and she hung suspended...one second...two...an eternity. Above her, Kevin groaned as he approached his climax and with a sudden dive, Anna's body responded. She became an animal, fighting her bindings and pressing her body upward and against him to milk every drop from his cock — to milk every drop of pleasure from the orgasm they shared.

Spent, Anna gasped for air even as she grinned in satisfaction. Her mind floated in a haze of contentment. When Kevin finally lay down beside her and took her in his arms, Anna knew for a fact she'd found a piece of heaven.

Kevin would have loved to stay there all night long, but tied as she was, Anna's muscles would eventually begin to cramp and make her uncomfortable. When she shivered in spite of his arm over her, he bowed to the inevitable.

"Let's get you untied and warmed up."

Forcing himself out of the bed, he untied the silk scarves that held her limbs in place. When she was free, she rolled over and sat up, rubbing her arms and legs to get the circulation moving again while he piled the big comforter back up on the bed. She pulled it over herself and scooted up to lean against the headboard catching the pillows he tossed her way. Climbing in beside her, he took her in his arms again, liking the way she snuggled against him.

"So was it everything you expected?"

He felt her nod against his chest. "And more." She sat up to look at him. "I didn't expect the flogging to be quite so...relaxing. And then later, it wasn't relaxing at all. I swear I could've come just from the flogger alone."

She looked so eager and innocent, he had to smile. "You probably could have. Maybe next time I'll let you."

Anna waggled her eyebrows at him. "You think there's gonna be a next time?"

Kevin pulled her in close. "Yep. And a time after that, and a time after that, too."

"And if I don't agree?"

Kevin looked down at her face, her eyes twinkling with mischief. Taking her chin in his hand, he brought her face close to his. "Then I suppose I'll just have to kidnap you again."

With his gentle kiss, together they slid under the comforter, lying side by side, the lights of Christmas softly glowing around the room. Anna snuggled into the crook of his arm, laying her head on his shoulder and placing a small kiss on his chest, hugging him with her free arm. "You don't have to kidnap me to tie me up."

A weight he hadn't even realized was there fell off Kevin's shoulders. "Anna, I could very easily fall in love with a woman who enjoyed being tied up and taken."

"Could fall? Or are falling?"

Kevin shook his head. He should've known she would brook no wishy-washy commitment. He pulled her chin up so he could see her face. "Am falling."

She smiled, her eyes trusting and contented. Before snuggling back into his chest, she uttered only one word, "Good."

He laughed. "Oh, no, woman. You're not getting away with that. You have to tell me you're falling in love, too."

She shook her head against his chest. "Can't."

The word froze him like a bucket of ice-cold water. "What?"

Anna looked up at him with contentment and happiness in her eyes. "I'm not falling in love. I'm already there." She pushed herself up and kissed him, a gentle kiss that promised many more to come. "I'm already in love with you, Kevin.

And you're already totally in love with me. You just haven't gotten around to admitting it yet."

Outside, the church bells rang the midnight hour. It was Christmas, and Kevin wasn't alone. With an ironic snort, he realized he'd taken Tony's advice and found himself someone to spend the holiday with. He pictured his friend's face when he told him that this one he wasn't going to let slip between his fingers. As the last chime faded into silence, he looked down at the woman in his arms.

"Merry Christmas, Anna."

"Merry Christmas, Kevin."

Also by Diana Hunter

ഇ

Cabin Fever

Diamond Studs (*anthology*)

Ellora's Cavemen: Tales from the Temple III (*anthology*)

Hooked

Irish Enchantment (*anthology*)

Kara's Captain

Learning Curve

New York Moment

Secret Submission

Submission Revealed

Table for Four

About the Author

ဢ

For many years, Diana Hunter confined herself to mainstream writings. Her interest in the world of dominance and submission, dormant for years, bloomed when she met a man who was willing to let her explore the submissive side of her personality. In her academic approach to learning about the lifestyle, she discovered hundreds of short stories that existed on the topic, but none of them seemed to express her view of a d/s relationship. Challenged by a friend to write a better one, she wrote her first BDSM novel, Secret Submission, published by Ellora's Cave Publishing.

Diana welcomes comments from readers. You can find her website and email address on her author bio page at www.ellorascave.com.

Tell Us What You Think

We appreciate hearing reader opinions about our books. You can email us at Comments@EllorasCave.com.

WINTER'S ROSE
Ruby Storm

Trademarks Acknowledgement

Prologue

శు

Rose Marie hauled back on leather reins, forcing her mount to a skidding halt as she squinted her eyes beneath the felt brim of her hat. The blood drained from her normally pink cheeks as she stared out from the edge of the tree line to the western horizon. Her heart pounded and nausea roiled her belly as she struggled against the power of the prancing animal beneath her.

Never taking her gaze from the man who sat atop the dashing horse as if they were one, she slid from the saddle unsure if her trembling knees would hold her upright.

Was it him?

Don't be ridiculous. A lot of men sit a horse like Kody...

She scuttled around a tree to better study the straight line of the man's back and the breadth of his shoulders. Damn! He was too far away to see his face. Her stomach rolled about as she watched the unknown horse crest a small butte and disappear. Sliding the hat off her head, she slumped against the tree and closed her eyes.

Kody. She had to be imaging things.

Her soft brow furrowed as she pictured him in her mind. It had been so long but his memory never left her restless nights. That same memory now prodded at her heart, but try as she might, she couldn't force it away, nor the intense feeling of longing that she'd fought every night since he'd walked from her life.

She had loved him so much.

Rose nearly cried aloud. Had? She still did — but there wasn't a damn thing she could do about it. Kody had made his choice and that was the way of things.

Shaken as if she'd seen a ghost, she remounted and reined her horse in the opposite direction. Before she tucked her hat over her thick blonde hair and kicked her mount into a gallop, she glanced longingly across the barren prairie. As much as she still wanted him, Kody's return to her life would be one hell of a complication, and was the one thing she didn't need.

She smacked the horse's rump with leather reins and headed home.

Chapter One

ℬ

Kody Winter's sparkling green eyes narrowed beneath the black brim of his Stetson as he studied the sign in a tinted storefront window. The hot Texas sun, abnormally warm for the Christmas season, heated the exposed skin of his arms. Shifting the weight of his trim jeans-clad hips to his opposite leg, the corded muscles in his arms rippled as he adjusted his hat and shook his head in amazement. It was hard to believe that he was here on a sidewalk in Bandera instead of in the middle of a covert skirmish in some remote location across the world.

Kody took a deep breath and waited for some intricate prodding of his mind to tell him he had made a huge mistake by not pursuing a military career. His superiors had done their best to persuade him to reenlist, but Texas was where he wanted to be. He was proud to have served his country over the last six years but was more than ready to rest his head in the same place every night. He took another breath.

Nope. No doubts. He'd done the right thing.

His gaze shifted again to the painted red door of the building. His lieutenant had told Kody more than once that every action was simply a matter of timing. Yesterday had been the perfect example. Kody really hadn't expected to find Rose Marie so easily. He'd seen her cross this same street and enter the building whose window he looked through now. The sight of her petite but curvaceous body and her thick blonde hair lifting in the breeze had shocked him so much that he'd almost rear-ended the vehicle in front of him. By the time he had parked his truck and hurried to peer through this same window, he'd seen her tuck a folder beneath her arm and lead a customer down the dark halls of Bandera's Botanical Spa. But where in hell had she been these last years? Kody had planned to start searching for her again, never contemplating the fact that she'd moved back to town after all this time.

She'd done it. She gone to school like she had said she would, had apparently gotten her degree in massage therapy and now worked in the field. One thing about Rose. When she made up her mind, she stuck to it.

Hence the ambush today. Lifting his Stetson, he traced his fingers through the slight waves already replacing the short cut of so many years and adjusted the hat once more. She would fight him, of that he was certain. Six years earlier she'd told him to go to hell when she discovered he had enlisted. In his own mind, the only way he could explain her sudden dismissal of him was that she'd taken his departure as a rejection of sorts.

But Rose had never left his thoughts. And when he'd returned home after his preliminary basic training for a quick visit, he'd gone looking for her. According to her father, Kody had discovered that she'd left Bandera with her sister. It was as if Rose had disappeared off the face of the earth, because with the few return visits over the next six years, the only thing he had found out was that the old man had drunk himself to death and Rose and her sister, Lily, had never come back.

Yup. Timing was everything along with a handful of sheer luck.

Seeing her yesterday had catapulted him into the past. All the intense roiling emotions that thinking of her always evoked had only intensified. He wanted another chance with her and the only thing that would cause him to step back would be if Rose had married. Last night he'd checked the phonebook, but she wasn't listed. That fact had set him on edge. So, to discover if she was still single he had called for an appointment and requested *Miss* Rose Leighton. He hadn't been corrected. Kody was sticking with the assumption that he still had half a chance.

He could simply have waited there on the street for her to arrive at work, but that would have taken the fun out of it. Kody's brain just wasn't wired that way. Maybe it was a throwback to his wild youth or his years in covert service, but he was going with the element of surprise. He was giving himself the advantage before she had the chance to tell him to go to hell again.

He reached for the door and entered the strangely scented front office. The lights were low and a fluted Indian melody filtered softly into the room from hidden speakers—strange music for an area where fiddles and lonesome cowboy tunes could be heard on every dial of the radio. His green gaze cast about. The ambiance would set anyone at ease. However, he wasn't just anyone. He was a man on a mission.

A smiling young woman who sat behind the desk greeted him.

"Hi there. I'm Laura. Can I help you?"

"Yes, I have an appointment for a massage."

"Your name?"

Kody watched her gaze trickle over him as if he were a piece of candy about to be eaten. He stepped up to the counter. "John Anderson."

The young woman opened a folder and picked up a pencil. "I see you've requested Miss Leighton as your masseuse today. She's just about finished with another client."

Miss... Once again, the confirmation that Rose was still single.

Glancing up, a smile lit the receptionist's face as her eyes flowed over the top half of his body.

Kody wondered if she even realized she ran the eraser end of her pencil across her full bottom lip as she stared, pink-cheeked.

"Are you here for a massage because you're having a problem area or are you just looking for the relaxation sequence?"

Problem area? Yeah, he had a problem area. It was Rose Leighton and the stiff backbone he expected to run up against. He leaned one elbow on the counter and pushed his hat farther back on his forehead. Flashing a smile, he winked. "I've been back up on a horse—something that I haven't done for a while. Guess I need a little relief for my legs and backside."

The receptionist smiled a bit wider beneath the bounce of her feathered eyebrows and blushing cheeks as she scribbled his answer. After asking him a few more questions in regard to his health and marking little square boxes on her form, she finally stood with the sheet of paper in her hand. "Mr. Anderson, why don't you follow me and we'll get you set up."

He trailed after her down a dimly lit hallway ignoring the exaggerated swing of Laura's hips. Instead, his gaze flicked over a couple of closed doors knowing Rose was behind one of them. Just a few seconds more and he'd be safely nestled away.

The woman entered a room at the end of the hall and swept an arm to indicate the empty and dimly lit cubicle. "Feel free to leave your underwear on and slip under the blanket facedown. Miss Leighton will give you a few minutes to get ready."

"Thanks."

"Enjoy your rubdown."

"Oh, I will," he replied, slightly surprised by how the woman's voice had become huskier with her last remark.

He tossed his hat onto a chair and tugged his T-shirt out of his pants and over his six-pack abs. It took a moment longer to slide his tight boots off, but as soon as that was done, he shucked off his jeans and slung them over the back of a chair. But just before he slid between the warmed sheets, he stepped back and slid off his shorts.

A grin curved his mouth upward as he settled on the table. Rose was in for the surprise of her life. He yanked the sheet up over his ass and lay facedown. His smile immediately widened. As he stared down through the opening of the headrest, he spied a cartoon taped to the floor for a patron's enjoyment. It was a picture of a man lying facedown on a massage table as the masseuse emptied his wallet from a pair of hanging pants. Surprises. Kody loved them. He took a deep breath and closed his eyes to wait.

His mind drifted back to years earlier and a vision of Rose mucking out the stalls at his family's ranch, her blonde hair pulled back in a no-nonsense ponytail and an angry scowl always in place because she figured the world was out to get her. But that look could change. Kody remembered that all too well. All it took was one kiss and her blue eyes would smolder to a darker color. It was at that moment Rose would forget her lot in life as she kissed her employer's son with abandon and with the heart of a wanton. At first, Kody was only trolling for another sexual conquest and Rose possessed the perfect innocence to easily be wooed by his charms, or so he'd thought. What he'd discovered was a woman who'd met every one of his sexual challenges, one who spurred his senses and wormed her way into his heart. Over the course of that summer six years ago, he'd fallen in love. A youthful uncommitted love, but love nonetheless.

As the years passed, he'd never been able to rid his mind of her throw-her-head back laugh, how wonderfully erotic Rose's naked skin felt against his, or how her eyes turned tempestuous cobalt as he coaxed her body through an orgasm. He couldn't wait for her to show.

Another full three minutes passed before he heard a light tapping on the door.

"Mr. Anderson? Are you ready?"

His heart picked up a beat. It had been so long since he'd heard her voice. A shiver raced up his spine at the remembered sound. "Come in," he stated quietly.

The door opened, then shut softly. A flip of a switch and fluted music filtered into the room.

He was on his belly, his face hidden from Rose's beautiful blue eyes. Although he couldn't see her, he knew she was close. His skin prickled, his heart rapped against his ribs and his cock stirred. Oh, yeah, after all this time, Rose was close by.

"Mr. Anderson? Before we begin, are there any problem areas you would like me to center on? I see you've been riding after a period of inactivity?"

The last was more a question than a statement.

He swallowed away a smartass reply and answered with a low, slightly timbered tone. "That's correct."

"Well, then, I guess I know what's hurting on you."

The laughing lilt of her voice flowed around him. As much as he wished it could go on forever, he knew that wasn't going to happen. Damn, she was really going to be pissed that he was pulling one over on her. He was eager as hell to come head-to-head with her indignation.

"Just relax."

Her soothing voice coaxed a quick flow of heat through his groin. It was going to be damn near impossible to remain unaffected by it. Already, he could feel himself hardening. This could be nothing but trouble...

* * * * *

Rose poured a bit of scented oil onto her palm. Rubbing her hands together to warm it, her gaze flowed across the broad expanse of the man's shoulders. Whoever John Anderson was, he was a tall man and looked to be in perfect physical shape. A mellow warmth curled inside her belly, then sprang to life.

She gave herself a mental slap. There were professional behaviors and standards, ethical and legal practices applied to massage therapy and never once had she experienced the hot, sexual yearning that quickly spun through her — not with *any* client.

Gritting her teeth, she walked to the head of the table, hesitated and steeled herself to slowly rub her palms down each side of his spine. His smooth skin rippled like water beneath her touch. Her eyes closed for a moment to simple enjoy the hard muscles beneath her fingers. Instantly she was ashamed at the immediate urge to bend forward and feel the heat of his skin against her cheek. Mr. Anderson was a client, yet her stomach flopped about and her heart continued to race with sexual undertones. Her womb clenched and she was appalled at her reaction.

Stop it! Too long without a man, Rose. What she felt was just a normal response to one hell of a fine specimen of a man — wasn't it? Whatever it was, she damn well better dismiss it. But a second later, her eyes drifted shut as she traced patterns across his back once more, enjoying the sensual, primal feeling of innate power within his muscles.

Silently, she moved to the side of the table, started again at his broad shoulders and kneaded down to his waist, wondering the entire time what her physical reaction would be when she worked the muscles of his thighs. Her gaze drifted back up to the dark waves lying against the back of his neck. Instantly a vision flashed through her brain.

This guy's hair was close to the same color as Kody Winter's, shorter than he'd always worn it, but it had the same deep chestnut color. That quick thought made her knees weak and shaky. Lately, she'd been thinking too much about Kody. Years had passed since they'd split, yet his memory still had the power to crack her normally firm resolve that she would never let a man affect her the way he had done. The leftover hurt just wasn't worth it.

Silently, she continued to massage the broad expanse of skin beneath her fingers, and decided once again that life just wasn't fair most times.

Her head tipped to the side. How weird. Touching the guy on the table seemed too familiar, too…wonderful. She was instantly grateful that he had decided to remain quiet. Most times her patrons rattled on through the first part of the massage until she'd relaxed them to silence, but this guy had absolutely nothing to say.

Once she was done with his back, she carefully moved the sheet and uncovered one well-developed leg, cautious to tuck the material between his slightly spread thighs and not expose his backside. A small intake of breath preceded the slow breath she let out. His leg was hard as stone. Whoa, this guy really was a great representation of the male species.

What in hell was going on with her? It was a struggle to remember that she worked muscles called the iliotibial tract, the long muscle running from hip to knee, and also the semitendinosus and gastrocnemius muscles… She forced the technical terms into her mind to halt the tingling that raced from her fingertips and up her arm. Eventually, she would have to work his gluteus maximus. She inhaled a little deeper this time and wondered if she'd be spending the night behind bars for inappropriate behavior with a client.

Stop it!

She forced herself to massage the muscles above the inside of his knee for another five minutes of silent, self-imposed torture until the moment of reckoning was upon her. Biting her bottom lip, she moved her fingers up the side of his leg and gently and professionally exposed a bit of the man's right gluteus. Jesus, he was completely nude. What the hell was the matter with Laura? Hadn't she told him to leave on his underwear? And just as she had expected, his buttock was hard and molded to a perfect curve. Normally she would tuck the sheet close to the client's midline, but because of the continued nagging heat and the fact that he was totally naked, there was no way she was doing that. Hopefully her client would think he'd gotten his money's worth with her simply working the outside of his hip.

Reaching for the oil once more, her gaze flickered across his exposed skin. Immediately her heart began to pound when she spied the edge of a birthmark on his ass cheek. Her hands instantly stilled.

A picture of the small butterfly-like mark on Kody's ass flashed through her brain.

Impossible.

Her eyes slammed shut. It was just a coincidence like the day before. Her brain was definitely working overtime.

Drawing in a ragged breath, she moved closer and began to knead the outer hip muscle, but her blue eyes anchored on the partially exposed reddish spot.

She had to make the comparison.

Did she dare? Her fingers moved in slightly larger circles, each time slipping the sheet a little more to better see the mark.

Rose's fingers stumbled like a clumsy dancer for only a split second. She stifled her gasp just before it echoed in the dimly lit room and kept on kneading. Her jaw tightened like a steel trap.

Kody, you son of a bitch…

She wasn't fooled for a moment that he didn't know who massaged him. Rose knew that she had been requested. For some unfathomable reason, he was back in Texas and had somehow discovered her employment, made an appointment under a false name and now was here. That's just how he did things. Why, she didn't have a clue, but when Kody wanted something, he always tipped the scales in his favor. For some reason, he'd planned this ambush instead of simply picking up the phone. But then he'd probably known she would hang up on him — if he had been able to find her. How dare he, after all these years, think he could still play his games?

The lump in her throat spiraled straight to her stomach. Chewing again on her bottom lip, her mind raced. Slowly, an evil grin turned up one corner of her mouth. She would show him she was someone to reckon with and not the naïve young girl of years ago. He'd played with her one entire summer. She wasn't about to give him another chance.

Instantly, her gentle demeanor disappeared and was replaced with barely leashed anger. He'd think twice in the future about pulling the wool over her eyes. She used the knuckles of two fingers to dig into the flesh at the back of his leg where she knew it hurt from riding and slowly manipulated the strip of muscle until she reached the curve of his ass, deriving a great sense of personal satisfaction when his pained groan echoed quietly around her. Ha! After years away from the ranch and horse riding, she knew the exact areas that hurt on him. An evil grin widened her mouth. Rose knew all about pains in the ass and she was determined to be his biggest.

The son of a bitch. To hell with professional standards.

Using her thumbs she pressed firmly into the tight right cheek of his ass, finding the exact spot that had bounced against the saddle and almost giggled aloud when she heard a muffled grunt. She dug in harder, almost wincing when his body started in pain against the onslaught. Good. She hoped he hurt like hell. Professional standards were the last thing on her mind as she put all her weight behind her fingers and went after him.

She heard another muffled gasp. His body flinched against her onslaught and she knew he tried his best to remain unmoving on the table, but it was becoming quite a struggle on his part. His torso stiffened and one of his legs bent slightly at the knee as if he were going to slither away from the torture. Rose's teeth clenched, she gave no quarter and only dug in harder.

Suddenly Kody flipped to his side with a pained gasp and firmly snatched her wrist.

She opened her mouth to spew out his name, but nothing came out. The blood drained from her face as she stared down into the green eyes she had thought to never see again, but her heart leapt with excitement. Swallowing twice, she licked her bottom lip and finally found her voice, however tremulous. "You'll have to get up earlier in the morning to fool me, Kody Winter."

That same old heart-stopping grin curled Kody's lips upward.

"I figured as much. I'm paying for a massage, not a beating."

Rose jerked her wrist but his hold was firm. "If it's a massage you want then you can get it from someone else. Let go of me."

He only grinned wider. "I'll take my chances with you."

She snorted and tossed her head. "Brave man, aren't you? By the time I'm done, you won't be able to walk. And that's a promise." She watched his gaze lower to skitter across her breasts and felt the stain of a blush heat her cheeks. Damn! Rose didn't have to look down to know her nipples peaked hard beneath the stretched jersey material of her shirt—and the son of a bitch enjoyed the view.

Finally, Kody's eyes moved back to hers. His hooded, lusty gaze narrowed as he easily pulled her closer and wrapped a free arm around her waist. Now he had her half lying across him with her breasts smashed against one side of his chest. "You're not even going to say hello?"

She was powerless to stop her hungry gaze that flowed across his square jaw, over a broad shoulder and down to where his fingers gripped her wrist. Ah, those fingers could seduce her skin and start a fire burning in the pit of her stomach. Damn him. It was as if six years of absence had never happened. "What do you want?" she asked through clenched teeth.

Kody's smoldering eyes darkened as he pulled her closer. "I want a massage."

"I have the right to refuse service. Let me go and get the hell out of here or I'll call the cops."

"Give me a break, Rose Marie. I'm not doing anything wrong. Just greeting an old friend who used to love my arms around her."

Rose swallowed again and wondered if he could feel the quick beating of her heart through her pulse. "Up yours, Kody. Let me go or you're going to be sorry."

He stared into her eyes, loosened his fingers around her wrist but refused to free her waist. Rose immediately braced her palm on the table beside him, straining away from the warmth of his bare chest.

"One question, Rose."

"I said let me go."

He shook his head. "Not until you answer my question. I want to know something. Can you massage away the ache of a broken heart?"

Their eyes locked again. Seconds passed, ticking away but unnoticed by either of them.

Damn, her heart thumped wildly and her crotch felt on fire. Broken heart? *He* claimed to have a broken heart? That's not how Rose remembered it.

"Why did you come here?" she finally whispered.

"Because I missed you." He took in the light freckles that splattered the skin of her nose and cheeks, knowing the velvety softness he would find if he trailed a finger across them. At the moment, honesty seemed the best policy. "Not a day has passed since I left that I haven't thought about you."

"Sure thing, Kody. Like I would believe that. I don't know what you think you're accomplishing here, but I've moved on."

How his hand ended up cupping the back of her head, she'd never know. But he drew her mouth to his, slanted his head and slowly captured her lips and she was powerless to pull away.

There it was. That remembered feeling of Kody's kiss, like a branding iron marking her forever. Her eyes fluttered shut as she drank in the moment, feeling his tongue probe against her closed mouth with more scorching demand than subtle permission. Her lips parted and instantly she felt the flicker of his tongue against hers, drawing her into a seductive dance that she remembered all too well.

Her knees trembled and threatened to give out. She held on tighter as a quiet purr rolled in the back of her throat. There was nothing but the two of them. No music, no sound except the blood rushing past her ears—only the fresh scent of him filling her nostrils.

Her head spun. She wanted the kiss to go on forever. He was the only man who had ever been able to turn her into a quivering mess. Her muffled groan met his when Kody guided her hand over the linen sheet to the outline of his hard cock. He cupped his fingers over hers and helped her stroke the steely length as his hips ground with the slow tempo.

"Rose…" he whispered against her lips. "You still have the power to do this to me. Only you, Rose. God, I missed you…"

"Kody…" Her fingers burned at the touch of him even with a sheet between his throbbing flesh and her hand. He was wonderfully hard and ready. The remembered passion of how he could make her feel when he slipped deep inside her had Rose's knees shaking. It had always been so magical, so sensually delightful, so…

Suddenly her head jerked back and despite his grip around her waist, she managed to dip out of his hold with the agility of a cat. "Stop that!" she hissed.

Good lord, what had she been thinking?

He was up just as quickly with the sheet draped around his narrow hips and his long legs hanging over the edge of the table.

She tore her eyes away from the light dusting of hair beneath his navel that disappeared beneath the sheet, but was drawn back to the hidden bulge at his crotch. Good god, he sat there with a full-blown erection. She groped for her client file as she struggled for air.

"I'm getting out of here," she managed to choke out.

Kody grabbed her arm as she sprinted for the door and slid off the table. "Don't go, Rose. I'm sorry."

"Lower your voice!" she hissed again. "Kody, you're going to get my ass fired if my boss suspects that you're prancing around in here naked and kissing me like it's perfectly natural to do so."

"It is perfectly natural—"

"Shhhhh!" Rose jerked her arm free from his hold and gasped aloud when Kody lost his grip on the bunched material in his hand. In a blink, he stood naked with a thick erection that just about brought her to her knees.

He simply shrugged and made no attempt to fix the situation. Instead, he cocked one knee and placed a fist against his hip and stood there in all his naked glory.

Rose spun away, stared at the door and pressed a hand to her heaving chest. "Honest to god, Kody. If I get fired you'll be the sorriest man in Bandera. Cover yourself up before I open this door," she hissed out.

He scooped up the pile at his feet and quickly wrapped it around his waist once more, not wanting to be responsible for that possibility. Their conversation would just have to wait until a later time—and there *would* be another time because he was going to force it.

"Okay, I'm covered up."

Her hand reached for the doorknob.

"Rose..."

"Goodbye, Kody."

His eyes flicked over her rigid spine. "Don't be pissed. I figured if I didn't come here you would do your best to keep me at arm's length."

"Well, you were right."

"Come on, Rose. Just agree that you'll see me again."

"I think I've seen enough." Her shoulders rose and fell with a settling sigh. "I'm going out now. Don't you dare ask for me again at my workplace. Just get dressed and get out of this building."

"But…" His words trailed off as she yanked open the door, closed it behind her without a glance in his direction and left him alone.

His head fell back as he closed his eyes. "Fuck. That sure as hell didn't go the way I wanted it to."

Snatching his shirt from the chair, he tossed the sheet onto the table. Rose Marie Leighton hadn't seen the last of him.

Chapter Two

ℵ

Rose leaned her head against the swing's rope and stared up into the starry night, using a toe to keep her moving gently. Normally she loved this time of night, especially when the evening was blessed with a clear sky. She could sit here for hours and listen to the coyotes howl far up in the hills. Even better were the low nickers coming from the corral. Rose lived with her sister, Lily, and her brother-in-law, just on the outskirts of Bandera. Theirs was a cozy little home with enough acreage for Lily to board horses for the locals. Rose sighed heavily, though.

As much as she'd tried, she couldn't capture the usual contentment of the evening.

From the moment she'd realized that it was Kody lying on the table, her emotions had been in a tumultuous uproar. Things were finally working her way and now he had stepped back into her life and she'd reacted to him as if they'd never split.

She was settled for the most part and she wanted to keep it that way. After Kody had walked out on her, she'd moved to Nevada with her sister and husband, gotten her act together and attended night school for massage therapy, never thinking she'd end up again in Bandera. But only a few short months ago when her sister's husband, Mark, was transferred back to his company's San Antonio office, Rose had packed up and moved back with them because she couldn't afford her own place. Things were better now. She'd planned over the last year to buy her own home, and had steadily saved money for a down payment—something Lily was none too happy about.

Rose and her sister were like two peas in a pod and Lily loved having Rose with them.

The kitchen screen door creaked behind her, breaking her train of thought. Rose glanced around and smiled as Lily approached. Her sister's tall, trim figure, so different from Rose's compact and petite body was wrapped in a terry robe.

"I came out to check on you," Lily stated quietly. "It's almost eleven."

Rose sighed, glanced back up at the night sky and decided a small lie was in order. "It's peaceful out here tonight. I was just enjoying this unusually warm weather."

Lily strolled to a small bench, sat down and crossed her arms as she followed her sister's gaze and looked upward. She let a moment go by before asking a question. "What's going on with you, Rose? You were quiet tonight, yet agitated."

A wry grin touched Rose's mouth. Lily always went straight to heart of any matter. In fact, she was surprised the question hadn't come earlier. She chewed on her lip and finally met her sister's eyes. "Kody Winter is back in town."

Lily's head nodded slowly, belying the fact that her heart instantly stepped up a beat at the declaration. "For a visit?"

Rose shrugged. "I don't know. He didn't say."

"What?" Lily sat forward. "You talked to him? Where?"

"At the spa. He came in today. Never did tell me how he knew I was there, but you can damn well bet someone told him. He used a different name and requested me." Her jaw tightened at the thought. Damn him.

Lily ran a hand through the long hair at her temple. "So what did he want?"

Rose snorted. "I never gave him a chance to explain." How could she? She'd been in a hot lip lock with him, but Lily wasn't going to know that. "Dammit, Lily. I'm finally getting my life on track and now he appears out of the blue. I know Kody. He'll be back, even if it's here knocking on your door.

He found out where I worked easily enough. Somehow he'll figure out where I live."

"How do you feel about that?"

"Don't you dare let him in. I was done with him when he left me standing in the dust."

Lily shook her head. Rose talked the talk, but she didn't fool anyone. She'd only been on a couple of dates over the last few years. And that just wasn't natural for a twenty-four-year-old woman. Especially when that woman looked the way her sister did. Rose was beautiful with her petite, curvaceous body and that fresh-from-the-farm look.

Lily shrugged a sigh. She also understood Kody. The man would eventually appear on her doorstep. "He won't be put off just because I refuse to let him in. He's come looking for you for a reason. Are you sure that you want to send him away?"

Rose's head snapped up. "Don't even go there, Lily. I'm not allowing him back in my life. He walked, plain and simple, and I never heard a word from him." She wanted to scream with frustration. Damn Kody—he was turning her world upside down again. "I can't trust him. He's a damn liar, Lily. He never looked back once he left. Hopefully we can keep him at bay until his leave is over."

"People change, Rose."

"That might be true, but we're just too different and too much time has passed." Her chin came up as she stared across the yard. "That was the problem in the first place. Kody belongs to big ranching society around here. And his soul is filled with wanderlust. He was hopping around the world doing exactly what he wanted to do and I was back here...shoveling horseshit to find enough money for technical school, then on to an illustrious career of cleaning rooms at a Nevada hotel to keep...keep the money coming in until I earned a degree."

Lily heard the sudden break in Rose's voice, realizing that Kody's unexpected appearance had affected Rose more than she would admit.

The swing did a crazy eight as Rose leapt off the seat. "I can't let him back in my life and you know why."

Lily stood and enveloped her trembling sister with a warm hug. "I know you two ran in different circles, but he's bound to run into someone who knows about... Are you sure?"

Rose laid her head on Lily's shoulder as she hugged her. "No I'm not. But I do know I'm not going to be Kody's plaything again." She hugged her sister tighter. "Everything could change. I just know that right now I can't let him back in. I won't take the chance of ever being hurt like that again."

* * * * *

Kody winced when he got out of his pickup and slammed the door. The one side of his ass hurt like hell from Rose's maniacal fingers the day before and every damn time he'd had to get in and out of his truck today, he'd been reminded.

To top that, he had to figure out a way to see her again, get her to listen to him and hopefully get back into her good graces—or least head in that general direction. If the past held true, it definitely would be a flip of the coin. She would either tell him to go to hell or fall into his arms.

Stretching his back, he headed for the barn with a slight limp. Damn, once he did manage to talk some sense into her, he was going to demand the massage that he'd paid for but hadn't received.

Thinking about a nice hot shower, he just about stumbled when the woman of his thoughts stepped through the open doors of the barn. He blinked and shook his head, but Rose was still there. Floored, he picked up the pace in her direction and tried not to limp.

Rose kept her chin up as she watched him stride toward her. She watched the small puffs of dust his boots raised and wished she could disappear into the breeze the same way. Her gaze drifted back to his suntanned face.

God he was even more handsome than he'd been at twenty and damn if that didn't just piss her off. His shirt clung to his muscular shoulders, molding around the leanness of his belly, and his narrow hips were sexy as hell in the washed-out jeans. They actually clung to him like a second skin. Not sure if coming to the ranch was the smartest thing she had ever done, she knew it was too late to change her mind and head for the hills.

She'd come out to the ranch because she didn't know where else he would be. Surprised that no one was around, she'd decided to wait because eventually he would discover where she lived. She didn't want any interference in her life and was going to make that very plain to him before he ambushed her somewhere else. Better to meet him on her terms than be a constant nervous bundle of energy until he appeared again. She met his questioning gaze and drowned in his nearness. Clearing her throat, she straightened her petite form, hoping to appear taller and more resolute.

"Hello, Kody."

He tipped back his hat, hooked one palm on his hip and nodded his head. "Rose. You're the last person I expected to see. I was thinking of giving Mark a call tonight. He's the only one who seems to have a phone number listed. Hey, are he and Lily still together?"

She ignored his question. Just like him to pretend that the years hadn't separated them. "I know you, Kody, and I knew you'd most likely try to contact me again. I'm here to tell you I'm not interested. Let's leave it at that."

"Seems odd then that you drove all the way out here just to tell me that. Hell, darlin', I was hoping we could make magic again."

When he took a step closer, she took one pace back. Anger instantly flared in her eyes. "Well, *darling,* you're gonna need a wand and a rabbit to make that happen."

Kody glanced heavenward. At times, Rose's tongue was as sharp as a new blade.

"And don't roll your eyes. I drove out here because I don't want you loitering out in front of the spa when I'm working. That little stunt you pulled yesterday could have gotten me fired. And I don't want you bothering my sister and her husband either."

"So Lily and Mark got married? Good for them. They belong together."

Rose heaved an exasperated sigh. She hadn't planned on giving Kody any kind of information. "Just stay away, would you? You and I were finished six years ago and I don't care to bring up the past and start over again. Just do what you're doing here, enjoy your vacation, then head back to...to some jungle or wherever the hell you go." Suppressed anger tensed her body and drew down the corners of her mouth. She wanted to run like hell—anything so she wouldn't have to stare into those gorgeous eyes of his, but she wasn't leaving until she'd exacted a promise from him.

Deep dimples dented his cheeks when he slid off his hat. He dusted the top of it with one hand, but every nerve he owned was honed in on the woman before him. "Well, Rosie dear, what I'm doing here is not so much a vacation as it is a new lifestyle."

Her spine straightened as she eyed him. "What do you mean?"

He shrugged and rolled his shoulders. "Well, you see, I'm planning to buy my own ranch. I'm not going anywhere. I'm parking my ass right here, for good. Kody Winter, country squire and operator of my own spread."

Her mouth sagged open. She blinked and unbelievably could not come up with one retort to spit back. This was something that hadn't even crossed her mind. Kody? Here for good?

He reached up and used a finger at her chin to close her mouth. "The flies are gonna get in if you're not careful."

She slapped away his hand and found her voice. "What about all your training—the years you spent away from this very spot because you wanted more out of life?"

"I realized that everything I wanted is right here in Texas. Now that you're standing here, I'd say I hit the mark."

"You're unbelievable." With a toss of her blonde head, she darted around him, but he stayed her flight by reaching out a hand and gently curling his fingers around her arm. A fire seethed in her eyes. "Let me go, Kody, or you're going to be sorry."

"Seems I've heard that more than one time over the last twenty-four hours."

"I should never have come here to try and talk sense into that thick head of yours. I wanted your promise that you would leave me alone, but I can easily see you're going to be nothing but trouble."

"That's not true. I don't make trouble anymore. I fix it."

"You're an idiot if you think I believe that."

Somehow he had to get her off the defensive. "All right, Rose. Just let me tell you something." She made an attempt to shake him off, but his grip was firm. "I know what you're thinking."

"Then why aren't you protecting yourself?" she spouted back in a quick instant.

Man, she was bullheaded. "I'm not the same person I was. Let's stop this. We've been in each other's company for only a short time yesterday and only a few minutes today, and all we've done is exchange smart-assed barbs. Jesus Christ. We meant something to one another at one time. Can't we at least be civil? I'm sorry for showing up the way I did yesterday. I just didn't think you'd stand and talk nicely to me on the street. Don't go. You came all the way out here for a reason, one I don't want to listen to, but I promise I will if you'll accord me the same chance and just hear me out."

"There's nothing for us to say."

"I think there is." He took a deep breath and eyed her. "We're not teenagers anymore." He let go of her arm, trusting his instincts and the subtle softening in her eyes that she might just listen without running. "Okay, if I promise to behave myself, would you come in while I clean up? I'll only take a few minutes. We can sit on the porch, have a drink and talk. Like old friends. Nothing more."

"What are your parents going to think?"

"They're not home. It'll be nice and quiet."

Her mind screamed no, but her senses had come alive when he'd grabbed her arm. She stared into his sincere gaze. Clean up? Why? She loved how his clothes carried the scent of clean, fresh prairie air. Even though his hat had worn an oval through his thick hair, the ends still curled in the breeze and fluttered about his ears. His square jaw was darker than yesterday with the sun's burning rays and the shadow of a beard. He was kick-ass gorgeous, yet he wanted to clean up. He was perfect the way he was. Mentally, she shook herself back to awareness.

Rose wanted to tell him no. She wanted to walk away and let it be done, but if she gave him the chance to enter back into her life, she could lose too much. He would take it away a slice at a time, not because he was evil but because Kody would have no choice. And he didn't even understand that himself because he didn't know everything about her. Damn, she'd worked too hard and had been through too much over the past years to every let someone like him rule her heart again.

She closed her eyes and took a settling breath. He was right. They were adults and if she didn't quit reacting like a hotheaded teenager, she'd never get him to back off. Even though she felt like she held a live grenade in her hand, she finally nodded and met his gaze squarely. "All right. But I'm holding you to your promise, especially after yesterday's little escapade."

Kody grinned like the idiot she'd stated he was, and he placed his hand over his heart. "I promise. No shenanigans. Come on, I'll find you a soda before hopping in the shower."

* * * * *

Rose strolled about the living room, amazed that nothing had really changed since the last time she'd been in the Winter home. The log ranch house had always struck awe in her mind and it still did. The richness of the place was hard to miss. Expensive tile covered the floor, leather furniture abounded and artifacts and paintings from all over the world adorned the walls.

Nothing like the shack she had grown up in.

Rose remembered a time when her home, however small, had been a haven for her and Lily. That was until her mother died far too young, only to leave two small girls with a drunken father who spent more time loving his alcohol than the two daughters who needed him so badly. Neither she nor Lily had ever had any sort of parental guidance from the drunkard. And when most people thought they were such good girls with high morals because neither had ever been in any kind of trouble, the truth was that both she and Lily had been scared to death of their father. Each had suffered through more than one bout of his physical abuse and they'd learned early on that any sort of "fall from grace" just wasn't worth the black and blue marks when discovered.

She rubbed away the goose bumps that covered the skin of her upper arms as her gaze flowed about, then rested on the grand staircase leading to the second floor.

"Whew…" The soft uttering followed the quick beat of her heart. Her face sank into her upturned palm and she waited for her pulse to slow. The last time she'd been here, she'd gone up those stairs. It was the night she'd lost her virginity to Kody.

Her mind swam back to an earlier time that same night and how she and Kody had had their own little party right here in this living room because Kody's parents had been at an auction and wouldn't be home until the following day. Both she and Kody had drunk too much. Somehow, they'd ended up in his room on the second floor because the make-out session between them on the leather couch had become explosive.

Cupping her forehead, Rose leaned her elbow against the fireplace mantel and closed her eyes. The memory of that night was burned forever in her brain. An eighteen-year-old virgin, panting and reckless because of the boss's enigmatic son with sparkling green eyes had teased the breath from her lungs with warm, full lips. He'd expertly unhooked her bra and sucked on her nipples until she'd moaned and wiggled beside him. Soon, she'd found herself naked on his bed and his fingers doing things between her legs that had driven her wild. And then? A hard bulge pressing against the bare heat of her pussy, begging entrance. Rose had spread her legs and pleaded to be fucked — Kody had readily accommodated her.

Her eyes lifted and she cast her gaze to the staircase again. She might have never been back between these four walls again, but that summer was filled with seductive, hot nights in Kody's arms whether in his car, rented hotel rooms or under the great expanse of the Texas sky.

Even now, those memories of all the energetic, hot sex could reduce her to a trembling mess.

Her pussy clenched tightly as her mind drifted back to all that had led her to being naked beneath him that first time and to his stiff cock breaking past the barrier of her virginity. She had cried out in pain. But soon that pain had given way to a hot flush of sensual trepidation, then to a glorious night of Kody pounding into her tender body. They had fucked on the bed, fucked in the shower and when he'd demanded that she suck his cock, she'd gone down on her knees. No matter what he'd asked for, she had accommodated him. Kody had been a hot and demanding lover. Was he still like that?

Rose gripped her forehead, telling herself that she had to quit thinking about the past and just focus on the future—one that didn't include Kody Winter. He would eventually leave her again for greener pastures and she simply wouldn't put up with that sort of rejection. Once was enough.

"You don't have a headache, do you?"

She spun at the sound of his voice. To look at him with hair still damp and cheeks flushed from the hot water after she'd just been daydreaming about making love with him was just about too much for her to take. She forced her eyes away and sank into a chair. "No, I was just waiting for you."

"You looked pretty deep in thought. And whatever it was has your cheeks stained a pretty pink. Hopefully you were thinking about me." He crossed the room, ignored her scowl and set down two plates. "I'm hungry as hell and didn't want to eat in front of you." He sat on the other side of the coffee table and scooped up a handful of chips.

Her stomach growled when she eyed the thickly layered sandwiches. Hell, she'd hardly eaten a thing since yesterday afternoon. "Thank you. Oh, and don't flatter yourself. I got some sun today." Her nose raised a notch. He flustered the hell out of her, but she was pretty proud of her waspish response.

She picked up half of her sandwich and nibbled on the corner, peeking at him from the corner of her eye. Yesterday morning, she'd awakened, completed her regular morning chores, then headed for work never expecting that she'd have a run-in with Kody after all these years. Shouldn't she have known somewhere deep in her psyche that the day was going to be like none other? Now she sat here with him as if six years had simply disintegrated into dust. She must be losing her mind.

Chapter Three

ॐ

Kody attacked his sandwich, concentrating on the salty taste of honeyed ham in order to control the urge to leap across the small wooden table and flatten Rose to the cushions. She'd probably beat the hell out of him despite her small stature, and then run for the hills. No, he'd behave himself and ignore his half hard-on. He had her talking civilly and at the moment couldn't ask for more. Rose saved him from trying to figure out where to start by breaking the silence.

"Where are your parents?"

Kody wiped his mouth with a napkin as he swallowed. "They're on a Caribbean cruise."

"Are they coming back soon? Christmas is only a few days away."

Kody shook his head. "No. They're planning to get back the day after New Years."

"Must be strange to celebrate the holidays with only your brothers." She remembered his two older siblings. She didn't know them all that well, but one thing she was sure of. Kody was the black sheep and had always marched to his own music.

"They've got other plans and weren't going to make it to Texas this year anyway. Probably part of the reason my mom and dad decided to head on out for the holidays. At the time they made their cruise reservations, they didn't know I was coming home. I don't think they would have left if they weren't assured I'd be here when they got back." *Ah, here it comes*, he thought as he watched the play of emotions on her face.

"Why did you muster out?"

He shrugged. "I told you outside. I want my own place. Surprised the hell out of my folks. I might even talk them into selling me a share in this homestead because they're thinking of retiring." His eyes cast about. "I decided I wanted to be here. I missed this place. I did what my parents demanded and now my years of service are done." He shrugged. "That type of life isn't for me. Toward the end, I began to feel claustrophobic just thinking about spending my days under constant supervision. You know what? Every day that I've been home, I've been surer about my decision. This is where I'm supposed to be."

Rose was certain what he stated was true. She never had understood how he'd let his father talk him into leaving the ranch in the first place—or for that matter, Texas. Kody was the type of man who blended with the wild landscape— always had and always would.

She had pined away for him when they'd split and had thought she was over him. Rose had discovered something the moment he'd stepped from his truck and it was rather disconcerting to realize she had been dead wrong. But her past emotions and what she'd felt for him—still did—had nothing to do with the present. Rose needed to maintain a hard exterior against those feelings. If he was home permanently, there was a good chance she would have to leave Bandera. Somehow, she'd find employment and could live off the money she'd saved to buy a house until she got back on her feet.

"Let's cut to the chase, Kody. What exactly did you think was going to happen when you came looking for me? Wait." She held up a hand. "I know that answer. You made it rather clear yesterday." As soon as she said it, a blaze of desire wound its way through her. Not once since she'd walked out on him the day before, had she forgotten the wondrous feel of being pressed against his chest.

He tossed his sandwich onto the plate and leaned back in the chair. "Let me ask you something. Why did you come here this evening?"

"Because you came looking for me yesterday and I was none too thrilled."

"Shit, Rose. Are we going to start playing games again? Fine. I came looking for you because you were the biggest reason I wanted to come back." Her eyes narrowed, but he plunged on without giving her a chance to speak. "Now just listen to me. I know we parted on bad terms. Why, I'm still not too sure. Maybe we were too young." His suntanned hand scrubbed over his clean-shaven jaw as he thought about what he'd just said.

Rose's lips formed a straight line beneath her glittering eyes. "And just because we're older, you think we can pick up again? Kody, you made your choice six years ago, and it wasn't me."

"We were kids, Rose. Now I'm a man, one who would like you to give me another chance. That arrogant rich boy is gone." A wry smile touched his lips. "You know, I think part of the reason my parents insisted on me leaving for the service is they knew it would change me, mature me. I was pretty wild at the time—even got myself kicked out of college. I never was serious about this ranch or the people in my life and took what I wanted."

"Myself included," Rose butted in. She blinked back the burning behind her eyelids and suddenly understood that Kody's presence affected her like a kick in the stomach. Rose never cried anymore. She had done too much of that when he'd left. Since seeing him the day before, she hadn't been able to get rid of the lump in her throat. Taking a breath, she plunged on. "We're much too different. I don't run within the same circle of people that your family does."

"You're looking at the past and comparing it to present day, but I've changed. I needed to become much more responsible. When I left, Rose, I was nothing but a troublemaker. I was the youngest son who didn't have a care in the world." His palm came up to stop anything else she might say. "I take that back. I did care about something. That something was you, but my parents pushed for me to leave. Suddenly, I wanted to go. In the beginning, I thought of the service as an escape, a big playground with rules I was sure I could get around. It wasn't until I almost got kicked out the first month that I started questioning my own morals. My father flew out to California, pulled some strings in high places and told me to get my shit together or never come back. He was serious and that one statement has stayed on my mind all this time. I don't know. Maybe I'm wired differently than most people. I liked danger, I enjoyed pushing myself to the limit."

Rose could well believe what he'd just said. Kody's devil-may-care attitude, his bad boy persona had attracted her like a moth to the flame. No matter what he stated, however, there was still a bit of the old Kody that would never disappear. He'd shown that side yesterday by pulling the stunt at the spa. He'd stood there as naked as the day he was born, and all she had wanted to do was climb back onto the table with him. She blinked to bring herself back to the present.

"I thought about you all the time," Kody stated quietly. "I tried contacting you when I came home for a few days after completing my preliminary basic."

"Sure you did. I don't believe that for a second."

"Your father never told you?"

"No. You know what he was like. Even if you really did want to find me, Frank Leighton only worried about himself and the bottle in his hand. *If* you left a message, he was the last person to do so with."

Kody's eyes rounded in surprise at Rose's vehemence. "I knew he was no prize. I really had hoped that life had changed for you and Lily."

"Well, it didn't." Her head came up. "I don't want to talk about him. I want to get things settled between us. I want to hear your promise that you'll respect my decision about us."

"I can't do that, Rose."

Her hand sliced the air in anger. "And why can't you? You should just head back to...to wherever the Navy could send you because nothing is going to happen here. I'm not a plaything anymore."

Man, it was hard to maintain his temper, but he wasn't going to butt heads with her. Half the reason he was so attracted to Rose was her ability to be exactly who she wanted without a damn care in the world what anyone else thought. He had always loved her independent spirit. "What are you talking about? I never treated you badly."

Her eyes flashed. "Saying goodbye and thanks for the great summer wasn't playing with me, wasn't treating me in a shitty way?" Rose shook her head in disgust. "At the time, I thought you really cared for me. We weren't too young. I knew what I was about back then. It just angers me that I let you string me along until a better offer came up."

"Wait one minute. I didn't string you along."

Rose crossed her arms with a jerk. "The hell you didn't. You constantly talked about the future back then and made it sound like I was a part of it. Then suddenly you enlisted, something you'd never spoken about. You didn't ask me to come with you, you didn't ask me to wait, and you never asked me how much I cared about you. And contrary to what you said about my father, you could have kept trying to contact me."

"I did. I called every chance I had. It was about two months later that your father said you'd left town with Lily and he didn't have a clue where you were." He would never inform Rose of how the old man had also said he didn't care much if he ever saw his daughters again. "I kept calling until one day all I got was a recording that said the phone was disconnected."

Rose squirmed on the cushion. The phone was disconnected because her father's overindulgent lifestyle had finally killed him that fall. Rose had stayed in Nevada while Mark and Lily had come back to clean out the house and put it up for sale. "You think I'm comparing past and present, Kody. I'm not, I'm separating them. And right now, I have my own life that doesn't include you. I would like to keep it that way."

"Are you seeing someone else?"

"That's none of your business."

"Then I'm going on the assumption that you're currently available simply because you won't discuss it."

Rose silently sputtered. What did he think? That she was like some mare on the auction block? Before she could shoot back another retort, however, Kody's eyes locked with hers.

"I'm not giving up, Rose. And I'm not leaving Texas. Eventually, we'll be running into one another."

That one statement scared the hell out of her. It took all of her grit to stand slowly instead of leaping off the couch and racing to the door. "I'll just make sure I head in the other direction when I see you coming." She said it, hoping to placate him for the time being. His presence was going to make it difficult to stay on in Bandera. Earlier she'd thought coming to the ranch had been a mistake. Not now. Now she knew for sure what his intentions were as far as she was concerned. Rose had some hard decisions to make.

She shrank back when he stood. "I'm leaving," she whispered as she stared up. "Just stay out of my life, Kody. No way am I going to have my heart broken again by the likes of you." She turned to flee, tossing aside her earlier resolve to appear calm and collected. She had to get away from him before dissolving into tears and making a complete fool of herself, but he was only a step behind her.

Before she could yank open the door, Kody reached out and pulled her to his chest. "Would you quit trying to run from me all the time? I'm not letting you leave until we talk this out. Not when it was youthful misconceptions that separated us."

Being held so close to him that she could feel the beat of his heart further cracked the hardened resolve she'd worked so hard to maintain. Feeling his fingers around her arms and having his warm breath swirl about her face immediately brought back the hot yearning that wouldn't go away. She clawed to the surface of sanity.

"The bottom line is you walked away from me and didn't look back until it was too late. You shredded my independence and stomped on my heart. You...you might think it was misconceptions back then," she shot out, "but it was reality and I've learned to live with it."

Kody struggled against his rising temper. "Just quit being so damn mouthy and let me talk!"

"Mouthy?" she spewed out. "I'm just standing up for myself. I'm no man's doormat, Kody, even if I was only the hired help around here at one time. Hey, face the facts. Your family would never allow me into your life on a full-time basis anyway. I'm not polished enough. I'm only good enough to clean horseshit off their stable floor."

"Oh, Christ. Get off your 'poor me' soapbox. My family isn't like that and you know it. Besides, they have nothing to say in regard to how I feel about you." His head tipped to the side and he studied her angry face. "There's more to this than you're telling me, isn't there? So why won't you even give me a chance? Spit it out, Rose."

"Why I won't is none of your business," she snapped.

"Goddammit!" The oath exploded from his lips.

Her body started at the sound.

"The past happened. Fuck all that, because there's something much more important to think about. You can't tell me that being in the same room doesn't affect you like it does me." His voice suddenly lowered as he stared into her flushed face. "I love Texas. I missed it like crazy. Yes, that was part of the reason I refused a military career. But a bigger reason was you. Those first few years when I had a chance to come home on leave, you had left the area. I couldn't discover anything about you—not where you'd gone or who you were with. I told myself that I would get over you. At times, I actually thought that I had. But when it came down to making a final decision, I couldn't sign a contract. Why? Because every night I saw your face when I closed my eyes. I had to go for what I wanted most in life."

Rose mentally scratched about for something to say. She didn't dare digest Kody's declaration. "How did you find me?" she asked through a clenched jaw. It was an extreme struggle on her part to maintain an aloof air with Kody in such close proximity. Her heart was bouncing all over the place.

He looked confused at the turn of the conversation. "What difference does that make?"

"I want to know." Rose *had* to know. How much was Kody aware of? How many details did he actually know about her life?

"I planned to start talking to people in your old neighborhood. But yesterday I saw you park in front of the spa and head inside."

"So? I could have been going in for a massage."

"I hung around outside and saw you pick up a folder and head back with a customer. It was easy to see you were employed there."

"You hung around outside? That sounds more like stalking to me." At least he'd found her by accident. Thank god he hadn't contacted any acquaintances.

His chin dropped to his chest. He would have counted to ten, but he didn't think he had the time. Taking a deep breath, he met her wary eyes. "Why are you being so stubborn?"

"I told you, Kody. Because…because I never want to hurt like that again."

In that instance, Kody spied the real Rose beneath the raucous, tough exterior she wore like armor. He had to make this work, but at the moment, the only thing he could think about was kissing her.

And that was exactly what he did. Yanking her tighter again his chest, her surprised eyes were the last thing he saw before he pulled her lips to his. She struggled in his arms, but his mouth tore at her defenses with a slow, pleading demand to allow him back into her life. Over and over, sucking at her lips, forcing them open so he could explore the remembered warmth of her mouth.

The taste of his lips chipped away her defenses, kiss by fervent kiss. Too long. Too many years without his arms. Too many lonely days without him. She was lost and at the moment didn't care. Every emotion she'd ever carried inside her heart rose to the surface as she wrapped her arms around his neck and clung tightly. Rose returned the heated kiss with a passion that surprised them both. Clutching his broad shoulders, she pressed closer and gave herself fully to his firm, moist lips.

She felt his desire, hard and insistent against her hip when he backed her against the door. Dipping down, Kody placed one arm around her waist as he devoured her mouth and swung his hips forward to press the hard ridge of his cock against her.

Her moan filled his mouth. Her body answered him back with a surge of her hips. Her fingers scraped through the thick softness of his damp hair. The anger, the heartbreak, the years of wishing for him—it was forgotten as they chased one another's lips and breathed in the scent of the other.

A strangled groan from Kody's throat rumbled across Rose's cheek as his lips burned a path to her neck. Her senses reacted hotly to the flicking thumb over the raised bud of her nipple beneath the thin cotton of her shirt, and to the strong hand at her waist that slipped down to cup a supple buttock. She could barely breathe, let alone open her mouth and insist that he stop. Her head fell back against the door. Her eyes fluttered shut and her mouth sagged open as she relished the touch of his hands on her body and his moist lips nipping at her neck. She shouldn't be here, but she didn't care. She just needed to be in his arms for this one, hot moment.

Kody tore at the snap of her jeans, his fingers fumbling to yank down the zipper that stood in the way.

She knew where he was going. Kody always took what he wanted, but she needed to be used. She would pick up her anger when she left his home...but for now? She had paid for this moment with six long years of loneliness. More than ever, she wanted Kody to fuck her hard, to slam into her body until she shuddered with passion. What his rushing fingers promised, was simply too hot to pass up. Her hand slipped through his hair to the back of his neck once more. She tugged his mouth back to her swollen lips just as Kody's hand slid carelessly between the flat of her belly and the waistband of her bikini underwear in search of her clit. Her knees nearly buckled and her belly muscles tensed. Remembered desire coursed through her, spiraling from her pussy in a hot jagged line to her breasts.

She gasped when his hand clamped her mound tightly within the confines of her jeans. Once more he sought her lips, flicking his tongue, sweeping the warm cavern of her mouth with promise when she opened to him. Her gasp echoed around them when he split her wet pussy lips with a thick finger, drew her moisture across her clit, then thrust into her cunt. Her muscles clamped down hard, her fingers pulled at his hair and her hips ground against each plunge, sucking at him harder and harder. Two fingers now, filling her hard and steady. She could barely breathe.

"Come for me, Rose," he whispered between licks. "God you're hot and tight." His fingers worked faster as the pad of his hand ground against her swollen clit. "I want to fuck you, but first this… First I want to feel you shudder in my hand." He drove his fingers upward, pinning her against the door.

Rose's orgasm exploded and if Kody hadn't had his arm around her and his fingers inside her, she would have slid to the floor. He stroked upward, time after time, coaxing her entire body through the frenzied shudder that threatened to never end. Her breasts ached, her stomach clenched, and her womb throbbed in response as the pulses squeezing around his fingers. She was delirious with the ecstasy pounding through her blood.

"Touch me," he groaned.

They licked at one another's lips crazily as her hand flailed to squeeze his cock. Kody's breath shot out of his lungs as she wrapped her tiny palm around his jeans-clad erection.

The fingers inside her quickly found the same rhythm as her hand and, immediately, Rose clamped hard against the pressure inside her, her hips writhing in frustration. Her clit throbbed hot beneath his touch and Kody worked it mercilessly. He refused to stop the wondrous and unexpected encounter no matter how much he wanted to be inside her, fucking her firm and steady.

His breath was harsh beside her ear. It rasped heavier when her hips began to grind harder. And as her body pulsed around his fingers once more, Kody lost control of his emotions and the hot flames that licked through his belly. He let the heat roil with her firm strokes around him. His hips jerked forward and cum filled his shorts. The intense, sizzling, and mind boggling realization that she'd driven him over the edge of control, stunned him completely.

Somewhere in Rose's mind she stumbled upon the fact that Kody's rhythmic throbs and wild moans meant he had come with her. She squeezed her fingers and licked at his mouth with gasps as her second orgasm cooled. Her head sagged against his chest, her eyes closed, and she panted wildly. Kody's hand left her ass and rested against the jamb as he tipped his head and settled his cheek against her perspiring brow. His hot, quick breaths rustled through the soft waves of her hair.

Slipping his hand from the confines of her underwear, he dipped his head to gently caress her lips with his own. Silently, he rested his hand on the slight curve of her hip to pull her closer to his body. He took another deep breath. "I just couldn't let you walk out that door."

His breath flowed across her heated cheek, bringing a strange sense of security along with it.

"Come upstairs with me, Rose. It's been so long."

The second floor? She opened her eyes and her gaze shifted to the winding staircase. Kody had just promised her a night of passion if she would walk up those steps with him. She couldn't think. He was too damn close for her to make any sense of what had just happened.

Her palm came up to rest against his chest. She was immediately sorry because his heart thumped as wildly as hers. Yanking her hand away, she dropped it to join the opposite one as she zipped up her jeans and snapped them shut. "I-I can't. I have to go, Kody," she whispered. "Please. I have to think about this."

"Rose…"

"Let me walk through that door. I…I promise I'll call you. I'm just…so confused. Please, Kody."

Her blue eyes sparkled with unshed tears as she stared up, and something in those bright depths touched his heart. Kody pushed away, but his fingertip drifted across her cheek. "I'm certain of one thing, Rose. I'm not sorry it happened."

Keeping her face turned away from the gentle sea of green, her hand flailed to find the doorknob. Much to her surprise, Kody beat her to it. He silently opened the door and let her walk out onto the porch. Thank god. But his words stopped her for a short moment.

"All I ask is that you call me, Rose. Don't let it end here."

She paused with her hand on the rail before taking that first step down. Her shoulders rose as she breathed in the night air. "Christmas is in four days. I've got obligations I have to take care of, but I will call." She closed her eyes not daring to glance at him over her shoulder. Hopefully Kody would be appeased and wait for her to phone him, thus giving her enough time to make an escape if that is what she needed to do.

"Good night, Rose." His voice drifted past her, creating a deep-seated yearning to simply turn around and step into his arms.

Her eyes fluttered open. "Good night, Kody."

* * * * *

Lily glanced up when Rose entered the house. Closing the book in her hands, she placed it beside her on the couch and waited for her sister to speak.

Rose stood tentatively in the arched doorway to the living room, her eyes darting about until she found the courage to meet Lily's wondering stare. "You didn't have to wait up, Lily."

"It was getting late. I was worried."

"I know. Sorry I didn't call." Rose shrugged. "I rode around for a bit after I left the ranch."

"How did it go?"

Rose shook her head. "How does it ever go with Kody?" Her confused gaze lifted. "I felt like I was eighteen again, Lily. He wanted me to stay. He wanted to…" The fingers of both her hands drifted through her thick hair. "He kissed me — among other things."

"You didn't…" Lily left the rest unsaid.

"No, I didn't." A streak of remembered passion burned inside her belly. "But I was so close." A wry smile lifted the corner of her mouth as she shrugged off her jacket. "Although, does having his hand down my pants count?"

"Oh, Rose..."

Shrugging, Rose turned and placed a hand on the thick wooden railing that led to her second floor bedroom. "Once he kissed me, I couldn't say no." She took a heavy step and then another as she shook her head in bewilderment.

"Rose, wait." Lily hurried to the bottom of the steps. "Maybe you should rethink this. If he wants you back, maybe you should give him a chance. It would be the perfect solution."

Rose turned. "For who? Kody? And what happens if it doesn't work out? I wanted to believe tonight that maybe it could. For a few short moments, I pretended." She shook her head. "There's so much at stake, Lily. So much to risk." Again, she shook her head. "I just don't know what is the right thing to do."

Rose could feel Lily's silent but nonjudgmental stare as she continued up the staircase. Once at the top, she entered through a closed bedroom door. The light from the hallway shone across the room and settled on the small sleeping figure huddled in the middle of the bed. She crossed the carpet and sat on the edge of the mattress. Her hand automatically reached out to caress the soft hair of her little boy. Travis muttered in his sleep and tucked his teddy bear closer. Leaning over, Rose kissed him gently on the cheek.

"Mommy..." Travis mumbled.

"Hi, baby." She tucked the blanket close around his shoulders.

"I missed you."

She smiled and kissed him again. "I missed you, too. Sorry I wasn't here to tuck you in tonight."

"Can you sleep with me? How many days now until Santa comes?"

Rose picked up his hand, folded a chubby little thumb into his palm and smiled. "Only this many. Four more days, honey."

"That's a long time."

She smiled. "Christmas will be here before you know it." Suddenly she needed Travis' tiny frame tucked close. "Scoot over. I'll cuddle with you a bit." Once settled beside him with his quilt wrapped around them both, Rose almost asked her young son if he would like to take a big adventure and find their own home. She decided against it. Not yet. Why risk ruining a four-year-old's Christmas with adult insecurities when she had no clue what the future held?

Rose pulled Travis closer and breathed in the scent of his freshly washed hair. Good old Lily had seen to her nephew's needs. A stab of fear pierced Rose's heart. She depended upon her sister and Mark so very much. The three worked as a team as far as Travis went, and Lily and Mark had never judged her when she'd discovered she was pregnant. They had begged her to contact Kody and let him know, but Rose's fear of rejection had finally made them back off.

Rose hugged Travis so hard that the little boy uttered a mumbled protest. What was she going to do? She was frightened to strike off on her own, but staying could change things in so many different ways. She nuzzled her son's hair after his breathing had turned soft and regular once more. He was the most cherished thing in her world, but Rose remembered Kody stating emphatically, and more than once, that he never wanted to be saddled with children. Fatherhood just wasn't for him. Had he changed? What if he decided that no, he didn't want a son and Travis discovered someday who his father really was? Rose had lived the horrible rejection of not being wanted or loved by a parent. She would never let Travis experience those emotions. And what if Kody wanted Travis in his life, but not her? He might be so angry at discovering her deception that he would make her life miserable.

Then there were Kody's parents. Rose had simply been the hired help, not refined or cultured like so many of the women she'd seen attending some function at the ranch. Rose just couldn't get over the very real possibility that they would want Travis but not her. She could never live through one day if they took her to court. Kody not only had his own financial resources, but he had his family's money behind him if they decided to join forces. She could never fight them because she simply didn't have the wherewithal to do it.

Rose had nothing.

She squeezed her eyes tightly and kissed the back of Travis' head. She had nothing but the small boy in her arms. Travis was hers, completely. He was the one thing in this world that no one could take from her—or so she'd thought until Kody had reappeared. Fear of the unknown such as she'd never experienced shot through her mind. She clung to the little boy and waited for it to abate.

She reached up to wipe at the tear trickling down her cheek.

Late into the night she continued to struggle with her emotions. A gentle voice told her that maybe she should give Kody a chance. He said he had changed. More grown up, more the man who knew exactly where his life was going. Could someone actually transform that much?

Rose sighed deeply. She covered Travis' shoulders with the quilt, rolled to her back and stared at the ceiling, praying for an answer and the guidance to do what was right. She should never have agreed to move back to Bandera.

Chapter Four

๛

More than once the next morning Rose picked up the phone then hung it up again. She wanted to hear the throaty huskiness of Kody's voice, yet she didn't. One thing was certain. He would plead to see her and she wasn't too sure she could say no. All morning long the memory of the hot sexual encounter the evening before was ever present. Kody had more than proved he desperately wanted to pick up where they'd left off. She shook her head in amazement. The more she fought to rid him from her mind the more she wanted him. It was crazy and insane and there was absolutely nothing she could do to squash her yearning.

She was just putting a bag together for Travis' daycare when Lily stuck her head inside the little boy's room.

"Are you going to need me to pick up Travis today?"

Rose glanced up from where she kneeled on the floor with her son's knapsack in her hands. "No, I don't have any late clients, so I'll stop and get him."

"Good," her sister replied as she held out her arms for a hug. Travis skipped across the room and was enveloped in a warm embrace. "I've got new customers arriving with their horse today. They just called. They can't get here until later this afternoon."

Rose settled back on her thighs and watched her son in Lily's embrace. At that moment, it hit Rose just how much Travis resembled his father. His hair wasn't as dark, but he possessed the same green eyes and Kody's full smile.

Lily glanced down at her nephew and gave him a final squeeze. "Why don't you run downstairs and tell Uncle Mark goodbye? He's going to leave for work shortly." She crossed her arms and stared at her sister after Travis disappeared. "Are you going to be okay?" Lily asked quietly.

Rose shook herself from her quick trance and got up from the floor. "Yes, I'm fine."

"I know you don't want to hear this, but I thought about Kody and you all night. Something happened between the two of you six years ago and it happened again last night. Don't you think that bears some thought? If he still feels so strongly, I think you owe it to him to tell him about Travis."

Rose's jaw hardened. "You know why I'm not telling him, Lily. I'm not taking the chance. I couldn't fight Kody if he took me to court even for partial custody. Besides, I can't believe he's changed that much. It's just a matter of time before the arrogant rich kid shows up. He'll love me and leave me again. And worse, there's an even bigger chance that Travis will end up feeling unloved and rejected by a father just as we were. I'm not putting him through that."

"You're not giving him enough credit. You don't know if six years of military life has matured him or if he would drag you through a court hearing. Besides, he wants you back or he would never have come to the spa."

Rose picked up her son's bag and turned to stare at her sister. "And what," she stated with a voice quiet and determined, "happens if the two of us don't work out? Travis will be pulled in all different directions. I don't want that for him." With a jerking motion, she punched Travis' teddy bear into the bag and buckled it. "He's the only thing I have in this world that I can call completely mine and I won't chance him being hurt."

"That's where you're wrong, Rose. Travis isn't completely yours, not really."

"Yes he is!" Rose stated emphatically. "Please, Lily. Try to understand. Maybe I just need to find my own place somewhere. I'm thinking about taking Travis far away."

"What? Don't be ridiculous. You can't just up and run."

Rose shrugged. "I'm keeping my options open. How can I stay now that he's back for good? I made a mistake returning to Bandera with you. I never worried about his parents because they didn't know me that well."

"What are you going to do if he calls?"

"I'm going to tell him I'm busy. Besides, he won't call. He doesn't know where I am. So far. And if he does discover where I live and you do talk to him, you can—"

"I don't want to have to lie, Rose," Lily stated firmly.

The bag fell from Rose's hands as she cupped her face. Frustration burgeoned inside her. "I...I don't know what to do."

Lily gathered her trembling sister into her arms. "I'm sorry for badgering you, honey. I do understand where you're coming from. You just have to trust in the future. Kody is back. Give him some of your time. See where all this might go. You just can't up and leave."

Rose heaved a rattling sigh, left the comfort of her sister's arms and took her hand instead to lead her down the steps. "There's nothing in the world, Lily, that I would love more than to be able to trust in the future. I can't."

"Yes you can, Rose. You just don't know it. All I'm asking is that you keep an open mind. Just say you'll think about it. Please. I hate seeing you this way."

To simply end the conversation, Rose nodded her head in agreement, but nausea roiled in her stomach.

* * * * *

Fifteen minutes later, Rose dropped Travis off at his daycare and proceeded to work. Once she'd parked her car in a small lot around the corner from the spa, she hurried down the sidewalk. Rounding a building, her gaze settled on a pickup parked in front of the spa, and on the man who leaned against the grill. His arms were crossed and one booted ankle rested lazily across the other. The Stetson he wore rode low on his brow and even though she couldn't see his face, Rose's heart picked up a beat.

Damn! What was Kody doing here? She marched forward, her fingers gripping her purse strap. At that moment, he glanced up and instantly straightened with a languid smile that still had the ability to heat her blood.

Rose's jaw clenched tightly as she snapped to a halt in front of him. "What are you doing here? I said I would call."

"Good morning to you, too."

Rose rolled her eyes heavenward and took a deep breath. "Listen Kody. I asked that you not come down here to the spa."

"I'm not in the spa. I'm just parked outside enjoying the sunshine."

"That's bullshit and you know it."

"Was it also bullshit when you said you'd call? I wasn't too sure and I didn't know how to get hold of you so I figured this was the best place."

"It hasn't even been twelve hours since I left the ranch." Heat rose to her cheeks as soon as the words were out of her mouth. Damn him. Thinking about the evening before was the last thing she wanted to contend with—especially when his presence had her emotions jumping all over the place.

"I didn't want to chance missing your call. Something came up and I have to head out of town tomorrow. I also wanted to ask you to dinner tonight."

Her jaw slackened in surprise. Just like Kody to plunge right in. "What makes you think I'm available? I told you I had commitments."

Kody shrugged. "Change them."

"Absolutely not."

"Change them."

Rose struck a pose with her fist against her hip, her eyes flashed and she raised her chin a notch. "Listen here, Kody

Winter. I haven't given us seeing each other enough thought to make any kind of spur-of-the-moment change in any of my plans." What a lie. All she'd done was think about him. And as upset as she'd been the entire evening before, sparring with him now made her feel alive and able to overcome anything. No way was he going to discover that though. She glanced at her watch. "It's almost nine o'clock. I've got a client who will be here in about ten minutes and I have to get to work. Just go home and I'll call you when I'm ready."

His eyes widened in feigned surprise. "Still bullheaded, aren't you. Okay, I'll just wait right here until you make a decision." With that said, he leaned against the fender of his truck, took a toothpick out of his T-shirt pocket and stuck it between his lips. "Stick your head out the door when you're ready and let me know what time I can pick you up."

Rose gasped at his audacity. She adjusted the purse strap on her shoulder with a jerk and sent him a shriveling glare. "Fine. Stay out here all day. I couldn't care less." She spun on a dime and headed inside the spa without another word.

When she slammed the door, Laura glanced up.

"Morning, Rose. Your appointment is already here. I set up Mrs. Hill in room three. Hey, that's the same guy out there who was in here yesterday. Um, Anderson I think?"

Rose stuffed her purse behind the receptionist's desk. "Yeah. If he comes through the door, call the cops."

Laura leaned to the side a bit and studied Kody through the window. "I'll call them only to borrow their handcuffs. Man, what I wouldn't give to run my hands over his belly."

"Laura!"

"Do you know him from somewhere?"

Rose picked through the files on Laura's desk and slipped Mrs. Hill's beneath her arm. "He's an acquaintance from a long time ago."

"What does he want?"

"To take me out to dinner."

"Oh, cool. In my dreams. Where are the two of you going?"

"*I'm* not going anywhere," Rose replied with a bit of exasperation.

"Doesn't look like he is either. What's he doing just standing out there?"

"Waiting for my answer."

Laura sighed and settled her chin on an upturned hand. "Ahhh, how romantic."

"How idiotic is more like it. Did you say room three?"

"Hmmm?"

"Room three? Mrs. Hill. Remember?"

Laura dragged her gaze from the front window. "Yeah, room three. I've got appointments set up all morning for you."

"Then I better get to work." Rose turned on her heel, but despite her firm resolve, she peeked a quick glance over her shoulder. Kody still leaned against the pickup, his head back and his eyes closed to the bright sunshine as if he didn't have a care in the world.

"Idiot," she mumbled beneath her breath just before she walked down the dim hallway.

* * * * *

At ten o'clock she finished with her first client and headed for the front lobby to collect the next one.

"Your knight in shining armor is still out there," Laura giggled when she looked up.

Rose turned and stared out the front window. Kody now perched on the edge of his truck's hood, talking with a meter maid. His head fell back as he laughed at something the woman said.

Gnashing her teeth, Rose took a deep breath. "I hope he's got sunscreen on because it's going to be a long day out there." With a pasty smile, she asked her next client to follow her to a room.

At eleven o'clock, history repeated itself. Only this time it was Laura standing on the sidewalk offering Kody a cup of coffee with the dazzling smile of a woman with a crush. Rose was appalled, but she didn't dare go out the door and chew on either of them in front of clients who sat waiting for appointments.

Rose hadn't seen her employer yet but knew he was in the building somewhere. Lloyd was going to start wondering about the cowboy who had parked himself in front of the building. Damn Kody.

At noon, Rose finished up with her third client. As she walked down the dimly lit hallway, Lloyd's voice called out to her from his office.

"Hey, Rose. Want to come in here for a minute?"

She paused with a hesitant step and wondered if she should check the front window first. Instead, she backtracked and entered her boss's office.

"What's up, Lloyd?"

He scribbled something on a piece of paper then looked up with a smile. "Are you going out for lunch?"

"I haven't decided yet." She wasn't stepping out the front door until she knew if Kody had left or not.

"Well, I would suggest that you do. And take your cowboy with you. Laura said he's been out there since nine this morning. He asked if I minded him loitering out front."

Rose's cheeks flushed. "You talked to him?"

"Yeah. Nice guy. Knows a lot about football. Anyway, I don't think he plans to leave unless I call the cops or you agree to go on a date."

Good god. "I'm sorry, Lloyd. I don't normally encourage this type of behavior. I'll ask him not to bother me at work."

"What's the story with this guy? He's not dangerous, is he?"

Maybe sexy dangerous, Rose thought. "He's harmless."

"Are you going to go talk to him? He's got the clients whispering in the lobby."

Rose nodded. "I'll take care of it."

"Have a nice date," he mused without looking up as she left his office.

Rose marched by Laura's desk and ignored the young woman's giggle. She opened the door and stomped out into the sunlight.

Kody was stretched lazily across the hood with his hands cushioning his head. One knee was bent and his hat covered his eyes.

"You're a pain in the ass, Kody."

He struggled to an elbow, pushed back his Stetson and sent her a winning smile. "So what's it gonna be?"

The force of his sex appeal slammed into her. He looked like he was in the middle of a Ford truck commercial with his masculine sensuality and lazy drawl. "Would you just leave?"

"Only if I get a promise out of you to have dinner with me." In one graceful leap, he was off the hood and standing far too close.

Rose backed up. She crossed her arms and looked up at the sky. Her slender foot tapped out a beat on the hot sidewalk. Myriad thoughts raced through her brain. As much as she'd like to give him a knee in the crotch, maybe Lily was right. Maybe she should give him a chance. Hell, maybe she didn't have a choice because it looked like he wasn't leaving anytime soon.

If she did agree to dinner, Rose knew exactly where the night would end up. She was no dummy, she'd be in Kody's arms.

Why not? Why not take something back? The night before, Kody had whetted her sexual appetite with his big body, easy smile and deliciously talented fingers. The force of her own emotions hit her hard. He was like a drug, like a sweet piece of remembered candy.

Rose's gaze met his. She studied the emerald green of his eyes and his firm, shadowed jaw. If she hadn't been trying to make a point with him at the moment that she was totally sick of his behavior, she would have drifted a fingertip down his cheek and across his full bottom lip. She closed her eyes for a mere second and made a decision.

"All right. If I have to say yes in order for you to get the hell out of here, then yes is the answer."

Kody let out an embellished whoop. "Six o'clock? Where do I pick you up?"

"You don't. I'll meet you somewhere."

"I never have a woman meet me somewhere."

"So you've asked lots of women on dates?" She stared and waited for an answer.

Kody shifted a bit and figured he better back off damn quick. "Do you want to pick me up?" He watched her jaw clench as she digested his question. "You pick me up and we'll head on out to Pepe's. It's close to the ranch and you won't have to drive me back from Bandera at the end of the night."

"That's quite an assumption."

"What?"

"You're assuming that if we ate somewhere in Bandera, that I'd be giving you a ride home afterward. There's a good chance you'd probably be walking."

Kody fought off the smile that threatened to break across his face. He loved every minute of her obstinacy. "Pepe's it is.

Six o'clock. I'll be waiting." He tipped his hat and rounded the front of his truck. Just before he dipped inside, Kody swept off his Stetson and held it across his heart, flashing Rose a smile at the same time. "Darlin', until we meet again."

A small bit of weight lifted from her shoulders as she watched him drive off. Maybe Lily was right. Maybe giving Kody a chance was what she needed to do. She turned to step back out of the sun. If things didn't work out, at least he still was unaware of where she lived.

* * * * *

"Mommy? You look pretty."

Rose smiled and set down her brush on a small dressing table. "Well, thank you, honey."

"Where you going?"

"I'm going out for dinner."

"You coulda ate with me."

She ruffled his soft hair and stood. "Then I would have been too full to eat later on."

Travis flopped on the bed and watched Rose strap on her sandals. "Who you going with?"

Rose smiled at her son. "You're full of questions, aren't you? I'm just going with some friends. Auntie Lily will be here to tuck you in. Are you okay with that?" A part of Rose hoped that Travis would put up a fuss, thus giving her the excuse she needed to take off her skirt and blouse. There were very few nights in his short life that she hadn't been home to ready him for bed. Tonight would make two nights in a row. If he objected, she could stay home and maybe her excited nausea would disappear. Hell, if she kept feeling this way she wouldn't be able to eat anyway.

Travis flipped off the bed. "I guess it's okay. Uncle Mark and I are gonna feed the baby horses."

So much for an out. Rose glanced at her watch. "Walk me downstairs then. If I don't get going, I'll be late."

* * * * *

Kody watched Rose's car turn into the driveway from his vantage point on the porch. With an eager step he headed down the stairs to greet her. She didn't get out but merely waited for him to round the front fender and let himself into the passenger seat. Glancing to his left, he flashed a sexy grin and pulled the seat belt over his shoulder.

She returned his greeting with a hesitant smile. "Sorry I'm a few minutes late."

"No problem. I'm just glad you're here." His palms brushed over his solid thighs as his eyes swept her informal, but neat attire. "You look really nice, Rose. I'm going to be the envy of every guy tonight."

She blushed lightly, put the car in drive and headed back out of the yard. "I hardly think so, Kody." More likely she was going to have to fend off women on the make. He was drop-dead gorgeous in his black jeans and black leather jacket. Glancing sidelong at him for a quick second, she had to tear her gaze away from the thick waves at his temple. No cowboy hat tonight. His hair was perfectly styled, his square jaw shaved and the lightly scented cologne he wore already drove her to distraction. Being with Kody was like playing with fire and though she'd struggled with keeping this date, Rose suddenly discovered that she wanted to be singed by his hot fingertips until she burst into flame.

Kody kept up the conversation the few miles to Pepe's. Rose responded with tight responses as she continued her internal battle while gripping the steering wheel. By the time she'd parked the car and they'd gotten out, she couldn't imagine eating a meal—not with how her stomach rolled.

"Rose?" Kody questioned as he paused in front of her. "What's wrong?"

"Nothing," she returned while fiddling with her small clutch bag.

When he reached out and brushed her upper arm with his hand, it was all she could do not to flinch.

"You can say that, but I don't believe it for a minute. You're like a cat on a hot tin roof. It's a date. We're going to have dinner and do a little dancing. We won't revisit the past unless you want to. I don't bite and I've been told I do a great Texas two-step." He watched the uncertainty in her eyes. With a sigh, he stuffed his hands inside his jacket pockets and smiled. "I can't believe I'm going to say this, but if you would rather just take me back home and forget about tonight, that's fine with me. I want to be with you, Rose. I want to laugh like we used to and not exchange barbs all night long. I want you to enjoy yourself and not act like being with me is the last thing you want to do. So, it's your choice. You tell me what you want and I'll abide by your decision."

Rose knew exactly what she wanted, but that was the problem. She wanted to pick up where she'd left off six years ago. But Kody knew nothing about Travis, and Rose couldn't summon the courage to tell him. Not yet. Not when their relationship was so tenuous, no matter what he'd stated over the last few days. She took a deep breath. If she didn't give tonight a chance, she might never know how things could have turned out. She looked up at him again. He was so damn handsome, masculine and hard, yet full of boyish charm. A smile broke out on her face. Dammit, she wasn't going to cut off her nose to spite her face. "All right. Yes, I am nervous, but I really want to have dinner with you."

Kody wrapped his arms around her, gave her a little spin and followed it with a quick hug before depositing her to her feet once more. "That's more like it!" Cupping her elbow he led her across the parking lot to the brightly lit building. "I promise I'll behave and you won't regret your decision."

A soft snort sounded in the back of her throat. "You? Behave? I bet you won't make it an hour." When his hand dropped to the small of her back as he guided her through the door, his touch warmed the spot and sent goose bumps rippling across her skin.

Chapter Five

ဆ

Dinner went surprisingly well. Despite her qualms, Kody was the perfect escort—jovial and attentive. It was easy for Rose to bask in the attention. Of course she was well aware that he held himself on a tight leash, but at some point, the old Kody would appear to tease her senses because he thought she'd been lulled into a false sense of security.

She sipped her wine as he told her about the many places he'd traveled to and subconsciously wondered how many times he'd filled her glass. The waiter appeared, quickly cleaned the dirty dishes from the table and left them as the country western band began to play another song. She smiled as she watched his fingers drum across the white linen tablecloth. "Thank you for dinner, Kody. This is the first time I've eaten here. I'm pretty impressed."

He leaned back in his chair with an answering grin. "My dad used to haul us here all the time. Of course, it wasn't until we were closer to being adults that he trusted my brothers and me to behave. Normally, we just sat outside under the tent and ate the chuck wagon food. But it was always a great meal and filled us up." He tipped his head and watched a couple dance by. "Would you care to dance? They're playing our song."

She laughed, her cheeks flushed with the wine she'd consumed. "We don't have a song."

"Okay, let's pretend that we do."

Kody had Rose's hand in his before she knew it. "Come on. I promised you some dancing tonight." He coaxed her out of her chair and onto the floor. With a flourish, he wrapped his arm around her and dipped her backward. "Ready to dance?"

Rose's gaze skittered about and noted that people were watching them. "Stop calling attention to us. Fine. I'll dance."

His chuckle echoed in her ear when he pulled her to his chest and began to move about the floor, nodding and smiling at the faces he recognized. A few silent minutes went by as they waltzed about. "I wonder why people are still staring?"

"Because you're an idiot," came her muffled reply. He held her so close that she could hear the beat of his heart.

Kody threw back his head with a timbered laugh. "Good. Then I can get away with just about anything tonight."

She leaned back and stared him straight in the eye. "You behave yourself or I'll kick you in the shin. You promised." But even as she said it, her heart rapped inside her chest.

He tightened his hold and furtively managed to get his thigh nestled between her legs as they danced. The line of his cock bumped her. He wasn't even in a full state of arousal, yet the feel of him against her body caused a flash of memory of just how big and hard Kody could be.

He'd played this game with her all evening long. Charming to the edge of distraction, subtle touches like his knee bumping against hers, his hand drifting across her fingers, a hot look in conjunction with a smile meant to melt her wary heart. The shit. He'd accomplished what he'd set out to do. He'd wooed her before she'd even begun to realize she was completely under his spell.

Being honest with herself, she admitted that she loved every single minute. She would think about tomorrow when tomorrow came. For now? She was going to enjoy being in Kody's company. She was going to surprise the hell out of him.

When he tugged her even closer, Rose willingly entered the tight circle of his arms. She spied the bemused grin on his face. "Why are you looking at me like you are?"

"I'm surprised that you let me pull you closer. Makes me think that maybe I could kiss you and you wouldn't kick me in the shins like you threatened."

"See? I told you your good behavior wouldn't last," she laughed out. "All right, so kiss me. I promise not to kick you."

He stared down in surprise. "Just like that? Right here in front of everyone? Why the change in attitude?"

Her hand lowered from his shoulder and she let her fingertip drift across the front of his shirt. "I guess I keep remembering yesterday and how you made me feel. I'm not a little girl, Kody. You woke up something in me that I haven't paid much attention to lately. Just because I'm a woman doesn't mean I can't ask for what I want." She waited for an inner voice to tell her she was making a huge mistake, but it remained silent. Good. Last night simply wasn't enough. She wanted more than his hand in her pants. She wanted his cock throbbing inside her, pounding away. She wasn't drunk, not even close. The wine she'd consumed had just helped to soften the edges a bit. Rose knew exactly what she wanted. She reached up and pulled Kody's mouth close to hers. "I want you to kiss me. Then I want to go back to the ranch. Surprised?"

His stared down, wide-eyed. "What do you think? First you're telling me you don't want me in your life, then you're asking me to take you to bed. I won't lie to you. I had hoped at the end of the night we would be together again. No ghosts. No misconceptions."

She stepped out of his arms. The smile drifted from her lips. "I guess a small part of me hoped for the same thing. I guess if you're not going to kiss me here, I'll have to wait until we get outside."

He grasped her elbow, led her back to the table and retrieved her bag without a word. They wove their way through the crowd and across the parking lot, but when they got to her car, Kody took the keys from her hand. Pulling her close, he lifted her chin with the tip of a finger. "A kiss—as requested."

When Rose's lips parted, he was there to meet the dart of her tongue against his. He licked across her bottom lip, then swept the inside of her mouth.

Instantly, his cock hardened. There would be no battle between them on this night. "You won't be sorry, Rose." He kissed her again. She remained silent as he helped her into the passenger seat then hurried around to get behind the wheel. Once there, he leaned over and kissed her again. Rose scooted as close as she could and laid her head against his shoulder. She stayed that way until he pulled up in front of his house. And when he helped her from the car and wrapped one arm around her shoulder, Rose had an instant bout of uncertainty. As much as she'd shoved away the notion that she would simply enjoy the night and worry about the consequences in the morning, suddenly her conscience peppered her once more. The entire way up the sidewalk to the house, that voice spoke louder and louder.

They entered the house and immediately, he pulled her against him. Flattening her hands over the firm expanse of his chest, she met his hungry gaze. She had to tell him about Travis. The night would most likely end differently than she hoped, but she didn't want any secrets between them. No more. She would jump in with both feet and hope he wouldn't turn her away.

"Kody? I-I have to tell you something."

"Shhhh," he whispered. "There will be time for that later." Silently, he helped her shed her sweater then tossed his jacket on a chair. Once more, he pulled her against his body. His fingers brushed a soft path up her spine. "All I want to do is forget about everything except the fact that you're here now, in my arms. I love the fact that there won't be a battle tonight between us. Just you and me. That's all I want to think about." He dipped his head and gently kissed her mouth.

Rose's fingers curled into fists against his chest as she fought to stay on track. Just his few words had her rethinking her honesty. His lips nuzzling her cheek and his warm breath against her skin made it even more difficult. "But, Kody..."

He bent slightly, kept one arm around her waist and slipped the other behind her knees and lifted her into his embrace. Rose locked her hands behind his neck. "Kody, I really want to talk to you about something." Her heart knocked in her chest.

He shook his head and turned to the staircase. "I only want to hear one thing from your mouth, Rose. After that, I refuse to speak of the past and its problems. So, I will abide by only two things. If you say no, I'll walk you to your car even though that will be the hardest thing I've ever done in my life. If you say yes, I'm going to carry you up those stairs. I'll keep you so busy that you won't have a chance to think about anything else. So what's it going to be?"

Her gaze flowed across his mouth, so close that if she tipped her head only slightly, she would be able to kiss it. Slowly she met his smoldering gaze. Now was not the time because he wouldn't listen. Running the tip of her tongue across her lower lip, she reached up and cupped his cheek. "Yes."

His eyes fluttered shut for only a moment as he drew in a breath. "You won't be sorry."

Each step he took up the staircase was filled with determination. They entered his parents' master suite, much to her surprise.

Rose glanced with bewilderment but instantly any surprise she felt was flung away when Kody laid her on the bed and slid down beside her. His hand quickly tugged at her silk blouse, pulling it from the confines of her waistband. All the while he kissed her, each caress building her excitement. His hands were everywhere, unbuttoning the blouse and tugging it from her shoulders to expose the smoothness of her skin. No hesitation on his part. He knew exactly what he wanted. She had said yes and apparently he wouldn't allow her a second reassessment of what the next hour would hold.

Rose quickly forgot about everything except his promising touch. She wiggled her hands between them as she tugged at the snaps on his shirt. Kody raised himself on one elbow and let her drag a sleeve over his opposite wrist, but not once did his lips leave her skin. It didn't matter if it was her cheek, her mouth, her neck—his lips blazed a path wherever they went.

Once he'd yanked his shirt off, he rolled to his back, dragging Rose with him until her body slid deliciously across his. He dragged the blouse from her body and with one flip of his fingertips, her bra was undone and tossed away. Again he rolled, pulling her willingly beneath him and allowing him access to her bare breasts. Both hands cupped them, pushing them upward toward his seeking lips. He sucked hard on one nipple, nibbled his way through the valley between her soft mounds, then suckled the other between hot flicks of his tongue.

Instant heat trickled through her belly. A rush of ecstatic liquid dampened her panties. Kody still had the power to turn her into a quivering mess and god, she still loved him.

His mouth dipped until his lips brushed a moist kiss across the velvety skin of her exposed shoulder. "I want to fuck you...here...now. It's all I've thought about." When her head tipped back slightly, his mouth paused against her neck. "I can feel the blood pumping through your veins. God, I missed you so much..."

"Kody..." she mumbled against his hair. Her fingers wove through the soft thickness, her back arching as she pressed her hips upward against his hard cock. "I want you to fuck me. I want you to make me lose reason. It's been so long."

He trailed kisses between her breasts and lower as his hands worked her skirt over her hips. "I want you naked. I want to kiss you everywhere...your stomach, your thighs...your pussy..." His fingertips were back at the waistband of her panties. Slowly he began to slide them down.

He paused to kiss the soft curls between her legs, which evoked a trembling in her limbs. His mouth blazed a damp trail down the length of one slim thigh as he dragged her panties over her ankles. Rose's mind clouded with passion as she quietly watched him stand at the side of the bed to unbuckle his belt. His shuttered eyes locked with hers as he retrieved a condom from his pocket, then shed both his pants and his underwear at the same time. His cock was rock hard, the base nestled within dark curling hair.

Rose's breasts ached with instant desire and moisture pooled sweet between her legs.

He ripped open the condom and held out his arm. "I want you to put it on."

She nodded her head slightly, scooted to the edge of the mattress and tentatively encircled his cock with one hand. It jumped at her touch. God, he was hard. And soon, he'd be pumping inside her. With a hesitant smile, she started at the top of his cock and began to roll the condom over the tip.

The air from his lungs whisked over her face. Holding him tightly, she glanced up again.

The look in his eyes had changed and it was because she had his cock in her hands. Feeling a bit more powerful, she got the condom rolled all the way down the steely ridge of his shaft, then she gripped it with both hands and slowly stroked him, sensuously, loving how his hips moved in time with her motions.

"God, that feels wonderful." His eyes closed as he stood there and let her milk him until he couldn't take any more. His hand suddenly clasped hers and stalled the motion. Soundlessly, he gently pushed her to her back as he slid over her. He wiggled just enough until her pussy lips cradled the hard line of his cock. Capturing her hands, he dragged them up onto the pillow, teased his cock against her slit once more and lowered his mouth to steal a kiss.

"I want to fuck you so bad. Right now. But that comes later."

Her mouth turned up in a soft smile. "So what comes now?"

"An orgasm for you. Then another. And then another."

She could hardly breathe. Her fingers clutched his tightly. She remembered the hot feeling of anticipation from so many years ago. Nothing had changed. He still had the sexual power with his nude body and quiet promises to make her sigh with abandonment. It had always been like that between them. He took and she gave willingly.

"I'm going to tease you until you're wiggling and pleading for me to fuck you. But I won't. Not yet because I have all night. I won't behave, Rose. I won't ask you what you like. I'm simply going to drive you insane."

"Kody..."

He pushed away and slipped lower over her body until his mouth was at her breasts. He sucked at her raised nipples, his hands massaging the tender mounds while her fingers drifted through his hair once more. Each sensual kiss was torment because his caresses sent an aching need straight to her pussy. Kody lightly ground his lower belly between her spread legs, teasing her as he nipped at her nipples once more.

"My skin is wet from your pussy. You're dripping, Rose, and I haven't really even started to do the many things I have planned."

"I can't wait, Kody." Her eyes fluttered shut when he lightly nipped her breast. "God that feels so good."

"It's only going to get better. That's a promise."

As soon as the words were out of his mouth, he slipped lower, scorching a trail with his mouth to her navel. Rose's legs spread wide with eagerness. He was going to eat her. Oh god, she was going to burst into flames. Her lower body surged upward with a subtle, sensual invitation, but he ignored her plea and kissed her satiny hip, nibbling until the skin goose bumped beneath his lips. Slowly, he licked closer to the center of her body, but dipped past her glistening pussy and pressed a tender kiss to the inside of her opposite thigh. He nipped again, then dragged his nose softly through her pubic hair and back.

Her cunt was on fire, the muscles clamping at nothing. Her clit throbbed. She wanted his mouth sucking at her clit, biting her, his tongue buried inside. "Kody…please…"

"Not yet." He rose to his knees, spread her thighs and stared at her pussy.

A shot of pure ecstasy shot through her lower body. She didn't fight his actions, only strained to keep her legs wide.

"This is how you'll be when I fuck you. Open wide…wet…hot…easy for me to slip my cock into you." His hungry eyes met hers. "But not yet." He forced her legs flat upon the bed. He massaged one of them, his thumbs rolling in small circles as he worked his way to her ankle. "I was going to make you give me a massage. After all, I paid for one and never got my money's worth. But this is so much more fun."

She lay with her arms spread across the mattress, her legs splayed wide and her eyes closed. She was speechless as she whirled in sexual bliss.

He continued to lightly knead the calf of one leg, and then the other until she began to squirm. His gaze swept up and settled on her pussy. With her legs spread so wide, he could see the droplets of moisture collecting along her pink lips. He wanted to be buried inside her, pumping his excitement out in hard thrusts, but his mouth curled up mischievously. He knew she wanted to be fucked. The quiet whimpers in the back of her throat, the minuscule jerks of her hips, her knees bending and unbending all gave away the sensual state she resided in.

His smile widened as he kneaded back up past her knees, over her thighs and to the outside of her hips, then down again.

Her eyes shot open when he forced her legs together. "What? Kody..."

Adjusting his position beside her, he used one muscular leg to imprison her thighs.

"What are you doing? You're driving me crazy."

He could feel how she subtly fought the slight bondage of the position.

"I want to watch you come, but not from my cock ramming you." His hand lowered to the vee of her legs. He slipped one finger into the tight space, feeling the sweet wet curls against the pad. She squirmed when it came in contact with her clit. When she tried to spread her legs against his hold, he shook his head. "You have to keep your legs closed."

"I want your cock in me."

"Not yet." He burrowed his finger farther down the crack of her pussy and only let the tip of it play at her opening, taunting her body because he didn't slip into her. Despite a slight struggle on her part, he refused to let her open wide and swirled his finger back up to tease her clit. "Come for me, Rose. Come without my finger in you. You're so fucking hot and wet. I can feel how swollen your clit is. Do you want to come?"

Her fingers curled around the edge of the pillow beneath her rolling head. "Yes. But I..." She clenched and unclenched at nothing.

He pressured harder against her clit. "Then let it go. You can't spread your legs. Just think about it. Think about the heat blazing from your cunt up through your belly. Think about me fucking you, think about my cock slamming your body against the mattress. Think about how badly you want to spread for me. Nothing would feel better than to be able to open your legs, but you can't." He rubbed her clit harder within the tight confines of his hold. Her struggle continued. Of course she wanted her legs open wide, ready to receive him and all he had to offer, but he wanted to be totally in control of her orgasm.

Suddenly he pulled his hand, relishing how her hips continued to surge against his tight grip. Her eyes snapped open, her mouth sagged wide. Rose already hung on the precipice of a hot orgasm — all he had to do was touch her clit and she would explode.

"Please," she gasped quietly. "I have to come. I can't stand this torture." Her heart pounded and the throbbing between her legs had become unbearable. She needed to release.

Kody lifted a finger and moistened it with his tongue, tasting the sweet essence that was Rose.

A shot of pure pleasure raced through her body at the intimate but primal gesture.

"Are you ready to come?"

Her head rolled quicker on the pillow. "Yes! Now, Kody!"

His hand brushed circles against the smooth tautness of her belly. Wordlessly, he let a damp finger creep inch by inch until it rustled through her pubic hair, taunting horribly as her hips began to swing to a steady tempo. And then? He wedged it between her thighs and pressed her clit hard.

Rose gasped as her body began to shudder. Her orgasm ripped through her, sending her tumbling into a sensual haze of wonder.

Kody fought his own excitement, knowing that when he finally did come, the sensation would be shattering. Yet, he staved off the urge and played between her legs until Rose's body rested limply on the bed. His heartbeat picked up when she ran her tongue across her lips to moisten them. She stared up with heavy-lidded eyes.

Kody dragged Rose to her knees. They faced one another, kissing wildly and running their hands over the other's skin until he broke away from the lure of her mouth and turned her to face the brass headboard. Guiding her arms wide, he forced her fingers around the rail. "Don't move." Sliding off the bed, he retrieved his belt, looped it around one of her wrists and through the rungs. "You're not scared, are you?"

"Do I need to be?"

He leaned over and kissed her waiting mouth. "I would never hurt you. Can I trust that you'll keep your free hand on the rail, or do I need to tie that one, too?"

A flush of sexual heat started at her toes and wound its way to her belly and sizzled upward until her breasts tingled. What did he have planned? Whatever it was, she would go along with it willingly. "I'll do whatever you say."

Climbing on the bed, he kneeled behind her. "Spread your knees wider."

The excitement pinging through her intensified. She was on her knees with her legs and arms spread wide. Secured by one wrist, Kody had assured that she couldn't wiggle away. She glanced over her shoulder and was shocked to see the lust burning in his gaze as he eyed her nude body. "What are you going to do?" she asked breathlessly.

He moved closer, slipped one hand around her to gently squeeze a breast as the other dropped to cup one firmly rounded buttock. "Remember I talked about the massage I was going to insist on? Well I've changed my mind."

His fingers plucked at her nipples. "Do you like this?"

Her head lolled and she closed her eyes. "Yes," she returned lazily.

"Just relax and enjoy."

Kody palmed her breast for a bit longer as he kissed the softness of her shoulders. "Your skin is like velvet. Even softer than I remembered. I love the scent of your perfume. It makes me hot and makes me want you." His strong fingers massaged a line from her ass to join the other at her shoulders. His thumbs worked magic in a path from her neck to her shoulder blades. He worked his way back down her spine and played with her ass cheeks until she bounced them backward.

"Do you like that?"

Did she like it? Moisture trickled a path down one thigh. Never had she experienced anything as sensual as his hands playing across her skin. The contrast of his warm fingers and the air cooling her wet pussy had an increasing effect on her already drugged senses, yet it was a sweet torture she never wanted to end.

His hot lips were back against her neck, licking and nibbling as his hands slid around her waist to brush circles against her stomach. Rose's belly sucked in tightly as she waited eagerly for them to move lower. His hard cock nestled against the small of her back. Suddenly it disappeared as he kissed his way down her spine and began to nip first one ass cheek, then the other. She couldn't stand it. She needed her ass more firmly against his mouth, but when she drew in one knee, his hand immediately forced her legs back apart.

"Keep your legs spread wide."

"But..."

The words died in her throat when he slipped a finger through her wet pubic curls, drifted lightly along the crack of her pussy, then on to flick at her clit. Her entire body jumped in reaction. Her chin dropped to her chest as she sucked in deep breathes of air.

"Do as I say. Keep your legs spread wide. I want to lick you."

How? He would have to... She gasped when he rolled to his back and wiggled upward until his head was between her legs. Her heart hammered in her chest when she felt his fingers wrap around her waist, and he dragged her pussy to his waiting mouth.

His tongue traveled through her wet slit, teasing, but then he stopped.

Her head fell back once more as she waited for the touch of his tongue.

"It's up to you, Rose. Show me what you want."

God, he was going to make her do what she needed to in order to come. And Rose needed to come badly. Her body was like a tightly wound spring. Bravely, she dipped down and dragged her pussy across his mouth. Kody rewarded her with another lick. She dipped again. This time his tongue darted into her hole, sending a shock wave through her system. Slowly, she lowered herself again and languorously moved across his tongue until her clit rested against his lips. "Nibble on it, Kody. Make me come."

He bit hard enough that she winced but the pain was so intensely pleasurable that she ground down again, determined that she wanted more. Kody easily complied.

"I-I want your finger in me while you do that," she demanded and wiggled above him, pressing her cunt into his face.

His hands grasped her thighs to keep her from moving. "No fingers, Rose. Just my tongue and my teeth. When I enter you completely, it's going to be with my cock." He pulled her down and teasingly flicked his tongue against her clit.

Rose floated in a wanton haze. Her fingers gripped the rail and she began to bounce against his mouth, loving how Kody simply let her do the work. He was in control, yet he wasn't. Rose's orgasm would be of her own doing.

Time after time she dragged her body across his face as raw sexual passion ignited in her belly. He refused to put his tongue inside her, sending her into a tailspin of need. But when he circled her clit with his lips and sucked the swollen bud into his mouth, she went wild. Her nipples ached and her stomach clenched as the seed of reckless desire grew, spreading through her womb and exploding through her blood. Rose gasped softly as wave after wave coursed through her. Kody squeezed the firm globes of her ass to hold her in place as his untamed tongue swept through her pussy lips, lapping at her cunt, drawing her orgasm on and on. Rose trembled, clutched the rail and rode the wave until it began to subside to tempestuous shudders of pleasure.

Kody slipped from between her legs and rolled to his knees once more and cupped her pussy from behind. Cream dampened his palm.

Rose's forehead rested weakly against the brass rail as she clung to it for dear life. She didn't know how much more she could take of this sexual torture. Her body was weak yet surprisingly far from sated.

"No more, Kody. I want you to fuck me. Please. I have to have you fill me. I ache for you to fuck me hard." Perspiration trickled down her scalp.

Kody grasped his erection and moved closer. Her knees were still spread wide and it was easy for him to run the head of his cock through her wet slit. Her body started and dipped downward to try and capture his length. Her free hand came off the rail in an attempt to guide his cock inside her, but Kody quickly grabbed it, forced it around the front of her body and pressed her fingers against her clit.

"Feel how swollen and ready you are for me?" he whispered beside her ear.

"Yes," she gasped.

"I'm ready to fuck you. God, I've been waiting for this moment."

His cock easily slipped into her wet cunt, filling her completely as he forced her finger to rub her clit.

"Oh god, yes!" she cried out. Her eyes squeezed tightly with pleasure as her ass rested against his belly. She wiggled crazily trying to get him to move.

That was when Kody began to slam into her. In and out with harsh strokes that filled her cunt. He let go of her wrist, wrapped the fingers of one hand in the soft length of her hair and grasped her hip tightly with the other to hold her in place as he continued to rock into her body. Rose met each thrust with one of her own, feeling she would be split apart but loving the intensely hot position. She rubbed her clit hard, sucking at his cock with her pussy, relishing the feel of his thick length pounding against her cervix. Stroke after stroke he carried her upward until the bed shook and the harsh panting of their desire thundered around them.

Rose flailed to grip the railing with both hands and rode his cock as another more intensely hot orgasm burst wide. She screamed and backed down hard, her pussy sucking at his cock. At that moment Kody answered her with a swing of his hips as he buried himself deeply and came in fiery shudders of ecstasy. Perspiration trickled down his back as his body curled about hers and his powerful orgasm thumped through his lower body. He kissed the soft expanse of her neck until the last tremor of passion cooled.

Kody finally pulled his cock from her. Rose's lower body slumped to the mattress, her breasts heaving with exertion and her wrist still tied to the rail. He reached up and with a quick flick of his fingers, tossed the belt to the floor. Sinking to the mattress, he gathered her into his arms and kissed her mouth until she groaned beneath him. Tenderly, he tucked her head against his shoulder.

They said nothing, only listened to the other's deep breathing as their hearts calmed and their shudders abated.

* * * * *

Rose buttoned her blouse while staring down at Kody's rumpled dark hair against the stark white pillow. Her body ached from the vigorous sex they'd had over and over until the wee hours of the morning. She wanted nothing more than to slip back beneath the covers and cuddle up to his hard body, but she had to go home. Responsibilities waited.

Each time she'd tried to tell Kody about the last six years and the wonderful little soul they'd created together, she'd been distracted by his seeking lips and wandering hands. And each time the correct moment to reveal that he was a father had drifted away to oblivion.

She couldn't tell him now. Not after the searing sex they'd shared and the fact that at some point during the night when they'd talked, he'd mentioned that he wasn't ready yet for a family. That was something to attend to in the future after he'd set up his own spread and gotten his ranch to become a paying proposition.

Rose carefully perched on the edge of the bed and let her eyes rove over the naked skin of his back. One long leg curled over the bedspread. He was magnificent and she loved him so much that it hurt. But not once had Kody mentioned the word love.

What was she going to do? Being with him again was every dream come true. Having spent the night, however, just made things more difficult. She should have told him instead of floundering about in a haze of uncertainty. She reached out a hand then yanked it back. Not yet. Just a few more days.

She had to leave, but didn't dare go without first telling him goodbye. Thank god tomorrow—she glanced at the clock—it was three in the morning. Thank god today was Saturday. She didn't have to work so he wouldn't be able to hound her at the spa before he left for the weekend. She wondered where he was going, but figured it didn't matter. It was Christmas Eve and she needed to help Lily prepare for the holiday. And she needed a day away from Kody's sexual allure to figure out what the future would bring.

Leaning over, she blew in his ear and nuzzled the tousled hair beside it and wondered if this would be the last time she ever did it. "Kody?" she whispered. "I have to go."

Slowly, his eyes opened. A lazy, satisfied grin lifted the corner of his mouth as he rolled to his back. "Go?" His hand came up to cup her jaw. "Stay with me." His gaze moved over her clothed body. "Christ, I never even heard you leave the bed. You wore me out."

Rose smiled. "Ah, I think it was the other way around. I can't stay. I have to help Lily with Christmas preparations."

"I want to spend Christmas with you." The request was honest and straight to the point.

"I-I don't know, Kody. Maybe we need to take a day and think about what happened between us."

"I know what happened between us and I don't have to think about it. In fact, I want to do it again."

Smiling, she punched him gently. "Go to sleep. I'll let myself out. I really have to go."

"No way." He stretched and sat up. "I'll walk you to the car."

"I'm totally fine saying goodbye here."

"Well I'm not." He glanced around. "Where in hell did my jeans go?" Dropping his long legs over the edge of the mattress, he rose, pressed a quick kiss against her mouth and retrieved his pants from the floor.

Rose stared hungrily at his bare ass, feeling desire course through her once again. Almost tempted to climb back into bed, instead she leapt up before she lost the internal battle that waged. An emotion akin to relief drifted through her mind when he zipped up his pants.

Kody closed the distance between them, pulled her close, and she cuddled against the warmth of his broad chest.

"Are you sure I can't talk you into staying?" he asked quietly. "Why do you have to leave?"

Rubbing her cheek against him, she tightened her grip around his waist. To stay and experience another breathless session of hot lovemaking would only make it harder to leave. A quick stab of pain pierced her heart at the thought. Maybe this would be the last time he ever spoke warmly to her and held her lovingly in his arms.

His mouth trailed kisses across her cheek until he captured her lips in a tender kiss.

As difficult as it was, she broke away and pressed a trembling hand against his chest. "I really have to go, Kody, as much as I hate to."

He nodded silently, took her hand and they walked quietly to her car. Once there, his fingers slipped beneath her long hair, cupped her neck and he kissed her. "I wish you didn't have to go. I'd love to haul you back inside."

Rose wrapped her arms around his bare waist and settled her cheek against his chest. A coyote howled and the sound of a soft whinny drifted across the yard from the paddock. The night had taken on a slight chill but Kody's warmth surrounded her. Rose would remember this one moment for the rest of her life. "Kody?" She leaned back. "If I don't see you until after Christmas, I hope you have a wonderful day."

He leaned his forehead against hers with a sigh. "I'd rather spend it with you, but I won't pressure you. Honestly, I'm serious this time. I feel so good about the two of us. Have a wonderful holiday. Hey, are you finally going to tell me where you live or give me your phone number?"

She stepped away, her hand trailing around his slim waist as she opened the car door. "I'll call you. That's all I can promise. Just give me a few days, okay?"

He nodded. "All right. Drive carefully. Say hi to Mark and Lily for me."

"I will." Forcing herself into the driver's seat, she cranked the engine, shut the door and waved. Rose watched him in the rearview mirror until she turned onto the highway.

Chapter Six

ᔕ

Rose threw herself into the day's activities and helped Lily bake pies for most of the morning for Bandera's annual Christmas party at the town Community Center. As she and her sister labored throughout the early hours, they laughed at Travis' antics as he played with a chunk of pie crust and jabbered about all the wonderful things that Santa was going to bring him.

Lily hadn't asked why Rose had gotten in so late, and the only information Rose had offered was that she'd had a wonderful dinner and an enjoyable time. In the early afternoon, however, when the last of the pies sat cooling, Rose's head began to ache horribly. Whether from the stress of needed decisions or the lack of sleep, she didn't have a clue, but she couldn't imagine attending the party when all she wanted to do was sleep away the day.

At one point, Rose glanced up and caught Lily staring at her. "What?"

"You look horrible. Are you okay?"

"I don't know if I have a migraine or what, but my head feels like it's splitting in two. I think I'll take a couple of pills and nap with Travis. I should be okay later on."

Lily's gaze drifted to where Travis stood on a chair and rolled doughy ropes with the ends of crusts. "That's probably a good idea for both of you. It's going to be a later than usual night for him."

Rose untied her apron. "In fact, I think we'll do that right now. Come on, Travis. We'll wash you up and I'll take a nap with you."

"Ah, Mommy, I don't want to go to sleep. I want to eat pie."

Rose smiled despite the pain that riddled her brain. "You can eat pie tonight when we go to the party. You have to get rest so you can have lots of fun. And then we'll come home, tuck you in and Santa will stop before morning to leave you presents. How fun does that sound?"

Travis leaned over and wrapped his arms around her neck. "Can tonight be our date? Just you and me and Auntie and Uncle?"

Rose kissed his cheek. "Most certainly. Come on, honey. Mommy is really tired and not feeling too good." She picked him off the stool and hiked him firmly on her hip. "Say goodnight to Lily and we'll be on our way."

* * * * *

Three hours later, Travis shook Rose awake. "Mommy? You have to wake up. It's time to get ready."

Rose's eyes fluttered open. She groaned and sat up. Cupping her head, she sighed with frustration when she looked at the clock. She didn't feel a bit better than when she'd climbed in for a nap. But she hauled herself from the covers, took his hand and left her son's room.

Three quarters of an hour later, she slumped into a kitchen chair. Travis was dressed and ready to go and following Mark about the yard. Rose had taken a few more pills, but they hadn't kicked in yet.

Lily eyed her from where she stood packing the pies into a box. "You sure don't look ready for anything. You haven't even showered yet. We're supposed to leave shortly."

Rose clutched her forehead. "Man, I haven't had a migraine in a long time. Honestly, I don't know how I'm going to make it to the party."

"Well, stay home then."

"I don't want to disappoint Travis. We have a date."

Lily placed her hands on her hips. "You're white as a ghost. Mark and I will take him. Hell, I don't want you sick tomorrow. It's not that big of a deal, Rose. It'll be the same people and the same party. I think he'll live without you."

Rose felt guilty as hell. Travis had talked nonstop about the party until she'd shushed him and told him to go to sleep. But how was she going to stand all the kids screaming and laughing when she felt so miserable? "He's going to be so upset, but the thought of just cuddling on the couch under a quilt sounds divine."

"Then do it. In fact, I'm ordering you to do it." Lily closed the top of the box and eyed her sister. "You haven't gotten a whole lot of sleep under your belt. Rose? I know you've had a lot to think about over the past few days…"

Rose rolled her eyes, then winced. "You don't know the half of it."

"Yeah, but I can speculate. I suspect Kody is half the reason behind your pounding head."

Clasping her hands on the table, Rose glanced up. "I'm sure you're right."

"I have to ask. Have you decided what you're going to do?"

"I love him, Lily. I guess I never stopped. I want him so bad that it's driving me crazy. Being with him is so easy, but he said something last night. He said he wasn't ready for a family. He doesn't want to be a father. So, despite my longing, how can I tell him now? How can this ever work out?"

However Lily was going to respond was lost when Mark and Travis came through the back door. Mark glanced at his sister-in-law. "Hey, you better get a move on. It's getting late."

Travis skipped across the kitchen and hugged Rose. "Yeah, hurry, Mom."

"Honey? I don't think I can go. Mommy's still sick."

"Aw, you can make it."

"No, really. I think I just need to lie on the couch and maybe sleep some more. You'll still have fun with Lily and Mark. I want to be all better tomorrow so I can watch you open your presents." That was all she needed to say. At the mention of Christmas, Travis totally forgot about their "date" and began to chatter about the next day's events.

Soon the trio left without her. Holding an icepack to her head, Rose sank onto the couch, pulled a quilt over her shoulders and closed her eyes.

* * * * *

Kody's body tensed when he spied Lily and Mark come through the double doors and into the center. His gaze darted back and forth between the couple and the door, waiting for Rose to come through. He settled back in his chair and smiled at the little boy who skipped between them. Cute kid. Here was another thing that Rose hadn't told him about. She'd held so much of her personal life close to her chest. Lily and Mark were parents and judging the kid's age, Lily and Mark must have gotten married not long after Kody had entered the service. He wondered if they would recognize him.

That might be a bit difficult when his face was hidden for the most part behind a fluffy white beard.

He gave himself a mental shake, finding it crazy that he was dressed as Santa Claus and would be asking little kids what they wanted for Christmas. He'd been bombarded by most of the children already as he walked through the gathering telling them all to get their lists ready.

Kody couldn't remember a time when his family hadn't sponsored a party for local kids. His father used to play Santa Claus. Kody's lips turned up in a smile. He'd never known his dad had played the part, not until he was older and knew Santa wasn't a real person. This year because his parents had decided to take a holiday trip, the Circle KW's foreman was called on to play the auspicious Saint Nick. Two days ago, however, the man had taken a spill off his horse and broken his leg. After a bit of pleading, Kody had been talked into taking the man's place.

An announcement came over the loud speaker that all the children were supposed to get in line because Santa was going to sit and hear their Christmas wishes. His attention was taken away from Lily and her family as he headed for the decorated chair of honor. Kody played Santa for the next twenty minutes until he glanced up to see Lily and her little boy next in line.

As a young girl climbed off his lap with a thank-you, Lily urged the boy forward. "Go ahead, Travis. Santa is waiting for you."

The boy walked straight up to him without the usual shyness he'd seen from so many other children. Kody looked down at the bright green eyes and dark hair thinking again that the kid was cute as hell. "What's your name?" he asked.

"Travis."

Kody patted his knee. "Well, climb up, Travis, and let's talk about Christmas."

The little boy scuttled into Kody's lap and stared up with wide eyes. "Where are your reindeer?"

"I left them parked on the roof." Kody grinned. The child's sheer innocence went straight to his gut.

Travis nodded as if what Santa had just said was the perfect answer.

"So, Travis. Have you been a good boy?"

"I've been the best so I could get what I wanted for a present."

Kody had to chuckle. "That's good to hear. What do you want for Christmas?"

"I want a PlayStation but my mom says I should play outside instead."

Kody glanced up and smiled at Lily. "Your mom has a good point. Little boys should be out in the fresh air and not sitting in front of a TV."

The boy's dark head nodded. "Mom always says there're a lot of good things in the world and we should spend time looking for them."

Kody tipped his head in wonder. Pretty awesome words from a youngster. "Well, what else would you like?" He just couldn't help but smile at the kid. He was plucky and quite the little gentleman.

"Um, maybe a new bike?"

Kody watched Lily smile at the boy's answer. Good. Now she knew what was on the kid's mind.

"Santa? Can I ask for something for my mom?"

"Sure thing." Kody winked at Lily who listened closely.

"Could you bring some money for my mom? She always says she needs more money. It makes her sad sometimes when she doesn't have money to buy stuff for me. She's saving so she can buy us a house."

Kody chuckled after another quick glance at Lily. "Your mom doesn't look sad now."

The little boy glanced around, slightly confused. "My mom is here?"

"She's standing right there," Kody said with a nod of his head in Lily's direction.

"That's not my mom."

"Oh, I saw you come in with her. I figured she was."

"Nah, that's my Auntie Lily. My mom didn't come to the party 'cuz her head hurts. Can you give my mom some money? You know her don't you? My mom says Santa knows everyone."

Kody's brow knit. "I guess I do then. What's your mom's name?"

"You're silly, Santa." He giggled. "My mom is Rose. She's real pretty."

Whatever Kody was going to say died in his throat as he stared down in shock.

Rose?

His eyes lifted to Lily's. Rose had a son? He dragged his gaze back to the little boy in his lap. Thoughts crashed inside his head as he struggled to comprehend what Travis had just innocently revealed.

Lily stepped forward. "I think your time is up, honey. We have to give the other children a chance. Tell Santa thank you."

Kody's hand tightened on the boy's waist. "How old are you Travis?" His heart pounded and a lump formed in his throat as he stared down into the round childish eyes—eyes that were the same color as his. Breathlessly, he waited, feeling like he stood on a cliff ready to topple over the edge.

Travis reached for Lily's waiting hand. Once he'd slid off Kody's lap, he turned a beaming grin on Santa. "I'm five. I'm going to kindergarten someday. Hey, Santa? I'll leave you some cookies. My mom makes good cookies."

"Thank…" Kody cleared his suddenly tight throat. "Thank you, Travis."

He watched them walk away, his mind spinning with bewilderment. He was stunned. He couldn't be wrong. Everything, the boy's age, the color of his eyes, his declaration that Rose was his mother—it all rang true and undisputable in his mind. Why had she kept this from him? Why? Especially after the evening before?

For the next thirty minutes one child after another sat on his lap, but Kody could hardly concentrate. His gaze rarely left the little boy who raced around with the other children from table to table, participating in all the many activities. He felt ill. He felt deceived.

The line of waiting children finally slowed and at last, the final child had sat on Santa's lap. Kody was off the chair in a flash and hurried across the room in Lily and Mark's direction.

They sat at a table with their heads close, laughing over something they'd said during their intimate conversation. Kody stopped before them wondering how he was going to ask the question he so definitely needed confirmed. Somewhere a part of him hoped it wasn't true, that Rose hadn't kept something so blindingly important from him all these years. But in his heart of hearts, he knew.

"Hi, Santa," Lily smiled up. Her head tipped as she stared at him. "Are you going to let us know who you really are?" she whispered conspiratorially.

Mark chuckled at his wife's query and placed an arm across the back of her chair. "That's supposed to be a secret, Lily."

"Can I talk to one of you outside?" Kody asked in a voice devoid of humor.

Mark straightened as he caught the seriousness in the other man's tone. "Is there a problem?"

"You know who I am, Mark." Kody reached out an arm. "It's been a long time."

Mark stood and accepted the extended handshake. He studied the features behind the thick fake beard. "I still can't figure it out."

Kody took a deep breath and never took his eyes from Lily's. "It's me. Kody."

Lily's mouth sagged open. Her eyes darted to her husband, then back to Kody, trying to find his features beneath the costume. "Kody?"

"Please. Could one of you step outside with me?"

Lily rose slowly, but her mind raced back to earlier when Travis had sat on Kody's lap and to what her nephew had inadvertently revealed. "Let me, Mark."

Her husband nodded and stepped away. Kody held Lily's elbow in a gentle grip and guided her through the doors. Seeing a group of adults standing on the sidewalk, he accepted their humorous jibes, then he tugged her to the side of the building.

Glancing about to find a private spot, Kody led Lily into an enclosed, dimly lit alcove. Reaching up, he dragged off the hat and beard.

"I can't believe I didn't recognize you," she stated quietly.

"If you had, would you have let Rose's son sit on my lap?"

Lily's face turned a pasty shade of white, but she didn't refute his question.

"Tell me, Lily. Who is Travis' father? I want to hear it from you."

She stuttered, trying to grasp the right answer.

Her reaction told him what he needed to know. "Never mind." Kody spun and smacked the wall with the side of his fist. Squeezing his eyes, he shook his head. "Why didn't she tell me?"

Lily cleared her throat and stepped closer.

Her hesitant answer filtered around him. "Rose wasn't your first choice. You picked something else besides her six years ago. You left her brokenhearted."

"That's fuckin' bullshit, Lily." It was all Kody could do to keep his voice low. "I had to do something with my life. Whether it was here in Texas or halfway across the world, she had no right to keep this a secret." Slowly he turned. Heated anger coupled with tremendous hurt darkened his eyes. "All this time I've had a son and I didn't know it."

"She didn't keep it to herself to hurt you."

"Christ, what the hell was she thinking?" His hand swept through his tousled hair. "Didn't she know that someday I might find out?"

"That's been her biggest fear, Kody. She didn't want to come back to Bandera. But she couldn't offer Travis a decent life on her own. Not until she had a good job and a steady paycheck rolling in. She took the chance here knowing that the town is big enough and you two really never had the same friends in common. She's not planning to stay here forever."

"Where is she?" He started out of the alcove.

"Kody, don't go off half—"

"Don't start lecturing me," he spouted as he cut her off with a rigid finger pointing in her direction. "Where in hell is she? She owes me an explanation and I'm damn well going to get it tonight. Are you going to tell me or do I have to go back inside and start asking people? Because believe you me, that's exactly what I'll do if I have to."

Lily sighed in frustration. She had no choice. "She lives with me." Crossing her arms, she stared at the leaf-covered cement, anything so she didn't have to stare at his tortured but angry eyes.

"Are you going to make me drag it out of you? Where in hell is your place?"

"Just give me a minute to explain a few things before you leave."

"Why should I, Lily? No one thought about me a few years back. Why try to cover something so deceitful now? The secret is out."

Lily began to get angry. "Just shut up, would you? You were the one who got her pregnant and left."

"Don't you think I would have made it right if I'd known that?" God, he thought of all the times he'd put himself in extreme danger. The little boy could have been fatherless forever.

"You might spout that now, but we'll never know the answer to that. Look what you were like back then. A hotheaded bad boy who thought only about himself. Besides, she didn't discover she was pregnant until after you'd gone.

I'm not saying any of this is right or wrong. I'm just trying to tell you how it was." She stepped closer and laid a hand on his arm. "All right, Kody. We both need to calm down and you need to listen to me. Rose was scared to death. She went through hell. She told our father even after I begged her not to. You know what that bastard did? He told her she had to get rid of it. *It*, Kody. Not a child, not a baby growing inside her. For as independent as Rose can be, she'd never, ever stood up to him in her life. Well, she did that time. She told him to go hell and no way would she give up her baby."

Kody's eye's fluttered shut for a moment. Thank god. He breathed deeply to clear away the haze in his brain. "I told her I came back after that first few months of training to find her. She was gone. It was like a big hand picked her up and just took her away."

"Mark took both of us away. When he saw Rose's black and blue marks he refused to let either of us enter my father's house again. Hell, Kody, we didn't have much anyway so it was easy to leave. Rose was in such a bad way that I don't think she really cared one way or another where she went."

"Bad way?" His heart thudded, his anger forgotten in a quick moment of panic. "Did he hurt her that badly?"

"She was a lot worse off mentally than physically. *You* hurt her that badly. She was dealing with leaving what was familiar and still dealing with your rejection. She so hoped for better things and with the fact that she was single and pregnant, it was a frightening task. Mark took us to Nevada. He found a job, we got married that same week and Rose signed up for night classes at the local community college. She paid for it by cleaning at a local hotel during the day. She refused to take any money from Mark, stating that we gave her a roof over her head. No matter how horrible she felt, whether she was tired enough to drop to the floor, whether her feet were so swollen that she could hardly move, she never missed a day of work or school. So Kody, if you think you're the one who has been cheated, think again. Rose was cheated too. She was cheated out of a husband to care for her and help her with the heavy load she carried on her shoulders. She didn't think she had any other choice. She did it all by herself and I'm so very proud of her."

His jaw clenched harder when his mind spun again with the many things he hadn't known. He was done listening. Anger built inside him once more. He wanted answers from Rose. "Where do you live?"

With a sigh, Lily rubbed her forehead. "Our place is the last small ranch before hitting the interstate on the south side." She squared her shoulders, her former weariness gone. Her round eyes narrowed. "I can't stop you from going there, but I will tell you something. If you hurt her, I'll come after you, and Mark will be right behind me. Nothing will stop us and we'll make your life miserable. That's a guarantee. She was only eighteen, Kody. Only eighteen and hurting so badly because she loved you so damn much and you chose a life without her. You keep one thing in mind when you see her. She still does love you no matter how she might come across. She'll say or do anything to protect Travis. So think about *that* before you march out to our place and play the wounded father." Lily spun on her heel and left him alone.

* * * * *

"What? He's coming here?" Rose clutched the phone. The blood drained from her face. "Lily! Why did you let Travis near him?" She jumped up from the couch and paced back and forth with a pounding heart. Suddenly she stopped, her hand cupping the back of her neck. "I-I'm sorry. I know it wasn't your fault. What am I going to do?" She listened for a moment with her head shaking. "No. He won't listen. If he's as angry as you said, he'll never forgive me."

Fear deeper than she'd ever known ripped through her. Rose had tried to tell Kody the evening before about Travis. But he'd stopped her words with kisses and the demand that he didn't want to talk. "No. Don't come home. We always knew this day might come. I-I can do this on my own. No, Lily. Please. Tell Mark no. Just keep Travis away for now. Don't come home until you call me. I don't want Travis here when Kody is ranting." She paused. "I love you, too, Lily." Hanging up the phone as a blaze of dread washed through her, she dropped her face into her upturned palms. The moment of reckoning was finally at hand, but she would go in swinging because whatever she might have found with Kody, it was over. He would never forgive her.

Rose paced in the living room, her eyes never leaving the front window and the long driveway leading up to the house. Kody was supposed to have been out of town. How he'd come to find himself playing Santa Claus was beyond her. One thing she was certain of was that he was angry as hell and she would pay the price by loving him and watching him walk away from her forever.

She nearly quit breathing when she saw his truck lights sweep across a field before lighting up the driveway. Racing to the front door, she yanked it open. She would not let him into the house. His presence in a confined area would take away her ability to keep the sharpest mind possible, and her brain was already fuzzy. She needed to stay resolute. Stepping out onto the porch, she straightened her spine and waited for his wrath.

Kody stepped from his pickup and slammed the door. She blinked, thinking she imagined the red suit and black boots in the glow of the yard light. Rose shook her head. She almost burst into hysterical laughter before getting hold of her chaotic emotions. Of course he was still costumed. He'd pinned down her sister with pointed questions after Travis had given away his true parentage and then headed straight for the house.

Kody never took his eyes from her as he marched up to the porch. She expected him to race furiously up the steps. Instead he stopped at the bottom and simply stared.

Try as she might, she couldn't read his features. A horse whinnied in a nearby paddock and a semi roared past on the road, but Kody said nothing.

Kody eyed her rigid stance as she glared across the porch. She reminded him of a lioness ready to protect her young and defend her lair. There was no doubt in his mind that Lily had called to inform her he was on his way out—and that he was snarling mad.

He'd been so angry thirty minutes earlier that if Rose had been at the hall, there was a good possibility he would have strangled her. His first instinct had been to spin out of the Community Center parking lot and race to Lily and Mark's to confront Rose about the secret she'd kept from him so long.

Instead, he had gotten back out of his pickup, found a window on the side of the building and watched Travis race around the floor with a slew of other children. With each minute that passed, the anger had left him bit by bit. He remembered smiling when the young boy stopped his racing about to help a little girl up from where she'd tripped and fallen to the floor.

Rose could have bowed to her father's wishes. If she had, life would have been so much easier for her. According to Lily, however, Rose had done whatever she'd had to do, always putting her son's welfare first. What she'd done was to protect her little boy and teach him about the good things in the world as best she could.

He sighed quietly now as he stared up. The air in his lungs filtered over his lips. Something else had cooled his hot temper. As he had stood watching his son through the window, he'd remembered that more than once the night before, Rose had tried to tell him something. But he'd always silenced her with hungry kisses.

A pang of guilt burned in his chest. At one point between the passionate kisses and bouts of hot sex, he'd also told her he wasn't yet ready for a family. The reasons why didn't matter. She'd become quiet and introspective after that, always assuring him that nothing was wrong no matter how he pried.

His eyes drifted over her once again. She was the reason he'd come home. And now there was another one. A little boy with green eyes and dark hair.

God he loved her. When all was said and done he would continue to do so.

"So now you know."

She said it with shoulders squared and her jaw tight, but Kody spied fear in her eyes.

He took one stair at a time and never took his determined gaze from hers. With each step she backed closer to the open door. Once Kody reached the top, Rose's arm came out to ward him off.

"Stay away from me, Kody," she ordered. "I did what I had to do. The last few days have been a huge mistake."

He advanced across the porch with purpose shining in his eyes. "I won't be put off so easily."

"I don't care what you say," she spouted, "I won't let you hurt him, or me."

Kody's hand shot out and snagged her arm when she bolted for the door.

Rose hauled off and smacked him with a closed fist as she fought to slip from his steely fingers. He grabbed her wrist and forced it behind her back as he yanked her to his chest. She kicked out, made contact with his shin, then struggled to escape.

"Let me go!" she screamed into his face. Fear produced instant tears that poured down her cheeks. "I love him and I won't let you take him from me!"

"Would you just shut up and quit beating the hell out of me?"

"Never!" Somehow she got her knee between his legs, but Kody was quicker and staved off her intended kick.

"Goddammit, knock it off, Rose!"

She squirmed against his tight embrace. Kody had had about enough. Without a word, his lips crashed against hers, silencing whatever else she might spew at him. His bruising kiss was harsh and seeking. Rose's body went limp beneath the onslaught as he forced his way inside her warm mouth. He continued to kiss her until he was assured she wouldn't bolt.

Finally, he tore his mouth from hers to stare down into her confused and watery gaze. "Christ, would you just listen to me?"

"Why...why did you kiss me? Don't do this to me, Kody."

"I kissed you because you've got the sexiest mouth of any woman I know and because I needed to shut you up. Listen to me, would you? I know you're scared, but you don't have to be. You were right to think I would be pissed as hell when I found out. I was. I couldn't believe you would keep something like this from me all these years."

Tears coursed down her cheeks. "I-I had no choice," she sobbed out.

"Yes you did." His fingers tightened around her arms. "You should have contacted me somehow."

"And what would you have done?" she asked as she swiped the wetness on her cheek. "You'd made your decision without even discussing it with me. I was nothing but a toy for you that summer."

The anguish in her eyes was like a punch to his gut. Kody wrapped his arms around her trembling body and pulled her against his chest. His eyes fluttered shut with guilt when he rested his chin against the soft cloud of her hair. She was right. He had toyed with her. No. The crazy wild youth that he'd been had taken what he could get.

How was he going to explain that to her and get her to believe it? "You're right. That's exactly what I did. But I cared for you, Rose. I didn't know how much until I left. You know that I tried to find you. And you know that one of the reasons I didn't stay in the Navy is because I wanted to be here." He leaned away, gently cupped her face and tenderly brushed away her tears with his thumbs. "I had to come back to find you. You never left my thoughts, Rose. Never. I felt we were always bound to one another. Now I know we are."

She reached up, clutched his arms and stared in disbelief. Her lips moved but no words came out.

Kody shook his head. "Lily told me about how you left with her for Nevada. I understand all of that. I understand the need you felt to be as far away from your father as possible. What I don't get is why you kept Travis a secret. I need to know."

Rose's mouth silently opened and closed again. Taking a deep breath, she wiped a tear once more. "I was afraid you would fight for him. I pictured you wanting him in your life but without me. How was I going to fight you in a custody battle? I had nothing, Kody. No financial resources, no connections that could help me. Then I-I was scared that he would discover who his father was and maybe you wouldn't want him. I lived with a father who thought I was nothing. I couldn't take the chance of him experiencing that pain. He's so precious to my heart...so innocent in all of this."

A shaft of pain pierced Kody's heart for what she'd had to endure. Once again, he pulled her gently into his arms vowing to spend the rest of his days making up all the hurt she'd had to suffer in her young life and the misconceptions over the past six years that had caused her even more pain. "Rose. I should have said this to you the first moment I saw you again. I love you. Do you hear me woman? I love you. I would never have taken him from you. But I do want to share him with you."

She clasped her arms around him and held on for dear life as quiet sobs left her.

"I'm going to work hard to get you to realize that. Give me that chance, Rose. Let me get to know him, but I want you to show me the way. I want us to be a family. My biggest desire is to have you both in my life."

"Oh, Kody," she whispered with a tremulous voice. Her arms tightened about his waist. "I'm sorry. I'm sorry for never telling you. I was young and frightened. All I ever really wanted was for the three of us to be together because I never stopped loving you. I never thought it could happen."

"No apologies, Rose. God…" he rubbed his chin against her hair once more. "I do love you. It's going to be fine. It'll be you and me and Travis. A family. I promise this will all work out."

Epilogue

ಬಿ

"I can't believe this is where you really wanted to be. Hell, Rose. We could have gone anywhere." Kody lay on the bed with his hands behind his head. He stared up at the ceiling and noted the tiny cracks that needed to be repaired. His attention, however, was drawn away instantly when he heard the bathroom door open as Rose stepped into the room. Rising up on an elbow, his eyes narrowed when he whistled in soft appreciation.

Her eyes glowed and she responded to the admiring gesture with a smile. "You like?"

"Oh, yeah, I like." His gaze coasted over the shimmering negligee, stopping at her full breasts defined beneath the silk, and then moved lower. The gossamer threads hugged her flat belly and outlined the slim length of her legs. She was absolutely gorgeous.

Rose struck a seductive pose. "See? We didn't have to go anywhere for a honeymoon. We can have just as much fun right here." A contented sigh left her.

Kody chuckled. "Having fun no matter where we were was never a worry as far as I was concerned." Lifting a hand, he beckoned her over with one bent finger.

Rose glided across the braided rug as he lifted the edge of the quilt and waited for her to climb in beside him.

"Oh, you're nice and warm," she laughed when she cuddled against his chest.

Kody slid a muscled thigh across her legs and stared down into a sea of blue. "I plan to get much hotter."

Rose giggled and locked her hands behind his neck. "Good. That's the reaction I was going for."

He lowered his mouth and kissed her. "You're such a tease," he chuckled softly. "Rather than here, though, we could have been lying on some beach in the Caribbean."

"You're something else, Kody. You've been wild to get Travis and me moved into this house. And now you want to go somewhere else for a honeymoon?"

"Hell, Rose. I knew you and I were a done deal before I even found out about Travis. I just never counted on your obstinacy about moving in with me until we were married. You can bet your sweet little ass that if I would have really believed you'd stick to your guns, I would never have waited an entire year."

"Ah, but it was a wonderful wedding, wasn't it? I loved the Christmas theme."

"You would." He nibbled her bottom lip because it was just too delectable not to. "And just so you know, you're going to pay for making me wait so long."

She giggled again and nipped him back. "You're just lucky I didn't make you wear a Santa outfit at the wedding. It would have been fitting."

Inch by inch Kody slid the silky negligee up her leg. His gaze devoured her smooth skin as he bunched the material around her waist. His mind wandered a bit, along with his fingers. Looking back on the past year, he couldn't complain too loudly about having to wait for the three of them to become a family. The time had given him the chance to cement a loving relationship with Travis and a chance for them to purchase their own homestead. He'd spent weeks planning a fantastic honeymoon, but in the end Rose won out. Only hours earlier, after the wedding, they had left their son at Lily's and promised to be back in the morning to celebrate Christmas.

The chuckle he let out was more a happy growl as he rolled on top of her body and nestled between her splayed thighs.

Rose sighed happily when he shoved the negligee higher over her abdomen and began to caress the soft skin of her belly. Her legs parted as he kissed his way through soft curls and swirled his tongue around her clit. Her fingers tickled through his hair. "I love you, Kody."

He paused to kiss her inner thigh. "I love you, too." His tongue moved back to lave her moist slit with a promise of what the night would entail. "I might not have the outfit you just talked about, but I do have an idea." He slipped back up her body and stared down into her loving gaze. "Want to play out a little fantasy with me?"

She laughed at the boyish hope she spied in his eyes, but couldn't stop the tiny shudder of anticipation when his cock pressed against her. "Good thing it's just you and me in the house. So what do you have in mind?"

He dipped his head and kissed her. Pulling back a bit, his mouth widened in a devilish grin. "Christmas might not be until tomorrow, but Santa is definitely going to come more than once tonight."

Also by Ruby Storm

ℰℴ

Cracked: Prelude to Passion

Diamond Studs (*anthology*)

Dragcon's Snare

Essence of Emerald

His Toys

Lucy's Double Diamonds

Mr. Fullservice

Payton's Passion

Perfect Betrayal

Perfecting Pearl

Sapphire's Seduction

Twilight Kisses

Virgin Queen

About the Author

❧

Picture Ruby Storm with her hair on fire! Yup, that's her every morning when she bounds out of bed and heads for her home office. Ruby thanks her lucky stars that she's a full-time writer and a part-time matchstick.

Although, there is a hint of a bulldog somewhere in there, too. Once she sticks her teeth into something, there's no turning back until it works.

Ruby loves to write, plain and simple. So much so that she took a leap of faith in herself and quit her 'professional' job, stuck her butt in front of a computer, and finally discovered what brings her true happiness. Her Romantica® stories for Ellora's Cave spans many genres: Contemporary, Futuristic, Fantasy, Paranormal, Time Travel and Historical. Be sure to check out her sweet historical romance series at Ellora's Cave's sister site, Cerridwen Press. All of Ruby's titles have received top awards for excellence in writing.

Some might think that the life of a writer is glamorous and enviable. This is what Ruby has to say about that: "Glamorous? Think of me in sweats and an old t-shirt just beneath that flaming head of mine, typing with one hand and beating out the fire with the other. Envious? Most times my 'new' job consists of long hours of dedication and damn hard work, cramping leg muscles from sitting too long, and a backside that for some reason is widening by the week. But I wouldn't change my life for the world!"

Ruby welcomes comments from readers. You can find her website and email address on her author bio page at www.ellorascave.com.

Tell Us What You Think

We appreciate hearing reader opinions about our books. You can email us at Comments@EllorasCave.com.

Why an electronic book?

We live in the Information Age—an exciting time in the history of human civilization, in which technology rules supreme and continues to progress in leaps and bounds every minute of every day. For a multitude of reasons, more and more avid literary fans are opting to purchase e-books instead of paper books. The question from those not yet initiated into the world of electronic reading is simply: *Why?*

1. *Price.* An electronic title at Ellora's Cave Publishing and Cerridwen Press runs anywhere from 40% to 75% less than the cover price of the exact same title in paperback format. Why? Basic mathematics and cost. It is less expensive to publish an e-book (no paper and printing, no warehousing and shipping) than it is to publish a paperback, so the savings are passed along to the consumer.

2. *Space.* Running out of room in your house for your books? That is one worry you will never have with electronic books. For a low one-time cost, you can purchase a handheld device specifically designed for e-reading. Many e-readers have large, convenient screens for viewing. Better yet, hundreds of titles can be stored within your new library—on a single microchip. There are a variety of e-readers from different manufacturers. You can also read e-books on your PC or laptop computer. (Please note that

Ellora's Cave does not endorse any specific brands. You can check our websites at www.ellorascave.com or www.cerridwenpress.com for information we make available to new consumers.)

3. *Mobility.* Because your new e-library consists of only a microchip within a small, easily transportable e-reader, your entire cache of books can be taken with you wherever you go.

4. *Personal Viewing Preferences.* Are the words you are currently reading too small? Too large? Too... ANNOYING? Paperback books cannot be modified according to personal preferences, but e-books can.

5. *Instant Gratification.* Is it the middle of the night and all the bookstores near you are closed? Are you tired of waiting days, sometimes weeks, for bookstores to ship the novels you bought? Ellora's Cave Publishing sells instantaneous downloads twenty-four hours a day, seven days a week, every day of the year. Our webstore is never closed. Our e-book delivery system is 100% automated, meaning your order is filled as soon as you pay for it.

Those are a few of the top reasons why electronic books are replacing paperbacks for many avid readers.

As always, Ellora's Cave and Cerridwen Press welcome your questions and comments. We invite you to email us at Comments@ellorascave.com or write to us directly at Ellora's Cave Publishing Inc., 1056 Home Avenue, Akron, OH 44310-3502.

erridwen, the Celtic Goddess of wisdom, was the muse who brought inspiration to storytellers and those in the creative arts. Cerridwen Press encompasses the best and most innovative stories in all genres of today's fiction. Visit our site and discover the newest titles by talented authors who still get inspired - much like the ancient storytellers did, once upon a time.

Discover for yourself why readers can't get enough of the multiple award-winning publisher Ellora's Cave.

Whether you prefer e-books or paperbacks, be sure to visit EC on the web at www.ellorascave.com

for an erotic reading experience that will leave you breathless.